"Not for all the gold in England ould I dance with you, sir."

lis eye twinkled and he smiled more sincerely, with a crooked expression that warmed something inside her. "I'm not offering *all* the old," he said, "but a significant portion could e yours if you're amenable."

proposition, sir?" She raised an eyebrow h the question. "Am I to run weeping at the ult or deal you a resounding slap? How do bets go that I will respond?"

o bets and no proposition. I have a very cent proposal in mind."

am already the object of ridicule," she told n frankly, withdrawing her hand from his. o find another to tease, who will at least rd you points for originality."

inclined his head. "Will you not grant me a all favor, at least, and take a turn about the r?"

haps this was an arranged jibe, compliments o her uncle. "Do you know Wardfelton?"

ave not met him yet, but I shall seek him mmediately if you will give me leave to ask him for you."

"For my *person*? Not only a dance? How droll."

"For your
equivocati

AUTHOR NOTE

All too often we judge on appearance alone. There might be a really wonderful person concealed beneath a less than perfect façade. As the hero and heroine of THE CAPTAIN AND THE WALLFLOWER discover, perceptions can change radically when one delves a bit more deeply and discovers true character and personality.

I write romance to entertain, but also to illustrate my heartfelt belief that selfless love does exist and ought to be celebrated! It is possible to find someone who would jump between you and a bullet, who would put your happiness before their own, and who would love you unconditionally. Some of us have found that person, and to those who haven't as yet I say, 'Keep an open mind, keep up the search, and don't forget to note what's beyond the surface!'

I hope you enjoy the journey as Grace and Caine discover the sort of love neither dared hope to find when they first stumbled into a marriage of mutual convenience. If you enjoyed *The Ugly Duckling*, *Cinderella* and *Beauty and the Beast* as a child, I think you will appreciate my grown-up story THE CAPTAIN AND THE WALLFLOWER.

THE CAPTAIN AND THE WALLFLOWER

Lyn Stone

First published in Great Britain 2012
by Mills & Boon, an imprint of Harlequin (UK) Limited.
Harlequin (UK) Limited, Eton House, 18-24 Paradise Road,
Richmond, Surrey TW9 1SR

© Lynda Stone 2012

ISBN: 978 0 263 89255 0

Printed and bound in Spain
by Blackprint CPI, Barcelona

A painter of historical events, **Lyn Stone** decided to write about them. A canvas, however detailed, limits characters to only one moment in time: 'If a picture's worth a thousand words, the other ninety thousand have to show up somewhere!' An avid reader, she admits, 'At thirteen, I fell in love with Emily Brontë's Heathcliff and became Catherine. Next year I fell for Rhett and became Scarlett. Then I fell for the hero I'd known most of my life and finally became myself.'

After living for four years in Europe, Lyn and her husband Allen settled into a log house in north Alabama that is crammed to the rafters with antiques, artefacts and the stuff of future tales.

This book is for my wonderful and courageous friend, Garland Whiddon Rowland. This is for all those discussions about what love is when we were teens still anticipating it. Oh, and for being my maid of honor once I found it! So happy that you found it, too!

Prologue

London
July 25, 1815

Caine Morleigh studiously avoided touching the cloth bandages covering his eyes as he waited for the physician to arrive. For five long weeks, his injuries had remained under wraps, the bandages changed by feel in pitch-dark to avoid further damage from the light. And to avoid revelation, he admitted to himself. Today, he would know whether his sight had been destroyed.

There would be so much for him to learn if that proved so. Already, he had begun counting steps from one place to another so that he could eventually get about the house unaided. He fed himself in private still, but was becoming good at it.

Control would not be beyond him. In time,

he would be able to manage the impediment, if forced to it. Damn, but he hated being dependent. Impatience warred with apprehension as the wait dragged on in the drawing room of his uncle, Earl of Hadley.

He heard his aunt Hadley gasp again as Trent, his best friend and companion, regaled her with prettied-up details of their final day on the field of battle. Caine paid little heed to the words. He'd heard it all before in considerably more graphic terms. Hell, he had lived it. Trent talked entirely too much, but his effort here was admirable, Caine admitted. It was Trent's way of lessening the tension and distracting everyone from the purpose of the gathering.

"We were wounded on the charge along with most of our brigade, most never to rise again! Caine fell beside me, unable to see, and I, my leg badly twisted, could not hope to walk. But did we lie there and die? No, ma'am! I served as his eyes whilst he got us to my horse. His horse had collapsed, you see, so we mounted double and rejoined the charge, galloping full speed. There was no going back...."

Someone cleared their throat and Trent, thank God, left off his narrative at the interruption. "Dr. Ackers and Miss Belinda Thoren-Snipes," Jenkins, the butler, announced.

"Show them in! Show them in!" his aunt exclaimed. Caine heard the rustle of taffeta skirts as Aunt Hadley approached and laid a hand on his shoulder. "I thought he would never come."

"How convenient they've arrived together," his uncle said. "I sent a note round for your Belinda to join us, too. I knew you would want her here."

Caine sighed, wishing he had not. He wanted to discover for himself whether he could see before he encountered his fiancée. If he was to be blind for life, she should not be held to the betrothal. For that reason, he had not initiated any contact at all since his return to London.

He had no trouble recalling how she had looked the last time he had seen her. He hoped against hope he would see her again. She was a blonde, rose-cheeked beauty, his Belinda. Her image had sustained him for nearly two years as he had faced the ugliness of war.

He heard approaching footsteps, the physician's heavier masculine tread interspersed with the soft click of Belinda's dainty shoes on the marble floor of the corridor. Did he actually smell the scent of her lilac perfume as she entered, or was that merely a fond brush of memory and expectation? Caine was convinced he loved her and had from their first meeting.

Despite that, he realized he knew very little about his future wife. He had courted her, of course, but not for long and always under the strictest of supervision. Their desultory conver-

sation then, and later her infrequent letters filled
with frivolous details of life at home, had not
told him much.

In fact, he did not know a great deal about
women in general, other than in the biblical
sense. That paid-for expertise was helpful only
in the bedchamber, but valuable nonetheless.
Perhaps that was all that any man could hope to
understand fully or, in fact, would need to know.

He employed respect with all females, regardless of rank, as well as chivalry and what charm
he had acquired. Common courtesy demanded
that much of a man, and rightly so.

He forced a smile to greet Belinda even as he
wished for her own sake, as well as for his, that
she were elsewhere this morning. Her scent of
lilacs, the essence he had recalled with fervent
longing in the midst of war, now nearly over-
powered the senses he had left.

"Captain Morleigh!" she said with obviously
forced brightness.

"How are you, my dear?" he asked, sick
with apprehension, holding his smile in place
by sheer force of will.

"Fine, thank you," she replied, the brightness
slipping, replaced by a tremor.

He noted that she did not return the question.
Her fear of the answer must be nearly as great as
his own, at being faced with the very real pros-
pect of having a blind husband to look after. He

would release her from their betrothal if it came to that, but she did not yet know it.

Caine identified the sound of the medical bag being opened.

"Could we get on with it?" he asked, impatience winning out. He wanted this over with, whatever the outcome.

"Certainly, my boy," the doctor answered, his tone entirely too sympathetic and tinged with worry. "Let's turn you away from the lamps to the soft light from the window."

Caine moved as directed and heard the others in the room, Trent, Aunt Hadley and Belinda, shifting positions, as well.

"Belinda, you must stand just there so that you will be the very first thing he sees!" his aunt said.

Belinda muttered her thanks as the doctor slid a scissor blade beneath the bandage at Caine's right temple and began to cut. He carefully peeled the cloth away and dabbed something wet over both eyelids, soaking them thoroughly. "There," he said finally. "Now open your eyes slowly."

Caine concentrated as he did so and sensed the doctor move to one side and expose him to the window.

He blinked, saw blessed light...and heard the screams.

Chapter One

❦

London
Cavanaugh House
August 25, 1815

"Spot the homeliest of the lot, Trent, and speak to her sponsor on my behalf." Caine Morleigh smiled at his friend as he handed his cane and top hat to the attendant. "She should look utterly frightful, perhaps be a bit dull of wit and wanting in every respect, or she won't do."

Trent sighed, rolling his eyes as he tugged at his gloves. "You don't have to do this. You're making far too much of that girl's reaction." He scoffed. "Porridge for brains, that one."

"That's as may be, but I have a more significant reason for this than the way *I* look." The receiving line had dispersed, and apparently they weren't to be announced, since they had come so late. He led the way, following the music down the wide corridor. He glanced inside a smaller room, which had been set up for card playing and refreshments, then turned and entered the ballroom.

He kept his voice low as he leaned sideways to continue his conversation with Trent. "I need someone who will require little attention, a woman satisfied to simply change her marital status and then leave me alone. I shall have more than enough to do as it is."

Trent huffed. "A woman who needs little attention? Is there such a creature? In my experience—"

"I know all about your *experience*. Now, stop blathering on and help me look."

The gathering at Lord Cavanaugh's was far from a crush, since it was past the regular London season and many had retired to the country. Decorations had been held to a minimum and this appeared to be a rather modest affair. Still the columned entry, the great expanse of highly polished floor and elegantly curved staircase needed little embellishment to shout wealth.

The musicians sounded rather good, though they were few in number compared to events he had attended in years past. He watched the dancers move through their measured steps without much gaity or conversation.

"Not much of a rout, is it," Trent commented

with a sigh of resignation. "I've seen more excitement at funerals."

"Suits my need perfectly," Caine responded. Most of the single women present would be the leftovers and their sponsors, hoping for a late-made match. Perhaps with a bit of luck, he could make one of the hopefuls content, if not happy.

Trent snorted. "Damned harebrained idea. You're obsessed with controlling every aspect of your life. Always have been. And it's not possible, y'know."

"I can but try."

"You're treating this like a military campaign, and you know how I hate taking orders!"

"Think of the compensation. You may go for the best-looking one for yourself. It's a small thing I'm asking of you," Caine said, applying his most reasonable tone. "*Asking,* not ordering. And as a friend, Trent."

"Fine! It's your own throat you're cutting. Your uncle was wrong when he put the condition on you to marry. I wouldn't do it if I were you. You'll have his title no matter what you do or don't."

Caine shrugged. "Yes, but it's the fortune that will go to Cousin Neville, plus the estates, since none is entailed. Think of all the people now employed by the earl who would suffer if Neville lost everything over a stupid game of cards or on a damned horse race. He could, and probably would, piss away everything the family has worked for these last two centuries."

"You don't know that he will. You haven't seen him since you were children."

"Oh, I've heard enough of his maddening exploits from my uncle. Knowing such things, I cannot imagine why he would even consider leaving *anything* to Neville, but Hadley seems amused by it all and oddly unconcerned. Therefore, I must prevent it however I can. So I will marry, as he stipulates. I don't have any strong objections. He is my uncle, after all, and I do care about his feelings. I should settle his mind before he gives up the ghost."

"But why must you have a woman who's desperate to marry?" Trent clicked his tongue, exasperated. "Not every female in London runs screaming from the room when she sees you."

"One certainly did."

"Well, *only* that one, and as I've said before, she's not all there." He tapped his temple with two fingers and shook his head. "Silly witch."

"Well, she's not *here,* either, which is why I came." Caine heaved out a breath of frustration and began strolling the perimeter of the room, Trent at his side.

"Watch how each miss gives me a look of repulsion as we pass, terrified I will take an interest." He shook his head. "Times such as this, blindness would be a blessing."

"Well, I'm damned glad you're *not* blind and you ought to be, too! Perhaps their regard is merely a reaction to your grim expression. Try smiling now and again. They could do far worse than you, and you know it. So you have a few scars. A wife would get used to that after the first shock of seeing them."

"I hope you're right." Caine stopped beside a towering plant and picked absently at one of the leaves. "But I think it best to choose a woman not prone to play the social butterfly. The most beautiful exist for it. I despise these sorts of occasions and would like to be done with them."

He hadn't used to hate social events, not when he'd been a young lieutenant, flirting, dancing, assessing the newest crop of preening lovelies, giving Trent solid competition. That's how he had found a little beauty of excellent birth, whom he had thought would be the perfect mate for a rising army officer. A young fool's mistake, that. Now he knew better.

He had been only third in line for the earldom then, with a military career underway. However, with the deaths of his father and a brother during the years Caine had served in the army, he was now set to inherit from the eldest of that generation, his uncle. He had not been born to the title, nor had he been trained for it. The responsibilities were enormous, greater than he had ever imagined. There was so much to learn. So much to sort out.

The old earl, who admittedly was not long for the world, demanded that his heir be settled and ready to assume his duties. That involved Caine's getting a wife immediately, so here he was, shopping. He surveyed the goods, evaluating faces, postures, attitudes.

This time he knew he must rely on different currency for the negotiations. The women he had been well acquainted with in his life thus far had proved rather shallow, valuing a handsome face, charm and practised manners well above anything else in a man. They left it to their practical families to ascertain whether their choice possessed the necessary means to support them.

Now he must find a suitable woman desperate enough to overlook his altered appearance and lack of social inclinations to settle for his prospective wealth and title. More important, as he had impressed on Trent, he needed one who would not impact on the time he would require to fulfill his duties as earl. The task of handling the earl's business matters already proved daunting. He must live up to it.

Trent's words troubled him. Did such a woman as he required actually exist? He continued scanning the ballroom, dwelling on the corners where the wallflowers perched, trying to conceal their hopes and dreams behind fans and half smiles. None of their smiles were directed at him.

Suddenly, his good eye landed on one in pale yellow, a painfully thin figure with lank brown hair, a colorless complexion and enormous, doe-like eyes. Caine immediately sensed in her a mixture of hopelessness and resignation, yet she somehow maintained an air of calm dignity he admired. "A definite possibility there," he muttered, more to himself than to Trent.

The girl was not precisely ugly, but it was certain no one would describe her as pretty. He felt a tug of…what? Sympathy? No, more like empathy. She did not wish to be here, either, most likely for similar reasons. Yet they must be here, probably striving toward the same goal— a suitable match.

These mating rituals were such a trial for any not blessed with the allure necessary to attract the opposite sex. At least he would have wealth and the title to recommend him. She had only her dignity apparently. If she were an heiress, she would certainly be better dressed, coiffed and bejeweled. Her pale neck and earlobes were completely bare.

If he could look past her surface, perhaps she would be willing to look past his. But he must put it to her in a way she would find palatable. He couldn't very well say "You look like a quiet, unprepossessing chit I could count on to not complicate my life any further than it is already."

Could he summon enough charm, persuasion and outrageous bribery to convince this one to have him? Yes, he decided, approaching her might be worth the risk of rejection.

"Yes, I think so," he said to himself. "That one, Trent," he said, nodding toward the candidate. "The one in the lemon-colored frock. She'll do."

"What? She's a bean stalk, Morleigh, and the beans don't appear to have developed yet."

"I'm not out for beans," Caine said tersely, his gaze still resting on the waiflike girl.

"Well, she looks like death on a plate. I doubt she'll live through the month, much less the rigors of a wedding." He nudged Caine with his elbow. "Besides, you said you'd let me choose."

"Don't be tedious. I believe she's the one, so go. Do what we came to do," Caine said simply, straightening his sleeves.

He hoped to have the selection completed with this one foray into society, because it was damned uncomfortable submitting himself to all these stares. He knew he wasn't that monstrous looking and that they were mostly curious, but it bothered him.

His left eye bore only a few scars, but those surely made everyone imagine the very worst of the one he kept covered. The right, he always avoided looking at in the mirror and concealed it behind a rather large eye patch whenever he was in company.

That was probably a useless vanity due to the well-broadcast observation of Miss Thoren-Snipes, his former fiancée. She had declared to one and all that he was a horrible sight that turned her off sick, a fright she would never forget, one that caused her nightmares.

To her credit, his aunt's reaction that day had verified that Belinda did not exaggerate by much. He made women faint, cast up their accounts and scream in their sleep. Avoiding that hardly qualified as vanity on his part. No, more like a gentleman's consideration, he thought.

Trent did not understand, and why should he? He had the wherewithal to pick and choose and take his own sweet time about it. No woman would refuse Gavin Trent, handsome as he was, a hero of the wars and witty as hell. Caine owed him his life, admired him enormously and wished him well. Envy had no place in a friendship as enduring as theirs. But Trent's eternal optimism and infernal teasing tried his patience to extremes.

The girl in yellow was now getting an earful from one of the other unfortunates, an overweight dumpling who seemed entirely too vivacious to qualify as second choice if he needed one. Her glance left no doubt about whom she had chosen to revile.

Caine wondered if perhaps he was overly sensitive and tried not to be, but he was unused to it yet. He had attended none of these functions since his return to London. He was grateful that he was still able to see and wished he could simply bypass mirrors forever and ignore how he looked. If not for this acquiring of a wife, he could be content with himself as he was.

The object of his future suit looked up and her very direct gaze again met his across the room. He should march right over and ask her to dance. Three times running. That would seal the deal. But not yet.

Caine snagged a glass of champagne off the silver tray of a passing waiter circulating among the guests. He raised it slightly, toasting the girl, and forced a smile as he spoke to his friend. "Go, Trent. Find out who she is. I'll wait here."

"You're certain you want to go through with this?"

"Yes, quite." He sipped the sparkling wine and concealed a wince. He preferred a stouter drink with some substance to it.

A quarter hour later, Trent rejoined Caine. "She's Wardfelton's niece, Lady Grace Renfair," he declared. "His lordship laughed in my face when I spoke with him. Told me she has no dowry. She's penniless. *Worthless* was the word he used to describe her, an ailing, aging millstone around his neck and none too bright."

"Aging? How old is she?"

"Twenty-four or thereabout. I inquired of a few others, as well as her uncle. Lady Nebbins, that old talebearer, told me the chit was orphaned at sixteen, engaged to Barkley's second son, a lieutenant in the navy, who died aboard *The Langston* six years ago. She lived as companion to the lad's widowed mother until that lady remarried. Lady Grace has been with Wardfelton for these past two years."

"Ah, good. Of suitable birth then. And something in common already, noble uncles with a foot on our necks. Perhaps she's ready for a change."

Trent hummed his agreement. "I don't doubt that. Rumor about town had it she was perhaps dead. People had begun wondering aloud whether she was deceased and how she came to be so. It's thought Wardfelton has trotted her out tonight to dispense with the gossip. I must say, she might yet make it a fact. To call her frail would be kind."

Caine smiled. "No matter. I can go forward with it then."

"Ah, well, there's a fly in the ointment," Trent informed him. He rocked to and fro as he spoke. "Wardfelton didn't take me, or my request on your behalf, seriously at all. He thinks we are making fun of his simpleminded niece and seemed to find it highly amusing that we should do so."

"Simpleminded?" Caine didn't believe it for a second.

Trent shrugged. "He doesn't think much of her, obviously. Probably exaggerated. I would remind you, you did ask for dull of wit."

"He didn't refuse outright to let me address her, did he?"

"No, he doesn't really expect you to," Trent admitted. "I spoke with Lord Jarvis, too. He says she is the daughter of the previous earl. Wardfelton's actually the third brother to hold the title. The second, Lady Grace's father, was a physician until he inherited. Only held it for a couple of years before he died of the cholera during the outbreak here, along with his wife. The girl was left home in the country and escaped their fate. And as I said, Barkley's mother took her in."

Caine nodded. "Ah, an earl's daughter. Uncle should consider the match entirely acceptable. If she is willing and I could obtain a special license from the archbishop, we could marry this week."

"You know what they say about marrying in haste."

"Never put off until tomorrow what you can do today," Caine retorted. He shoved his glass at Trent. "Hold this for me. Better yet, get me another with something more bracing than bubbles. Courting's thirsty work."

He left Trent standing there staring at the delicate crystal stem and went to ply his suit.

Chapter Two

Grace Renfair shifted her gaze elsewhere, determined not to look back at the man standing across the ballroom. His intense regard unnerved her. Why did he single her out so pointedly? Probably wondering who was so witless as to sponsor a creature such as herself.

She felt exposed, woefully underdressed and incomparable in the worst sort of way. No matter. She lifted her chin and paid only scant attention to the vile chatter of the girl beside her.

"I could never abide a man so tall and large as Captain Morleigh, even if he were handsome!" exclaimed Miss Caulfield. Grace did not reply, even to nod or shrug.

He was large, yes, but not frighteningly so. Grace thought he cut quite a figure when compared to the fashionably slender or the aging portly gents milling around him at the moment.

"He would frighten the life out of anyone! Belinda is well out of that match! She says he has turned unbearably cold and cruel since the war. Why, he probably slew dozens of people before he was nearly killed himself!"

Wasn't he *expected* to do that when he was a soldier? Grace ignored Miss Caulfield's comment. Would the girl ever change topics? No, she prattled on. "Look at his shoulders! All that swordplay, I should think. No padding there, I'd wager!"

Not a bet Grace would take. She had also noted that his features were well defined and rather stark above that square jaw and stubborn chin. The eye patch added a dash of interest, as perhaps it was meant to do, though if he had been wounded in battle, it probably was not simply for show.

The black evening attire topped by a snowy neckcloth looked impeccable, though his straight-shouldered military bearing was such that he might as well have worn regimentals. His height was remarkable, too, putting him at least half a head above the men around him.

"Yes, his looks are compelling," Grace said, before remembering she should not speak at all.

So why should she mind if he caught her looking at him, since everyone else seemed to be? Perhaps she should thank him for drawing inquisitive stares away from her.

When she finally gave in to curiosity and shot another glance in his direction, she saw this Captain Morleigh heedlessly interrupting the progress of the quadrille by walking directly through it. Now, there was a man who did precisely as he pleased. She would give anything to be that bold.

She had been once, but had changed so much she hardly knew herself any longer. The face in her mirror seemed a stranger, as did her almost-lifeless form swathed in the dated ball gown her uncle had provided. There had been no maid to dress her, to help with her woefully straight hair or even produce pins for it.

Her uncle had brought her here to show her off, so he said. She believed that to be true in the very worst sense and wondered if perhaps he thought he must. He had kept her a virtual prisoner for well over a year. Did anyone question where she was keeping these days and what had happened to her? Or did anyone remember her at all?

She had never made her debut, having been betrothed so early on. Then her mourning had been extended much longer than usual. She had lost both parents and soon after, her husband-to-be. The comfort of his mother, Lady Barkley, had been such a balm, she had been loath to give up the sweet lady's company. Not one to intrude on her dear friend's newlywed state, Grace had insisted on removing herself to the care of her only relative. Such a mistake that had been, and so irrevocable.

She and Wardfelton had gotten on quite well in the beginning. She even played hostess for several entertainments he had held at the country house. Then, literally overnight, things had changed. He suddenly turned into nothing short of a jailer, insisting she remain in her rooms except for a supervised walk about the enclosed gardens when weather permitted. Her meals were sent up. Her correspondence disallowed.

It seemed he thoroughly enjoyed humiliating and even frightening her in every way he could devise. She shuddered just thinking of the tales he had told of young English women disappearing, sold into white slavery, never to be seen or heard of again. Though not an outright threat, there had been warning in his eyes. Why, she could not fathom, but he obviously meant to keep her terrified and biddable for some reason or other.

Perhaps he feared being called to account for squandering her inheritance, if indeed she had ever possessed any such thing. She could not look into it herself and whom did he think would do so on her behalf? No one cared.

Well, her looks were gone now and she much

doubted any foreign sultan with proper eyesight would want to buy such as her. What more could Uncle do to her other than offer her up to ridicule as he was doing tonight?

Murder was still an option, even though he would be the most obvious suspect. She had pointed that out to him when he deliberately had left out that book of poisons for her to see. He had laughed at that, but she had sensed his unease. More likely, he intended to drive her to suicide so he would look blameless.

If only she knew someone here, she would plead for escape. But would anyone believe her? Would anyone care?

"He's coming this way!" Miss Caulfield announced. "Should we venture to speak to him?"

Grace knew she was being watched, for Wardfelton had told her she would be. He also warned rather adamantly that she was to hold no personal conversations with anyone present. She was only to been seen, not heard. Grace held her head high despite all that. He would not steal what little dignity she had left.

Nor would this man approaching with a patently fake smile upon his face. He stopped directly in front of her.

"My lady, please allow me to presume and introduce myself."

"You would be Captain Morleigh," she replied, to save him the trouble. She held out her hand and watched with interest as he lifted it almost to his lips. Damn Wardfelton. Let him do his worst. Damn them all. She was sick of living in fear.

"Lady Grace," he said, holding her gaze, as well as her hand. "I see that our reputations have preceded us. Such a pleasure to meet you. Would you do me the honor of the next dance?"

Grace cocked her head to one side as she continued to peer up at him. He bore a few scars from the war, pinkish and still healing, random marks upon his forehead and around his uncovered eye. They did proclaim the validity of the eye patch he wore that lent him his roguish air.

Misses Caulfield and Thoren-Snipes were so wrong. The man was not hideous at all. More's the pity. She had never trusted handsome men, especially *arrogant* handsome men who presumed too much, as he did now. She forced a half smile. "Not for all the gold in England would I dance with you, sir."

His eye twinkled and he smiled more sincerely, a crooked expression that warmed something inside her. "I'm not offering *all* the gold," he said, "but a significant portion could be yours if you're amenable."

"A proposition, sir?" She raised an eyebrow with the question. "Am I to run weeping at the insult or deal you a resounding slap? How do the bets go that I will respond?"

"No bets and no proposition. I have a very decent proposal in mind."

"I am already the object of ridicule," she told him frankly, withdrawing her hand from his, flipping open her fan and giving him the signal to leave her alone. "Go, find another to tease who will at least earn you points for originality."

He inclined his head. "Certainly no ridicule intended, my lady. I merely ask to be considered. I have some trouble in that quarter as you have no doubt heard." He cast a pointed look at her overfed companion, who promptly blushed and hurried away.

Morleigh returned his attentions to Grace. "Will you not grant me a small favor, at least, and take a turn about the floor?"

Perhaps this was an arranged jibe, compliments of her uncle. "Do you know Wardfelton?"

"I have not met him yet, but I shall seek him out immediately if you will give me leave to ask him for you."

"For my *person?* Not only a dance? How droll."

"For your hand in marriage," he said without equivocation.

A short laugh escaped in spite of her dismay. The man was either woefully desperate, quite mad or downright cruel. "I should give you that leave, my lord, and hold you by law to your word. It would serve you right for carrying this jest too far."

Amazingly, he stretched his hand closer, his expression totally devoid of sarcasm, his deep voice rife with sincerity. "Please do. I would be forever grateful. Perhaps we could dance and discuss it further?"

His madness must be contagious. Whatever he had in mind could hardly lower her any more in public estimation than did the way she looked tonight. And why should she care if it did? None of her former friends were in attendance, not that she had ever had many who would be here in town.

She had hoped at first to appeal to someone she knew to give her some respite from her uncle, but he had warned her no one would. In fact, she had nothing provable to complain about except his clearly implied hatred and her suspicion that, for some cause unknown, he wished her to wither and die. She could not run away again, for even if he were disposed to let her, where would she go and what would she do?

Revealing her fears to anyone and asking their interference might imply hysterics on her part. Wardfelton had accused her of that himself, cleverly attributing it to her martyring grief and self-induced illness. No doubt he had already broadcast that diagnosis to anyone willing to listen. Secluding her in a madhouse was a distinct possibility, and perhaps tonight was meant to set the stage for that.

Damn the man and his threats! This was no way to live, and she was sick of it. Why had she stood it for so long?

Let him do his worst. She probably would die soon one way or another. Sad, but that fact seemed oddly freeing at the moment. It wasn't as if she stood any chance of ever making another match or doing any of the things a young woman of means might undertake. She had no means. No prospects at all. Why not do as she pleased tonight and damn the consequences?

Without thinking any more about it, Grace placed her gloved hand in the captain's again. He swept her onto the dance floor and into a scandalously close waltz.

She was not so familiar with the steps, but he held her firmly and guided her as if they had practiced daily for weeks. Grace found it exhilarating, being held so near and whirled about so expertly.

After one turn around the floor, she looked up at him. "Why do you do this, really? You have already made us a spectacle, so honesty will lose you nothing."

His expression smoothed out. "Honestly? I need a wife. And I am guessing that you need a husband. That *is* why we are here, is it not?"

"You *do* know Wardfelton. He has put you up to this."

"We have never met, I vow it on my life. I will admit I sent Lord Trent as my emissary to ask Wardfelton's leave to court you."

"Oh, he would never agree to that," she stated, quite sure of it. Who knew what her uncle would do to her simply for having this dance and conversation?

"Well, he did not refuse, either. Probably too deep in his cups. I can only hope he's drunk enough to let me have you. Assuming you are willing, of course. Are you?"

She laughed a little. "What idiot steered you in this direction, I wonder? I've not a farthing to recommend me. I would come with nothing. Surely he made that clear enough."

"I come with everything you will need. Make your demands and I shall meet them."

Grace shook her head and kept a smile on her face, unwilling to let him see how painful it was to be toyed with in such a way. Yet she decided the best way to deflect this sort of jest was to laugh along with the jester. "Ah, well, if you put it that way... A thousand quid per annum, two maids and a shiny new phaeton. Oh, and diamonds, of course. A lady must have diamonds."

He gave a satisfied nod. "Done and done, my lady. Only, you shall have two thousand, all the servants you like, plus a matched team to pull the phaeton."

"Why, thank you!" she exclaimed with her widest smile. "But what of the gems, my lord? Does that break the deal?"

"No. Do you prefer blue or yellow stones?" He whirled her again, causing her stomach to flutter wildly.

"White diamonds," she declared, leaning back and challenging him with her eyes. "You know, this is most entertaining. For you, that is to say. As for me, I should like to kick you in the shins and spit in your face. Manners prevent, however, so if you would kindly lead me back to my place by the wall and collect whatever sum you have riding on this farce, I would be most appreciative."

He stopped dead still in the middle of the floor and stared down at her. The music faltered and the noise died down. With no apparent care for who was watching and listening, he took both her hands in his and brought them to his lips. "Lady Grace, you've quite stolen my heart and I cannot live without you. Would you do me the great honor of becoming my wife?" His voice was even deeper than before. And rather loud in the gathering hush.

A collective gasp shook the cavernous room. Someone dropped a violin and the strings pinged, the only other sound to be heard.

"Say you will have me, or my heart will break." A stage whisper if she had ever heard one. It fairly echoed round the room.

Grace barely resisted the urge to throw back her head and laugh out loud. She had not laughed that way in so long, perhaps she had forgotten how, but the urge was there.

She glanced over the group surrounding them and saw Wardfelton had entered the ballroom and was standing there with his mouth agape. She realized at that moment she would do virtually anything to discommode him further. And anything to get away from him permanently, even if it landed her in a worse fix. Well, here was her chance.

She recalled the old expression, *better the devil you know...* Balderdash, that wasn't so in her case. The devil she didn't know could hardly be any worse than Wardfelton. She had nearly forgotten what it was like to live without constant terror. And for some unfathomable reason, she had no fear of Captain Morleigh. None at all.

Grace looked back into the eye of the presumptuous man who held her hands. Here was no devil, only a slightly disfigured fellow who doubted his appeal to women so devoutly he would settle for the one he thought most desperate. Well, he had found her right enough.

The description of him that Miss Thoren-Snipes had passed around had been widely dis-

persed, according to Grace's companion earlier
this evening. Perhaps Morleigh suffered more
than anyone knew, especially if he was now
reduced to pleading with the least-agreeable
woman in the room to marry him.

He began to look hopeful then, taking her
hesitation for wavering, she supposed. It certainly was that. She felt him draw her closer
as he leaned down to speak privately. "All that
I promised you, plus independence," he whispered, then added, "no conditions attached."

"None?" Yes, he *was* mad.

"Well, faithfulness, of course," he said against
her ear. "We will vow that much when we wed.
But otherwise, you shall do as you please, go
where you will, act as you choose."

"Your word of honor?" she whispered back,
actually considering it seriously. She might be
trading one threat for another. Morleigh could
beat her, lock her away or possibly get rid of her
permanently as she was sure her uncle planned
to do. Even as she thought that, it seemed more
likely this man would simply leave her to her
own devices if she displeased him. Or even if
she didn't. It certainly was a gamble, but she really had nothing to lose.

"Then yes," she replied in a whisper.

"Louder," he suggested. "That will make it
official and irrevocable."

"I will!" she declared, flashing her uncle a

steely glare. "I would be honored to marry you, Captain Morleigh. My heart is lost and I simply cannot wait to be your wife." Who cared if that sounded like a line from some mawkish play. So had his loud proposal.

Morleigh kissed her hands, each in turn and signaled to the orchestra. "Gentlemen, if you please, a celebratory waltz!"

Stunned, shaken, still feeling the urge to laugh wildly, Grace followed his lead until the music stopped.

Lord, she felt dizzy, overcome with heat from the exertion. The moment he released her to applaud the music, she swooned. Her last thought was that she had finally starved herself into wild delusions. This night could not be real.

Chapter Three

"Fetch a doctor!" shouted Caine. He felt her wrist for a pulse and found one. It seemed steady enough and only a trifle weak.

No one came forward to help. Highly unlikely that a mere physician would be present at the assembly, so he scooped her up in his arms and strode out, barking an order to have his carriage brought round on the instant.

"Where do you think you're going with her?" Wardfelton demanded loudly. He followed them out the front entrance and scampered around to hamper Caine's progress.

"She needs a doctor. I know one. Stand aside. She's mine now."

"She is *not* yours!" The man's outrage seemed real enough. "I forbid this!" he shouted. "Put her *down,* I say!"

"Come with us if you're worried about her. Otherwise, stand clear!"

Half the attendees had followed them out to the steps and stood transfixed. Better than a horse race or a boxing match, Caine figured. More food for gossip at any rate. He needed the audience, so he didn't mind.

"Someone call the watch! This is abduction!" Wardfelton cried, wheeling right and left, searching for someone to interfere.

Caine faced him down, the lady's inert form between them. "Lord Trent is my witness. He spoke for me and you did not deny my asking for her hand. I have done, and with intentions most honorable. She is of age to accept without your consent. Lady Grace will be properly chaperoned by my aunt, the countess of Hadley, until she recovers and then we shall be married."

"This is absurd!" Wardfelton announced, still looking around for support amongst his peers.

"Is it? What is your objection, sir?" Caine noticed the carriage making way along the thoroughfare to where they stood at the edge of the steps. "I marry her not for money or property, for you and she both swear she has none. I admire her enormously and find her delightful."

He appealed to the crowd, whose female members had just uttered a sigh and were looking rather dreamy eyed. "Beauty is as beauty does, you know. And she does beautifully so far as I am concerned."

Another collective sigh and numerous eager nods of approval. As he meant them to, the women present were eating this up with a spoon.

His carriage now awaited with the door open. Caine turned sideways and stepped into it with his featherlight fiancée still in his arms, her head resting on his chest.

She had revived on the steps. He had felt the tension in her thin body the moment he had faced down Wardfelton, but she continued to feign unconsciousness. He didn't blame her in the least, and it did suit his purpose of keeping crowd sympathy.

"Don't come round yet," he warned her in a whisper as he waited for the footman to close the door. "Your lady friends are sighing at the romance of it all. Add that to their relief that I'm no longer in the market for a bride and we two could become legend."

"Thank you for a moment I shall never forget," she whispered back. "Even should you dump me in the nearest ditch, I would still feel beholden. The look on his face was priceless. I peeked."

He grunted in response as he shifted her more comfortably on his lap. "You are guaranteed more than a moment. Can you survive all this or do you plan to faint on me regularly?"

She shook her head. "No, it was merely the exercise. I've not danced in ages. Or eaten of late. Is there food where we're going?"

Caine relaxed. "I believe we can find something."

The carriage was well away from the crowd now. Grace sat up, moved off his lap and onto the opposite seat. She leaned forward and clasped her hands on her knees. "So we are going to your home now?"

"My uncle's house here in Mayfair, where you'll be properly chaperoned, as I promised."

She nodded. "All right. This is no jest, is it? You truly were not in collusion with him."

"With Wardfelton? You heard our exchange."

With a heartfelt sigh, she leaned back against the seat and closed her eyes. "Thank God."

"I'll send someone round for your things tomorrow," he said. He reached up and started to shift the patch from his eye, then stopped himself.

"Oh, go ahead. The binding must be dreadfully uncomfortable," she said with a flap of one hand. "My father was a doctor and I assisted with patients. I shan't be shocked by an empty socket."

Still he didn't remove the patch. He merely studied her in the carriage light. "You seem a different sort from the lot I've known."

"Truer than you could ever guess," she admitted, then stifled a yawn with her hand.

"Are you ill, Grace?" he asked, then seemed to realize his impertinence. "Sorry. May I call you Grace in private?"

"Address me as you like. I suppose you have a given name?"

"Caine," he replied, looking a trifle uncomfortable.

He had a strong face and very fine skin where it wasn't scarred. His hair was rather too long, but a lovely shade of brown and with a slight wave to it.

She imagined he had been far too handsome for his own good before his injury. In fact, he was even now, though he would never believe it should anyone say as much. "How were you wounded?" she asked.

For a full moment, he remained silent and she thought he would refuse to answer. Then he did. "Artillery fire." He gestured to his face. "A shell exploded nearby and I was struck by fragments. Killed my horse."

"But you survived," she said, fascinated and wishing he would tell more. "That's the important thing."

"So I thought at the time. Wouldn't you like to lie down? I'll make a pillow of my coat." He began to take it off.

"No, don't bother. Is it very far?"

He glanced out the window. "Almost there. How do you feel?"

"Exhausted, if you must know," Grace admitted. "But I shan't need a doctor. A good night's rest should put me right. And food, as I said before. I'm famished."

"Good God! Has he been starving you?" Caine demanded.

She laughed, giddy and a bit light-headed. "No. I've done it to myself."

His worried expression said what tact prevented. He thought *she* was the mad one. And given her present situation, perhaps he was right.

Caine would not second-guess his choice. That was not his way. He made decisions and lived with them. If one proved wrong, he worked it to his advantage as best he could. Never vacillate, never look back on what might have been. And now he had chosen a wife. Granted, this decision had been made more impulsively than most any other in his life, but he would stand by it.

He would stand by *her*. For some uncanny reason, he felt an odd kinship with the little Lady Grace and had from the moment he had first seen her across the ballroom. Odd.

Trent had followed them home and stood in the foyer behind him as he introduced Grace to his uncle's housekeeper, Mrs. Oliver. The older women curtsied even as she frowned at the newcomer. Caine could sense her disapproval, or perhaps it was only concern. The earl might mirror that when he met Grace, since she did not possess the appearance of a healthy breeder. No matter.

"Mrs. Oliver, could you arrange something to feed us?"

"The three of you, milord?"

"Yes, but nothing fancy. A simple tray in the breakfast room will do nicely. And a pot of strong tea for the lady."

"Only brandy for me," Trent supplied. He turned to Grace with a succinct bow. "I am Gavin Trent, friend of this nodcock you're now attached to."

"And his second this evening, so he tells me. Thank you for your assistance with the arrangements," she said with a curtsy.

"My pleasure."

"This way," Caine said, ushering Grace down the corridor.

"A lovely residence," Grace observed, sounding a bit breathless. "Your uncle is…?"

"Earl of Hadley."

She turned to him. "And you are his—?"

"His heir. Yes, you will one day be a countess. I understand your father was an earl, so perhaps you won't mind the station." Caine hoped she wouldn't faint again and took her arm in case she did.

"My goodness!" she exclaimed, her hand clutching her bodice. "Why *me?*"

Caine might not know much of women's minds, but he certainly knew better than to be completely honest in this instance. "You looked positively regal standing there. I was quite smitten."

She laughed out loud, a full-throated, joyful sound he hadn't expected. It was contagious and he laughed with her. Trent shot him a frown and, obviously not amused, went straight for the brandy decanter when the butler appeared with it.

They sat at one end of the breakfast-room table, Grace on his right, Trent to the left. "So, here we are," Trent said on a sigh as he poured a draft into three snifters. "What now?"

"Would you see about getting the license?"

"If you like." Trent gulped a swallow and winced at the burn. "But first I'll need information you haven't given me yet. Where will you marry?"

"Do you have a preference?" he asked Grace.

She gave a shrug and a small shake of her head. "Anywhere."

"The chapel at Wildenhurst," Caine stated. "It's close enough that Uncle can attend comfortably, but not here in town where we might be plagued by hordes of the curious. Have you friends you wish to witness or attend?" he asked her.

Again, that small, disbelieving shake of her head. She knocked back the entire contents of her glass and coughed.

"Easy there. Are you quite all right?"

She nodded uncertainly as if the full impact of the evening's events had suddenly hit her.

"No more plans tonight. You need to eat and then sleep. Tomorrow is soon enough for arrangements," Caine declared. He looked meaningfully at Trent.

Trent set down his glass and stood. "I'll just be off then." He held out a hand to Caine. "Congratulations on your betrothal." He bowed to Grace. "My lady, I wish you every happiness. And with that, a good night to you both."

Grace exhaled audibly. "Thank you."

Caine grinned at Trent's wry expression. "See you in the morning."

When they were alone, Caine sought to soothe Grace's concerns, since she surely must have a few. "Everything will be done for you and you needn't worry about anything."

A kitchen maid arrived with a tray laden with cold meats, bread, sliced oranges and a pot of tea.

"You may leave it," Caine told her. "I will

serve the lady." He proceeded to slather butter on a slice of bread for her.

She hurriedly rolled two slabs of ham and attacked the food without pause. Or anything resembling manners. Caine stopped what he was doing and watched with fascination as she ate. Eyes closed, she moaned softly and chewed rapidly.

After a few moments, she stopped and covered her mouth with her serviette.

"Too much, too fast?" he asked. "Perhaps you should rest a bit first."

"She should and that's a fact," Mrs. Oliver declared. Caine turned to see her standing in the doorway Trent had just vacated. The heavyset retainer marched forward and virtually lifted her charge out of the chair. "You come right along, miss."

He stood quickly to bid Grace good-night, noting that she plucked up the slice of bread he had buttered before being hauled away.

Caine sat down again when they were gone, eye fixed on the remnants of the cold supper without actually seeing it. Why would Grace admittedly starve herself, then gobble down food with such abandon? Had she lied about Wardfelton's treatment? Had the man withheld sustenance? And if so, whyever would he do such a thing?

This would bear some investigation, but there

was no rush. His little Grace would be perfectly safe now and hereafter. He would see to that.

For the first time since the morning of the battle that nearly blinded him, Caine felt a wave of calmness and well-being. He dearly hoped it would last.

The next morning, Caine awakened late, but fully alert and eager, for once, to face the day. He ascribed that to having a meaningful and interesting project other than the tedious business of straightening out his uncle's affairs.

Grace must take second place, of course, immediately after their marriage. Once he had grown accustomed to the new duties he would assume and felt confident he could handle them, he would investigate Grace's situation or have someone do it.

No sooner was he dressed and on his way downstairs than Trent arrived with news. Caine motioned him toward the library.

Trent began speaking before he even took a chair. "The archbishop will provide the special license to wed any place you wish," he announced immediately. "However, Jarvis says that you will still have several weeks' wait."

"I thought we could wed at any time thereafter." Caine made himself comfortable behind the earl's desk and began rearranging the papers he had been working on the day before.

"Well, these days, a special license has become a status affair and everyone wants one. So why not have banns called at the Wildenhurst chapel and do things in the regular way?"

Caine steepled his fingers beneath his chin and thought about it. "I had hoped to have it done sooner, but I suppose there's no great reason for haste."

Trent nodded his agreement. "He also said it might be wise for either you or the lady to repair to the country for the duration in order to establish residence. Though, that could likely be waived, since it was your home before the war."

Caine considered that for a moment. "Very well." Truth was, he didn't mind leaving London, but he would need to convince his uncle to accompany them. "Would you see to retrieving Lady Grace's belongings from Wardfelton's house for me?"

Trent sighed and threw up his hands. "I went by to accomplish that after I asked about the license. Her uncle refuses to part with a thread of hers, or to countenance what he's calling her abduction. He swears he plans to bring charges against you, but I doubt it will come to anything. Too many witnesses heard her accept your offer."

"I suppose the town's abuzz with last night's antics," Caine said.

"If that was your intention, it was wildly suc-

cessful. Still, public approval of your little romance doesn't help clothe the lady, does it?"

"No matter. I'll send for a dressmaker. Grace
will need a trousseau. But absolutely nothing
in *yellow*," he added with a shake of his head.
"Atrocious."

Trent was staring at the doorway and wincing. Caine turned to see Grace standing there,
wearing the awful garment he had just referred
to. "Sorry you heard that, but you must admit…"

She nodded thoughtfully, staring at the floor.
"I am well aware of how I look. No need to
mince words on my account."

Caine wished he could call her beautiful, but
he did not want to begin their relationship with
lies. She was not beautiful. The poor little dear
looked pitiful this morning, even worse than
last evening. Her light brown hair hung from a
middle parting in stick-straight strands, the ends
uneven about her shoulders. Pale as death, her
features seemed far too small for the large blue
eyes. Remarkable eyes. His heart went out to
her in that moment.

"It's the color yellow that I object to, Grace.
And only that," he said with conviction.

Trent cleared his throat, breaking the spell.
"Yes, well, if you two will excuse me, I have errands of my own."

Caine thanked him absently as he left.

"Mr. Trent is a good friend to do so much for

you," Grace said as she ventured farther into the library.

"It's *Lord* Trent, Viscount Trent. His father's Marquis of Alden. And yes, indeed he is my best friend." Trent had been that since they were boys. "We schooled together and served under the same command in the army. I would scarcely know what to do without him," Caine admitted.

She traced her fingers along a row of books before facing him with a sigh. "Would you grant me permission to go to the country alone while the banns are being called?" she asked.

"Not to Wardfelton's estate. Unless you've changed your mind about the marriage."

"Heavens no on both accounts," she answered with a little huff of laughter. "I will go anywhere you say *except* there, but I would like some time to myself before the wedding if you wouldn't mind."

"If you would be willing to take a companion and the dressmaker I mentioned, you could go on to Wildenhurst. It's one of Hadley's minor properties, but well appointed. And I could remain here. I understand that my company is probably—"

"Oh, no!" She frowned and shook her head vehemently. "No, I swear, it isn't anything to do with you at all!" For a moment, she looked at him with a plea evident in her expression. "You promised me freedom. I would like a taste of it."

Yes, he had promised. He nodded.

"There you are!" Mrs. Oliver came marching in, hands on her hips. "You come with me now, miss. You've not had your chocolate and toast yet and aren't even dressed proper for the morning, showing shoulders and such. Excuse us, sir, and go on with your business. I shall see to the little miss."

In spite of himself, Caine liked the old lady, overbearing attitude and all. Everyone in the household, regardless of rank, obeyed her. Even Jenkins, the earl's snobbish butler, didn't dare oppose her. How she had gained so much power, he couldn't guess, but she was one to reckon with. Still, he felt an urge to defend Grace. "Little Miss has a name, Mrs. Oliver."

"Well, she's Little Miss to me until she's a married lady. Got to look after young misses, we all do, till they grow up and marry."

Caine could see Grace hiding a smile behind her fingertips. So she understood and didn't mind the heavy-handed martinet. Perhaps she would enjoy being fussed over and looked after. "Go with Mrs. Oliver then and have a good day. My aunt and uncle will want to meet you, but I think we should wait until tomorrow for that."

"She'll be ready," Mrs. Oliver assured him. "Now, come along, luvvy, so I can put you to rights. A good feed and a hot bath should do the trick."

"Could I have eggs?" he heard Grace ask her as they left.

"And black pudding. Good for strength and such," Mrs. Oliver declared.

Caine smiled at Grace's groan. A fair beginning. They had two dislikes in common. Black pudding and Wardfelton. He toyed with his pen as his gaze lingered on the doorway. He wondered idly whether they shared any likes. And then, why such a question should occur to him at all.

Chapter Four

Caine promptly went to work, but found he could not concentrate. Impatiently, he pushed aside the account books for his uncle's largest estate. The figures were not in good order, but today there were more pressing matters.

There were inquiries to answer, orders for supplies and letters of instruction to be prepared for signature. He arranged the paper, dipped a pen in the inkwell and began to write.

In all his life, he had never thought to do anything but soldier. He liked the structure of army life in general, but had hated the chaos of battle and the incompetence of leadership. If not for his wounding and the earl's illness, he would have continued trying to rise in rank until he could displace some of that inefficiency. But now here he was, facing the ever-increasing responsibilities of an earldom. So many people were dependent upon his ability to manage well. And soon, so would a wife.

Thankfully, Grace shouldn't pose a problem or even much of an added responsibility. She would remain practically invisible, by her own choice, he expected.

She was easily led and apparently preferred solitude. An excellent match indeed with which to satisfy his uncle's demand and Caine's own need for time and space to acclimate to the nobility. Yes, he had his personal affairs arranged precisely as they should be. Well, almost. There were matters there that needed his attention before he could relax.

That afternoon, he put aside the earl's business for his own. A meeting with Grace's uncle was necessary and might as well be accomplished as soon as possible to get the unpleasant errand out of the way. He changed his coat, ran a comb through his hair, adjusted his eye patch and set off on foot for Wardfelton's town house.

The man was not at home, but the maid who answered the door did advise Caine where the earl might be found at that hour.

Caine had avoided the clubs since returning from the war. Before that, he and Trent had frequented White's on occasion. His leanings were

Whig, as were his uncle's. Apparently, Wardfelton preferred Brooke's, overwhelmingly Tory.

Things had worked out well, after all, he thought as he strode down St. James road. A public place would be better than a private meeting.

Caine used his uncle's cachet and feigned interest in joining in order to gain entrance. He strolled room to room. Attendance proved low in midafternoon, most of the cardplayers and drinkers still at home, readying for the next night's revels, he supposed. He found Wardfelton upstairs, sitting alone in one of the assembly rooms and reading a newspaper.

Grace's uncle certainly looked the part of an earl, though he, like Caine, had not been born to it. He was a third son. The elder brother had died accidentally, thrusting the title on Grace's father. Then the country doctor, cum lord, had perished of cholera two years later, leaving Wardfelton to inherit.

Caine assessed the man who had not yet noticed him. The suit appeared to be Saville Row, tailored to perfection, the linen snow-white. His black hair, stiffly pomaded, showed no gray. The waxed mustache curled upward in direct opposition to his thin, pale lips. His hands were smooth, long-fingered and as delicate as a woman's. Nothing else about him looked effete, considering that he was nearly the size of Caine.

Wardfelton looked up suddenly, glared at Caine and folded the paper into a neat rectangle. He did not speak and he did not stand. The gaze of steel held fast as his lips tightened to a straight line.

Caine pasted on a smile in an offer of civility. This was Grace's uncle, her only family. And though she obviously had no love for the man, nor he for her, it would serve no purpose to irritate him further.

"Good afternoon, milord," Caine said as he approached the table and executed a congenial nod in lieu of the bow convention demanded.

"You have no business in this club. Or with me," Wardfelton said, his tone flat. He slapped the paper on the leather tabletop.

"Surely I do, sir. We should discuss the contract. The marriage is in three weeks."

"There is nothing to discuss," Wardfelton snapped, looking past Caine, a deliberate cut. "I made it clear that my niece is destitute, without property or funds."

"I thought you might want *her* interest served, since I am *not* destitute. We should decide her portion, agree to provisions should I drop dead before I inherit."

Wardfelton sighed, rolling his eyes. "Very well. Sit down, Morleigh. I see I shall have to speak with you about her, but it's nothing that you'll enjoy hearing."

"Nothing that will dissuade me, either." Caine pulled out a chair and sat, certain that the man had suddenly decided to stifle his anger over Caine's appropriation of his niece and be reasonable. "Understand that we must amend today's contract after I inherit, for there will be more to settle on her then."

"I doubt either will be needed once I've had my say. What has Grace told you?"

"Very little," Caine said truthfully, unwilling to share how much he had divined from the bits she had revealed. "But I have heard that her parents died, as did her betrothed. She served as her fiancé's mother's companion, then came to live with you almost two years ago. Have you something to add?"

Wardfelton nodded and sighed again. He pressed his fingers to his brow. "I'm afraid I do. I had hoped not to have to reveal this. The grief affected her mind, Morleigh. I regret to tell you that Grace is quite mad. She conceals it at times, but she is rarely stable for long."

Caine froze, locked in denial. Of course it could not be true. Still, a shadow of doubt began to flirt, tempting certainty to desert him. Grace's response to him had been unexpected, definitely out of the ordinary for a young unmarried woman. There was that sudden faint. And she had expressed unusual candor on such short acquaintance with him. Then there was the fact that she had admittedly starved herself, no reason given.

She certainly seemed lucid enough, however, and he had witnessed no hysterics or incomprehensible tirades. How did this supposed madness present itself?

"I cannot blame you for what happened," Wardfelton declared. "Grace can be quite persuasive when she chooses and I do not doubt she fabricated some tale of woe to stir your sympathy. Some imagined plight to do with me. You see, I've had to keep her confined for her own safety, no choice about the matter. I thought it better than sending her to strangers in some institution."

Caine listened well enough, but observed even more carefully. His army command and dealing with all sorts of men had taught him that. Tongues could easily lie, but the body often spoke the truth. Wardfelton's eyes met his only briefly now and again, as if gauging whether Caine trusted what he was saying. The man often shook his head as if he couldn't believe himself.

"Yet you took her to a public ball where you knew she might embarrass you before the ton?" Caine asked.

"And so she did," Wardfelton said with a huff. "But I had to do it. Rumors were gathering. Some thought I had done away with her. As if I would harm my own flesh and blood! They have no idea how difficult it has been to care for her at home rather than relegate that duty."

"That must have been a difficult decision. Did you even consider it, putting her somewhere?" Caine asked, projecting sympathy he did not feel. Wardfelton struck the wrong notes in this song of woe. It simply did not ring true.

The earl pressed his fingers to his forehead, hand concealing his eyes, and groaned softly. "I am ashamed to admit that I did inquire. Not Bedlam, of course, but a licensed house in Houghbarton that provides such care. You see, Grace has wandered away twice and had to be brought home, kicking and screaming."

"But you decided against sending her? Why?"

"Even though our own king is so afflicted, poor devil, I dreaded the scandal to my own house," Wardfelton confided, his voice deep and sorrowful. "Madness in the family, you see... You understand my conundrum, surely."

"Indeed. An unfortunate situation for anyone to imagine," Caine remarked with a nod. He drummed his fingers on the tabletop, letting the silence gather, wondering what the man would say next to fill the void.

Once again and once too often for his act, Wardfelton heaved a sigh of regret. "So you must bring her back to me, Morleigh, or let me fetch her. No one has to know why the betrothal was dissolved. We can put it about that Grace herself had second thoughts."

Aha. The crux of the matter. Caine stood, now impatient to be away. "No, sir, that won't do. I said I would marry her. Once my word is given, I hold to it. Grace and I will wed, come what may."

The earl stumbled to his feet, almost upsetting his chair. "No! I insist… Wait. I implore you, Morleigh. Think, man. You'll be disgraced!"

"Better I than you, eh? You should be relieved. If Grace's madness is ever discovered, everyone will believe I am the cause. They shall have Miss Thoren-Snipes to verify once again that Morleigh's become a monster." Caine smiled. "I gave *her* nightmares!"

He looked directly into Wardfelton's eyes and read fear. Caine wondered at that. "Good day to you, sir. You may have your solicitor call on me regarding a contract and your niece's future."

Caine left him standing there, obviously dismayed.

On reaching the street outside, worry began to gnaw at Caine like a ravenous rat. Could there be a grain of truth in what her uncle said? Had Wardfelton's fear been for Grace, or for the earl himself, should his treatment of her be revealed?

The path to truth lay with Grace and her behavior. Caine hurried back to Hadley House to observe that, praying all the while that Wardfelton was simply a mean-spirited man trying to gloss over his abuse of a helpless relative.

Good lord, he should have listened to Trent. What had he gotten himself into with this hasty arrangement? But, as he had stated to Wardfelton, his word was his bond. His decision had been made. Grace was his now, for better or worse, whether that wedding vow had been repeated or not.

Caine felt apprehensive about talking to Grace, though he certainly needed to after his meeting with Wardfelton. The man must be lying, but his words had required careful reflection, in case Caine's reasoning about this was faulty.

He spent hours after returning home reviewing the visit with Grace's uncle. His preoccupation was so intense, he barely tasted the meal Mrs. Oliver brought him on his tray. He ate absently as he considered every word, every move, every sigh Wardfelton produced.

Caine denied himself that last element of consideration, the woman herself, until he had examined the rest in detail. That accomplished, he would now have to judge her for himself in light of her uncle's declaration. He was resolved that, mad or sane, he would never return her to Wardfelton, but Caine felt he should know her state of mind one way or the other.

Grace had been left to her own devices all day. How must she feel in strange surroundings among people she hardly knew? He wanted to give her no reason to reconsider their betrothal, least of all because of his neglect of her when she was most vulnerable.

The visit with Grace could prove awkward. Now that the matter of their marriage was settled, what would they discuss? Most of their conversation thus far consisted of fielding insults, arguing away her mistrust and convincing her that he meant business.

His trepidation annoyed him. She was only a little bird of a girl after all, hardly anything to dread. If grief had stolen her reason, then he would restore it if he could, keep her comfortably if he could not. He would see that she was as happy as he could make her and as free as possible. She would know that she was cared for.

Caine postponed calling for her. The evening would be soon enough, he figured. He resumed working, poring over numbers in the earl's accounts.

Late that afternoon, the butler interrupted the never-ending effort. "A Mr. Tinroy to see you, sir. He insists it is urgent."

"Show him in," Caine said, shuffling the paperwork into a neat stack and setting it aside, welcoming the intrusion, whatever it was. The visitor's name was unfamiliar. Perhaps it was Wardfelton's man.

"Thank you for seeing me, sir," the spindly little fellow said after Jenkins had introduced him. Hat in hand, he stood before the huge oak desk like an errant schoolboy called up for an offense.

"What is this urgent business, Mr. Tinroy?" Caine demanded, the former commander in him responding naturally to the man's subservient attitude.

"It concerns your betrothal," the man said with a timid smile. "I should say, the original one made with Miss Thoren-Snipes."

"Ah, a thing of the past then. What of it?" Caine replied, clasping his hands atop the desk and leaning forward.

"The thing is, she never officially ended it, sir. Her brother has retained me to speak on her behalf and tell you that, as a gentleman, you are obliged to carry through. He mentioned a breach-of-promise-suit if you prove unwilling."

"So she would sue?" Caine almost groaned at the irony. "How can one be a *gentleman,* Mr. Tinroy, when he has been quite publicly declared a beast? Please inform your client that unless she wishes a countersuit for defamation of character, the matter is best considered closed."

"Oh, sir, she meant no harm by her words. You know how young ladies natter on to one another when they are upset. But *never* did she cry off the engagement!"

No, she had *screamed* it off as far as Caine was concerned. He sighed, unclasped his hands and stood. "No contract was ever signed, because her brother originally opposed it. Of course, I was not heir to the title at that time. Perhaps that has inspired his sudden inclination to find me an acceptable match?"

Tinroy rolled his hat brim and tried a smile. "Oh, no, sir, not at all! It's merely that the young lady has realized her foolishness and had a change of heart!"

"So have *I*," Caine declared, rounding the desk and towering over the little toad. "Good day to you, Mr. Tinroy."

He watched the solicitor back out at a near run. Caine felt like dusting his hands and hoped he never heard the name Thoren-Snipes again in his lifetime. Greedy buggers, the lot of them.

After a day fraught with confrontation, he knew he had one more to face before he could rest. Grace. Only, this meeting, of course, was to be more in the nature of an evaluation to see whether Wardfelton's accusation held any semblance of truth.

He flagged a maid in the hallway and sent her up with a summons for Grace. They might as well meet here in the library. If she were a reader, they could discuss books. There, that was settled. He waited.

Grace appeared within five minutes, almost breathless as she entered the room. Had she taken the stairs at a run? Her hair was pulled back into a rather untidy bun at the nape of her neck and several strands had come undone. She raked them back with an impatient hand. "You wished to see me?" she asked with a nervous laugh.

"Yes, of course. Good evening, Grace," he replied as he stood and surveyed the change in her. It was not so remarkable. She wore a plain gray long-sleeved dress, not a good color for her, but better than the yellow. It was a bit short and so large it hung rather loosely at the waist. He figured she must have borrowed it from one of the maids. In fact, she looked like a young maid on her first day of work, sans apron and reporting late.

He could not help comparing her looks to the stunning, yet shallow, beauty of Belinda. Somehow, even in her plainness and disarray, Grace did not seem wanting. Surface attraction held little appeal for him, especially now. Grace's smile was sincere and she seemed honestly happy to see him. Lord, maybe that alone made her unhinged.

He smiled. "How was your day, my dear?"

She cocked her head and studied him for a

minute, then seemed to form a conclusion. "Interesting, indeed. How was yours, Captain?"

Caine sensed she was really interested instead of just being polite. "Honestly? I have had better." He indicated she should take one of the large wingback chairs beside the fire. He sat across from her in the other as he elaborated. "Business matters consumed me, being new to the chore of managing properties. I must have been born to soldier. That was never so difficult for me."

"Ah, but you love a challenge," she guessed with a sly grin that lighted her slender features.

"That's true enough," he agreed, noting that she had a foxlike manner, watchful, knowing, quick to respond. "Do you?"

She inclined her head and nodded once. "I suppose I do, come to think of it. We certainly took on this one without much hesitation, so it seems we have something in common from the start."

"Apparently."

The silence drew out between them. Caine wondered if there were any more to say. He had to think of something. "You seem quite… rested." Truth was always appropriate. Her eyes were brighter, such a true, clear blue. Like a cloudless sky at its best. "I take it that you slept well?"

She sat back in the chair, perfectly relaxed,

though her feet, clad in her soft yellow dancing slippers, didn't quite touch the floor. She swung them idly as he watched. "Oh, yes, and I haven't slept much of late, so that was a great relief. And the food here is remarkable!"

Ah, there was that prodigious interest in food again. "I shall commend the cook," he promised. "Have you already eaten this evening?"

"An hour ago. You were busy and Mrs. Oliver said I shouldn't wait for you. I understand your aunt takes a tray in the carl's chambers early in the evening to keep him company."

"Yes. We seldom dine together at table these days." Caine felt guilty that she'd had to eat alone. He should have joined her. But she must grow used to his being absent, since he would have little time to entertain her in future.

He grew impatient to end the exchange that was beginning to seem forced. And yet, he needed to evaluate her condition. Nor did he want her to feel dismissed. Or lonely. She had probably had far too much time alone in Wardfelton's care.

"I look forward to traveling to the country," she declared with another bright smile. "It has been a while since I have been anywhere at all if one doesn't count the trip from the manor to the house here in Town." She leaned forward, her expression animated. "Do tell me about your estate, the one where we are to go."

"Wildenhurst is not mine yet, though it is where I was born." Immensely relieved to have a topic he could expand upon, Caine let himself meander back to childhood. "It's the lesser of two properties owned by Hadley, the grander one being Hadley Grange, his seat near the Eastern Coast."

"A grand mansion, or perhaps a castle?" Grace asked.

He answered absently, "A country house, quite impressive and easily thrice the size of Wildenhurst."

"But what is Wildenhurst like? Has it a great history?"

"Well, I suppose it has that. The property was purchased by my great grandfather who had the house built directly over the site of an old monastery destroyed by King Henry. The stones lining the underground floor are still there. The rest is relatively new."

"You have a dungeon!" she exclaimed. "I love old things and places!"

Caine hated to dash her streak of romanticism. "Not a dungeon at all. It consisted of monk's cells originally, and with the new structure over it, it became a rabbit warren of storage rooms and a marvelous place for a boy and his imagination."

"Even better!" She listened avidly and Caine saw yearning for a real home in her faraway look. The place where she had played, laughed and loved now belonged to someone else. Perhaps one day she could think of Wildenhurst as hers.

He continued, "I think of it as home. My father managed it for the earl until his death. As I said, it's where I first saw light of day, where I lived until I went away to school and then where I took holidays. There are the greenest of hills to ride, a river at the back, trees in abundance and wildlife to watch. Gardens with flowers of every sort you can imagine."

"I *adore* flowers," she said, clasping her hands beneath her chin. "And herbs are a must. Is there an herb garden? Say there is or I shall make one for you."

Caine searched his memory. "I believe so. Yes, I'm sure of it." He went on. "The house itself is rather modest, comfortable and not too elegant, but with plenty of rooms. When I retreat to a place of peace in my mind, that is where I go."

"Oh, I know I shall love it!" she exclaimed. "Your description makes it sound heavenly. Why would anyone ever leave it to come to Town?"

He laughed, quite liking her exuberance and her optimism. Caine could use a dose of both, and hers were infectious. "Well, there is the season, of course. And meetings in the House of Lords, though I've yet to experience that and hope I shan't in the near future. Uncle could not attend this year, but remains in town now to be near his physician."

"I see. Well, I do hope you may spend some days in the country to restore your sense of peace after your time at war. It would probably do you a world of good," she said with a succinct nod.

He thought so, too, but did not see it as possible the way things were now. However, he agreed with her anyway. "I expect it would. You know you may take complete charge there if you like. My aunt has declared she will do no more with it. I think she always felt somewhat isolated in the country. For all intents and purposes, other than formally deeding it over, my uncle has consigned the place to me."

"On condition that you marry," she guessed with a wry purse of lips.

Caine nodded again. "With that stipulation, yes." He looked at her. "Grace, I sincerely hope you will be content. And I thank you for accepting my offer. This cannot be easy for you and I do appreciate that."

She laughed, a merry sound and not at all bitter. "I did admit I welcome a challenge. Here's proof of it. I hope you will be happy, too. There. We have set our goals—contentment and happiness, each for the other. So be it. Now, if you would excuse me, I believe I shall visit the kitchens, nick some milk and biscuits and retire. I understand tomorrow is to be a busy day."

Caine stood when she did and reached for her hands. "Good night, Grace. Sleep well."

"Thank you. I'm very grateful," she said with all seriousness. "I never thought to have such good fortune again in my life." She gave his hands a fond squeeze and let go.

Caine watched her leave, wondering how he could have dreaded her company. No one could be less intimidating than Grace. Or less mad. Wardfelton was a bounder and ought to be hanged.

Chapter Five

Mrs. Oliver had managed to find her another more appropriate gown to wear, though gray seemed to be the signature color for the help hereabouts. For a price, one of Lady Hadley's maids had parted with her Sunday best, a plain gray broadcloth with long fitted sleeves, a simple black pelisse and a close-fitting bonnet to match.

Grace met Morleigh at the earl's chamber door, where she had been escorted by Mrs. Oliver. He knocked gently as he spoke to Grace. "Don't be afraid," he said, smiling. "I think he's too weak to bite."

She mustered a smile of her own as he ushered her into the room. "Uncle Hadley, Aunt Hadley," he said in a formal tone, "May I present Lady Grace Renfair, my fiancée. Grace, Lord and Lady Hadley."

"Come closer, gel," the earl demanded just as Grace was in the midst of a deep curtsy. He beckoned clumsily, so she approached his bedside.

His lordship was a white-haired, florid-cheeked old fellow who had trouble breathing. He had a heart problem resulting in dropsy, Grace determined from the swelling in his arms and hands. That looked different from ordinary corpulence. His condition could probably be improved by a small concoction of foxglove. She had seen a number of gents in his fix when she had assisted her father in his practice.

It would be rude to suggest a dose of anything, however, since he had a physician in attendance who would surely take offense. The physician was frowning at her from his position in the corner of the room. Perhaps he wasn't reading her mind, but only judging her state of health at the moment.

Caine must have noticed the interaction. "Pardon me. Lady Grace, Dr. Ackers, his lordship's physician."

The man bowed. "My lady."

Grace nodded. "A pleasure to meet you, sir. My father shared your profession when we lived in Norfolk."

"Renfair? Oh, my, yes!" The man's eyebrows rose and his face livened with recognition. "I believe I knew him. *James* Renfair? He studied in Edinburgh?"

"Yes, he did!" Grace said, pleased to meet someone who had known her father.

The earl noisily cleared his throat, obviously to direct her attention back to himself. Grace immediately attended to her audience with the family, smiling her apology for the interruption to his lordship.

She did, however, decide on the instant that she would correspond with Dr. Ackers with regard to his knowing her father. And perhaps when they were better acquainted, see whether he would be willing to entertain Dr. Withering of Birmingham's research papers on treatments of the heart. Her father had found them invaluable.

Her mother had objected to Grace helping her father at first, but Grace had explained how foolish it would be to forego the opportunity to learn as much as she could about healing and tending the sick if she was to run her own household one day. She wondered if she would have the opportunity to treat anyone where she was going or if they would simply think of her as a useless lady.

"How is it you met the boy?" the earl demanded, huffing as he peered up at her from beneath hooded and wrinkled lids.

"At Lord Cavanaugh's ball, sir. He charmed

me instantly." Grace glanced nervously at the countess, who stood on the opposite side of the earl's bed, studying her carefully.

The countess looked pleasant enough, not much younger than her husband, at least a stone too heavy but blooming with health. Her hair and eyes were both as dark as a Spaniard's, though her complexion was very fair. Her mouth formed a little bow faintly lined with wrinkles. She wore a flattering green silk taffeta trimmed in black that was the height of fashion. Quite a beauty in her youth, Grace imagined.

"You are Wardfelton's child?" she asked Grace.

"His niece, ma'am, though my father held that title before he passed on."

The carl transferred his attention to his wife, reached for her hand and spoke in a near whisper, "Caine told us of her lineage, remember, my dear?"

"Yes, of course. Where are you staying?" the countess asked.

Grace glanced at Morleigh, wondering what to say. Did the countess not know what had transpired at the Cavanaugh's and that he had invited her here? Grace thought the events of that evening must be all over London by today.

"She is here with us of late, Aunt," he said. "However today, she's going on to Wildenhurst, where we will have the wedding in three weeks."

"The season must be over," the countess said, her free hand fiddling with her ear bob as she stared across the room at nothing.

"Almost over, Aunt. Soon we'll all be breathing the country air," Morleigh said, sliding an arm around Grace as if to protect her. "We should leave now."

"I haven't dismissed you, boy!" the earl exclaimed, shaking a finger in their direction. "What provisions did you make her? What of her dowry and such? Agreeable terms?"

"We are satisfied with the arrangements, Uncle. I'm handling the business matters until your health is restored, so you needn't worry. Everything's well in hand."

"The estates?" the earl asked.

"Thriving, sir. Bills paid, rents collected. Everything is as it should be."

The earl closed his eyes. "Or will be when you're wed. She'll do, then. Got to have a wife to be settled. A helpmate. Eh, m'dear?"

The countess nodded. Her smile was for the earl. They were still holding hands. Grace felt tears threaten at the sweetness of it all. She thought of all the years these two had been together and the bond they obviously had formed.

Morleigh quietly guided her out of the room and closed the door.

"He never dismissed you!" she whispered. "Will he be angry that we left?"

Morleigh patted her back where his hand rested. "No. He only likes to remind me now and then that he's still in command."

Grace liked the kind way Morleigh handled the delicate situation with his uncle. Here he was doing all the work of the earl and yet allowing the old gentleman to preserve his dignity.

The earl and countess had not seemed to notice that Morleigh's future bride looked like a mouse. At least they had not remarked on it. Grace was just happy not to have appeared before them as a molting duck in her old, jaundiced, limp, ruffled frock.

Grace was glad, too, that the audience with Caine's family had been a short one, so as not to tire his uncle.

She and Caine headed downstairs, since she was to leave immediately for the country. Caine had informed her it was a distance of only eighteen miles to Wildenhurst.

When they were halfway down the stairs, she saw that Lord Trent had arrived and stood speaking to the butler at the open door. He must be a constant fixture in Captain Morleigh's life. Mrs. Oliver had told her Trent was a born adventurer and a dear friend to Morleigh.

Trent was handsome, a real head-turner, though Grace had scarcely noticed that until now. He was nearly as large as Morleigh, though his features were slightly more refined. He was of fairer complexion and his chestnut-colored hair had a reddish glint. She quite liked his looks, but not the way he assessed her, as if he worried she might harbor some ill intention toward his friend.

She had been told he would bring Madame Latrice, the dressmaker, and a trunk full of fabric lengths for the trousseau.

"Your seamstress and Mrs. Oliver are probably waiting to board the coach," Caine commented to her as he saw Trent.

"Everything is happening so quickly," Grace said as they continued to descend.

He had hold of her elbow, a firm but gentle grip. "I know, but in a few hours you'll be settled and have plenty of time to rest and absorb it all." He patted her arm with his free hand. "I promise you'll have nothing to worry your little head about but the cut of your gowns and whether tea is on time."

Grace decided not to push him down the stairs. He was only a man and they were all taught that women needed coddling. She sighed. "I suppose it's not your fault, really."

"What isn't?" he asked, and she realized she had spoken her thought aloud. Oh, dear!

How could she be so ungrateful? Just because she was feeling renewed strength and boundless energy after deep sleep and a few decent meals was no reason to turn uppity. Captain Morleigh had her best interests at heart and he truly could not deny his ingrained, overprotective nature. She should be kissing his feet!

"Uh, it's no fault of yours that my shawl was left behind last evening. Is there a blanket in the coach?" And it was not even cool outside this time of year. How ridiculous did she sound?

"Not to worry. I have your shawl. Trent fetched it, so you'll be warm enough." He looked so proud, as if he had already procured for her all he promised her last evening.

She stopped, halting their progress for a moment. "About what you said as we danced…and all those things I asked you for?"

"You will have them, Grace. I always keep my promises."

"No! What I mean to say is that I was merely playing to what I believed was a jest." She lifted her hand in question. "Now, what would I do with a phaeton and team? And as for diamonds…" She scoffed.

He was smiling at her so fondly. "Then perhaps for the nonce, you'll accept a purse with pin money. It is a wife's due." He pulled a small velvet pouch from his pocket and placed it in her hand, folding his around hers.

"I'm not yet a wife," she reminded him, stunned that he had prepared this just for her. What a thoughtful man he was.

He laughed softly. "So practical. I'll deduct

this from your first quarterly allowance then if you'll take it now."

She shrugged. "Very well, if you insist. But I must ask what you want from me, aside from the faithfulness you require and an heir, of course."

"I never mentioned an heir," he said, sounding a bit surprised. And confused.

Grace rolled her eyes. "Well, that's a given, isn't it? If you're to be the earl, everyone *knows* you'll need at least one. Isn't that the whole purpose of marrying?"

His gaze dropped to the stairs as he seemed to consider it. Perhaps he dreaded the very thought of doing what it took to get the heir.

Then, without responding to her question, he took her arm again. "You should be on your way so as to arrive before dark. There'll be plenty of time to address details later."

Details? An heir was but a detail? "Yes, of course," she muttered, doubt setting in that she had made a wise choice after all. He had declared his need for a wife and was taking her without a penny to her name. Her looks certainly had not captured his heart.

So why had he married her if not to continue his line? A condition of the will, she supposed. Mrs. Oliver had hinted at something of the sort and he had all but confirmed it when they'd spoken of the ownership of Wildenhurst. But surely that was not reason enough to bind himself to a wife he had no intention of bedding.

She looked up at him, then allowed her searching gaze to travel the length of his body, wondering if perhaps he was incapable of relations due to some unseen injury. Was that why he had chosen her, a woman who would be too grateful to insist on her rights as a wife once the marriage was a done thing? No, she could not imagine him capable of such deceit. She would put that right out of her mind and forget it.

Madame Latrice and Mrs. Oliver had already seated themselves inside the coach when Caine handed her in.

"Goodbye for now, Grace," he said. "Take care you don't tax yourself these next few weeks and send word if you need anything."

Grace nodded and added a simpering smile for good measure. If he wanted a milk-and-water miss who didn't know bedding from biding, she supposed she could pretend. At least for a while.

What a pity that was all he desired, since she had spent the entirety of yesterday and last night looking forward to her marriage to him and imagining, even dreaming about, what it might entail.

Now that she had escaped Wardfelton's threat, she would be back to her old self in no time. However, Morleigh had arrived in her life as the answer to her fervent prayers and she would try to be precisely what he wanted whenever he was around.

She could not help but like his straightforwardness and felt quite attracted to him as a man, but he was obviously not interested in her as a woman, despite his playacting last evening. Perfectly understandable.

He had baldly stated that he needed a wife, but apparently wanted one in name only, probably one who would not bother him with her presence. Grace smiled inwardly, imagining herself as the invisible countess. What a role to play, but she certainly preferred it to playing Wardfelton's clueless prisoner.

The question she had to ask was whether she could keep up the act in future just to accommodate Morleigh. She was grateful to him, of course, but gratitude wasn't everything, was it?

She had always wanted to have a child, and if she were completely honest with herself, she wanted the man even more. However, she was not yet ready to explore too deeply the reasons for her odd reaction to him. Perhaps it was merely because he presented a challenge.

The coach rumbled over the cobblestone streets as Grace studied her companions. Mrs. Oliver appeared a comfortable grandmotherly type, short and rather rotund, dressed in her sturdy black wool. The ruffles of the mobcap beneath her plain bonnet framed graying hair, bright green eyes and sweetly rounded features. But though surely nearing fifty, the retainer possessed the strength of a man and the iron will of a mule. Nothing intimidated the woman. Grace quite admired her for it.

As for Madame Latrice, that one obviously felt her importance and dressed it splendidly. Grace judged her to be close to thirty, very self-sufficient and more than a trifle haughty. She wore a lovely traveling costume of forest green made of fine bombazine that rustled with every move she made. Her black bonnet sported dyed green ostrich feathers and a fringe of jet beads that dangled off the brim. Stylish to a fault. However, the prune-faced expression spoiled the effect.

Grace attempted conversation, but the woman seemed loathe to discuss anything, even her plans for Grace's new wardrobe. Mrs. Oliver merely raised one eyebrow and gave Grace a conspiratorial look.

The well-sprung coach afforded such comfort and traveled so slowly, Grace found herself nodding off now and again. It was twilight and they had come quite a ways when the coach rolled to a stop in the middle of the road. The horses neighed and she heard a man's shout. Then a shot rang out.

Madame screamed.

The coach door flew open and a man stood

there, holding a double-barreled flintlock pistol. "Get out, all of you!" he shouted. "Now, and look lively!"

Madame exited first, then Mrs. Oliver and Grace followed. She glanced around to see whether the man acted alone. No one else was in sight. She looked up and saw John Coachman slumped sideways on the box, reins still clutched in his fist.

"Which of you is Morleigh's woman?" the highwayman demanded.

"She is!" Madame cried, pointing a shaking, leather-gloved finger at Grace. "It's her! She's the one!"

The highwayman grinned at Madame, showing several missing teeth. He scanned Grace's length and shook his head slowly. "Don't think so. Easy t'see who's the fancy piece here. Beggin' yer pardon, ma'am," he said, sounding coy.

Then he shot Madame point-blank in the chest. She crumpled slowly to the ground as Grace and Mrs. Oliver watched, stunned. The gunman kept grinning as he reached into his pocket.

Grace knew at that moment he would not let them live. He was going to stand there, bold as you please, reload and shoot them both! She had to do something.

He wasn't terribly big, but she couldn't overcome him on her own and had no idea whether Mrs. Oliver would help her or faint dead away. But if he managed to reload, they had no chance at all!

Grace knew she must use the dirty trick Father had told her about, the last-ditch effort to save herself that he had declared every woman should know. Could she do it? What if she missed? There would be no second chance.

"Sir?" Grace said softly. "Look." She slowly began to raise the front of her skirt and petticoats to get them out of her way. She bared ankles, knees and even higher to entice him.

He looked, all right, and slowly began to walk toward her. She pasted on an inviting smile and waited for just the right moment. When he was near enough, she kicked for all she was worth, thanking God for the borrowed ankle boots she wore. He dropped the still-empty pistol, grabbed his essentials and buckled forward with a harsh cry of pain.

Mrs. Oliver snatched up the pistol and hit the back of his head with the butt of it. He fell like a tree, right at Grace's feet. Mrs. Oliver hit him again, several times, then stood away. "Think he's done for?" she gasped, breathless with exertion.

"Not yet. Give me the gun," Grace ordered. She knelt and fished in the man's pocket for the small powder flask and bag of caps and shot she figured he had been reaching for earlier. She hoped she recalled the correct method of loading. It had been years since she had done it and her hands were shaking now, but she finally managed.

"Take this and point it at him in case he wakes," she ordered the housekeeper. "If he moves, pull the trigger. And do *not* miss."

She hurried over to Madame to feel her neck for a pulse, but knew the woman was dead even before she touched her. Grace shook her head at Mrs. Oliver's silent question, then returned to check the highwayman again. His breathing had stopped and a puddle of blood surrounded his head. "He's dead," Grace said.

She lost no time climbing the wheel and mounting the driver's box to see about the coachman. "He's alive and coming to," she called down. Then of the driver, she asked, "How far are we from our destination?"

"Five miles or so," he rasped.

"You have a wound in your neck, John. Hold this end of your neckcloth over it tightly so it will stop bleeding. I don't believe it's serious, but I shall drive."

"You, my lady?"

"Of course. We can't have you bleeding to death."

"What of…them?" he asked, pointing down at the ground.

"I'll be back up in a moment, just lean back, sit still and keep pressing steadily on that cloth. You should be fine."

She scrambled down, catching and tearing her skirt in the process. "Mrs. Oliver, you and I will have to load the bodies into the coach. I'm afraid you must ride inside with them, but we only have a few miles to go."

"Can't we leave *him* here for the carrion eaters?"

Grace shook her head. "No, I think it best if we return him to London along with Madame Latrice. Perhaps he can be identified. Someone must have hired him to do this, Mrs. Oliver. Someone who knows Captain Morleigh."

"Aye, Lady Grace. Somebody paid him to kill *you!*"

Chapter Six

Grace still shook inside as a footman assisted
her down off the coach box. The Italianate fa-
cade of Wildenhurst manor looked impressive,
much like the home she had lived in before her
parents' demise. The house didn't intimidate her
and neither did the rolling meadows and beautifully landscaped grounds. What did strike fear
in her heart was the sudden assumption of responsibility for all of it. Morleigh had said she
might take charge, and Grace knew she must do
so at the outset.

None here would outrank her. Therefore, all
would look to her for a solution to this particular
problem, as well as for the ordering of the estate
in the earl's or Morleigh's absence.

She straightened her skirts, took a deep breath
and firmed her resolve. Prepared or otherwise,

she must assert herself. This was to be her home for the nonce, perhaps for good and all. "Might as well begin as I mean to go," she muttered under her breath. Then aloud, she asked the footman, "What is your name, young man?"

"Harry Trusdale, ma'am." He eyed her curiously, but did not presume to ask who she was.

"I am Grace Renfair, Captain Morleigh's intended. We were assaulted on the road and the coachman is wounded. Help him down and take him inside, then summon the earl's steward to me immediately."

Mrs. Oliver joined her, still eyeing the coach. "What shall we do about the uh—"

"Leave them as they are for the return trip." She turned to the two grooms who were holding the team. "You there, unhitch the horses here and have another pair brought 'round. We shall need a driver and another man to accompany him back to town. See to that, then await my written message, which you will deliver to Captain Morleigh at his lordship's house in Town."

She marched up to the front door that stood ajar. An elderly woman stood there, watching, mouth agape.

"Are you housekeeper here, madam?" Grace asked her.

"Mrs. Bowden. We were not notified anyone was to arrive today. I fear—"

"No need to fear, Mrs. Bowden." Grace

brushed past her. "We have a wounded man needing attention. Where shall we put him?" She peeked into the room to her right, a morning room with a divan, several chairs and a large round table in the center. "In here will do. Bring me strong spirits, whiskey if you have it, vinegar, needle and thread and any medicaments you have on hand. Heat water and have a bed prepared on this level. We shall have him moved once I've seen to him here."

Mrs. Oliver took her cue. "Look lively, Mrs. Bowden! Her ladyship won't abide delay. Summon some maids to fetch and carry." To Grace, she announced, "I'll see to the patient if you need to speak with Mr. Harrell. He'd be his lordship's factor."

"Thank you, Mrs. Oliver." She moved aside for the footmen to help the coachman into the room and onto the divan. "I'll have a closer look at John's injury first."

Mrs. Oliver closed her eyes for a moment and released a heavy sigh. "What a day this has been!" she murmured.

"It is not over yet," Grace reminded her in an aside meant only for Mrs. Oliver's ears. "Steady on until things are settled. We can fly to pieces later."

Mrs. Oliver grunted a wry laugh. "Just so. I shan't be calling you *Little Miss* any longer, my lady."

In the next hour, Grace tended the coachman's wound, apprised the steward of the incident on the road, penned a brief letter to Morleigh and ordered the coach containing the bodies back to London. She insisted that Mrs. Oliver retire to the upper servants' quarters and rest.

By that time, Mrs. Bowden had assembled the staff for introductions. Immediately after, Grace and Mr. Harrell interviewed several of the menservants and determined which ones were handy with weapons.

"Collect all weapons and the hunting guns, load them and arm yourselves," Grace ordered. "Post guards at all entrances to the house. No one is to enter unless you know them well and they have business here. If there is any question regarding that, hold them at gunpoint and report it to me. Is that understood?"

The men nodded, excited to have a break in their routine, she expected. Mr. Harrell assured her he would see to everything, and herded the men away.

"Now then," she said to Mrs. Bowden, "where am I to stay?"

"The rose room should do nicely, my lady. Jane here will show you up and draw a bath for you. Would you like to come down for supper or have a tray sent up?"

"A tray, please," Grace said on the instant. "And send it as soon as may be. Hearty fare and plenty of it, but it need not be grand. Whatever you have already prepared."

"But 'tis only beef and cabbage, my lady. I could—"

"I know, but tomorrow will be soon enough for Cook to show expertise. Tonight, I'd as soon not wait."

"Of course," Mrs. Bowden said, eyeing Grace askance. "Anything else you require, my lady?"

"Yes. Make certain that John is given restorative broth and red wine every two hours tonight. He lost a lot of blood. Also, please see to Mrs. Oliver's comfort. She's had rather a shock and an enormous demand on her courage. Were it not for her, we should both be dead."

Mrs. Bowden's mouth rounded and her eyes flew wide. "Mrs. Oliver saved your life!" she exclaimed in a whisper of awe.

Grace nodded somberly. "She dealt the highwayman a deathblow with his own pistol."

"I will see to her myself, Lady Grace! Poor woman must be fashed indeed! But you are an angel to think of the others so kindly when you had the fright of a lifetime yourself. Will you be all right in Jane's hands?" She darted a look at the plump young maid who stood waiting.

"Go along, Mrs. Bowden. Jane is highly capable, I'm certain."

Finally, Grace thought, she could afford to retire and collapse. The mantle of command slid off her shoulders in a heap. Had she filled her new role as a future countess? She hoped she had done her mother proud, as that woman had been saddled with a like situation years ago when Father had inherited. Grace recalled how graciously Mum had stepped from her life as a mere country doctor's wife into the exalted position.

Countess. Wife to an earl. Mistress of a large household. That would be her lot when Morleigh inherited. What a daunting thought. Even more daunting was the wifely part of it. Would she be a bride in truth to Caine Morleigh? She admitted she felt more anticipation than apprehension at that thought. She wondered just how he felt about it.

Her stomach growled loudly and she pressed a palm against it as she and Jane climbed the stairs. For now, she would concentrate on other pleasures. Like food.

"There's apple dumplings left, I expect," the shy little maid ventured. "Custard, for sure."

Grace laughed. The girl must read minds. "I think you and I shall get on like a runaway horse, Jane."

Caine cursed as he tossed Grace's letter on his desk. "Damn me, I promised to protect her!" He turned to the butler, who stood waiting in case he wanted to send a reply. "Jenkins, send some-one for Trent. Have them tell him it is urgent."

She had written that Caine must stay in London and not hie to Wildenhurst, as would probably be his first inclination. She guessed correctly there. It was all he could manage not to mount up and set off immediately and see for himself that she was unhurt. However, the danger to her originated here. She was also right about that. Whoever had sent that cretin to kill Grace would not yet know his minion had been unsuccessful, so she would be safe for a while.

This needed to be kept quiet until he could investigate. That might be difficult since the deaths of the dressmaker and the highwayman would have to be reported. Caine only hoped it would not appear in the news sheets and alert the mastermind that his plot to murder Grace had failed.

Who in the world would want her dead and why? Considering the highwayman's words, it obviously had to do with Caine's marriage to her. There was his cousin, Neville, who would be heir to the earldom if Caine did not marry and produce an heir. Getting rid of the prospective bride would prevent that. However, why not go directly for Caine? Perhaps because he would prove harder to kill?

Then there was Wardfelton. He had no love for Grace and it had already been rumored that

he had done away with her before he quelled
the gossip by bringing her out for all to see. Of
course, one could not accuse the man, a peer of
the realm, of attempted murder without solid
proof. How was one to get evidence of that when
the hireling was dead?

Trent arrived within the hour, appearing a bit
disgruntled at having been awakened so early.
He was shaking rain off his hat and handing it to
the butler as Caine met him in the foyer. "Damn
nasty out." Trent straightened his cuffs and blew
out a sigh. "What's the crisis of the day then?"

Caine got right to business. "A highwayman
attacked Grace's coach, killed the dressmaker
and wounded the coachman before the women
did him in. His body's in the carriage house
along with that of our unfortunate modiste,
whom he mistook for my fiancée."

Trent had frozen in place, his eyes wide.
"What!"

Caine continued. "I need assistance in identifying the corpse and discovering who employed
him to do murder. Have you time to help me?"

Trent snapped his mouth shut, thought for a
moment, then nodded. "Of course I'll take the
time. This is…abominable!"

"Come," Caine ordered. "We'll go and have
a look at him. I thought perhaps you could draw
a likeness of him and we could show it round in
quarters he might have frequented. I shouldn't

have called you out so early, but the sooner the better, before his features are too sunken."

"I'll need charcoal and paper," Trent said, hurrying along now that Caine had proposed the task.

An hour later, Caine looked from the drawing Trent had made to the actual face of the dead man. "Excellent. Even better than that one you did of Colonel Colbert for his wife. Amazing likeness, really. We'll put it under glass to protect it from smearing and then be off to make inquiries."

"What of the woman?" Trent asked. "Shouldn't you send her remains to her family and make some sort of explanation?"

"The undertaker's been notified and will come before noon to take both bodies. I've sent someone to search for her relatives and have prepared a letter for them when they're located."

"You've notified the authorities?" Trent asked, an eyebrow raised in doubt, obviously aware that no one was present and questioning the deaths yet.

Caine shook his head. "I will, but I'd like a head start on identifying the man before word gets out. I'd not like it known yet that the attempt was foiled."

"How was it, by the way? You said the *women* did him in?"

"Grace wrote that she and Mrs. Oliver overcame the man when he was reloading his pistol. I wish she had seen fit to give more details, but I guess it's sufficient for now to know they were successful and neither was harmed."

Trent grinned as they made their way back to the main house. "I'd love to have seen it. I expect Mrs. Oliver must have torn into him like a she-cat with kittens. Not hard to envision, is it!"

Caine could visualize it with no trouble at all. "I owe her more than I can repay. Perhaps a generous sum put by for her retirement would go a ways toward that."

"I dare say. Poor little mite you picked to marry probably just fainted again. Will you go and see about her?" Trent asked.

"I'm debating with myself on that. Even she realizes that the plot was hatched here in town and suggests I remain to investigate. Grace has a good head on her shoulders. She writes extremely well, concisely and to the point. Pragmatic girl, if I do say so."

Trent issued a wry laugh. "And in no way modest, is she? Taking credit for a part in downing a highwayman." He shook his head. "I can't see her doing much other than fluttering those thin little fingers and wilting to the ground."

Caine stopped and glared at Trent. "Leave off diminishing her! She's a brave girl, who's endured entirely too much."

Trent laughed again. "You've gone sweet

on her! God, Morleigh, you've been without a woman for so long any kind will serve!"

Caine grabbed Trent's lapel and jerked him to his toes. "I *chose* her, Trent. She's to be my wife. You keep your tongue behind your teeth or I'll have to knock them out!"

Hands up as if to ward off a blow, Trent backed away when Caine released his coat. "Settle down, man! You know I don't mean half I say and the rest is a joke. I *do* like her. She seems quite...well, polite." When Caine continued to glare a threat, Trent added, "Gentle. Well-spoken. Hell, Morleigh, I don't know her well enough to say more in her favor!"

"Don't speak of her at all then," Caine advised.

Trent straightened his lapel and wisely changed the subject. "Shall we go to Whitechapel first? We can show the sketch at the pubs. Perhaps he's a regular at one. Or the brothels. Haven't been to one of those since we came back to London, have you?"

Caine didn't trouble to answer that. He had thought about it, but somehow had not wanted a woman he had to pay for. There was too much pretense in the world as it was. And any woman who lay with him would have to pretend. Oh, they would do anything he wanted for pay, of course, but he was well aware that not one would look forward to it.

He wondered how he would deal with Grace in that respect. By only coming to her in the dark? Or granting her the right to refuse him? She probably wouldn't require either favor. His looks didn't seem to bother her all that much. She herself had brought up providing an heir. And she had said she was very grateful. He supposed he would have to resign himself to accepting her gratitude or else do without.

"Would you like me to go to Wildenhurst and see how she's getting on?" Trent asked, his tone conciliatory. "I promise I'll treat her with all kindness and care."

"No," Caine snapped. He didn't want his friend, or any other gentleman, foisting himself on Grace as a houseguest. "I'll go myself as soon as we have a name for the dead man."

Trent laughed and shrugged. "Sudden decision, eh? May I come, too?"

Caine shot him a nasty look. "Why do I put up with you?"

"Must be my good humor, since you have obviously lost yours. To think, you used to be such fun," Trent said with a weary sigh. He tugged on his gloves. "Shall we be off to the stews?"

Grace looked around the Wildenhurst library as she paused in rereading the letter she had just received from Dr. Ackers, the earl's physician. She had written to him the day after her arrival here. He said he had studied with her father more than twenty years before and was quite interested in his success with the heart patients Grace had told him about in her missive to him.

He replied that he would certainly obtain and explore Dr. Withering's papers on the subject and thanked her for the information. She was pleased that he would consider it and would write to tell him so. She had truly missed writing and receiving letters after Wardfelton had denied her the pleasure.

This room was the perfect place to do her correspondence, plan menus and simply sit and read. She had been struck immediately by the comforting familiarity. Her father's favorite retreat had possessed nearly this same ambiance and almost as many books. Few of these were medical texts, however, but many were interesting all the same.

In fact, Wildenhurst proved everything Morleigh had related and much more. Aside from the generous welcome from the staff, the house itself seemed to embrace her. Grace took an hour whenever she could find a free one, to explore the manor.

The four floors were simply laid out in rectangular shape. A modest vestibule lined with beautiful paintings led one to a highly polished, gently curving staircase. It also opened to the right into a lovely morning room and through that, the formal dining hall. Behind that lay the kitchen areas, containing the buttery, scullery, still room and the kitchen proper.

To the left, off the vestibule, Grace could enter the formal drawing room, an enormous space that had obviously been three rooms at one time, probably set up originally as a state apartment for important or even royal guests. Beyond that was a small conservatory that opened onto a flagstone terrace at the north end of the house.

Off the main corridor behind the stairway, she had found this wonderful oak-paneled library redolent of lemon-oil polish, sweet-scented pipe tobacco and the unique essence of old books. Floor-length windows swung open easily and led to the gardens out back.

She loved this room best of all. An interior door led to a small business room where the estate accounts were kept and managed. The rest of the ground floor consisted of living quarters for the upper servants in the household.

Up the stairs on the first and second floors were the family and guest bedrooms opening off the corridor that ran along the middle of the house lengthwise, as it did on all levels. The attic chambers for the maids occupied half the third level, while the other half contained a large area for proper storage.

Below it all lay the cellar she had yet to explore, but she had been told the menservants had

quarters in the northern end, while the root cellar, wine cellar and various other utility areas
held up the kitchens.

Grace was no student of architecture but she
applauded the Wildenhurst designer for his attention to convenience. This was no rambling,
added-onto conglomeration of wings wherein a
stranger might lose her way! Efficiency had a
home here and she hoped she had, as well.

The gardens were rather casually formed, rife
with roses of all description, but the herb beds
were in overgrown disarray. She planned to rem-
edy that as soon as time permitted.

Yes, she thought with a sigh, Wildenhurst felt
like home after only four days. She wondered if
Caine would allow her to stay on here after they
were married or whether he would send her to
some other property to live.

She had begun to think of him as Caine in
her own mind. It seemed so much more friendly
than either Captain or Morleigh. More inti-
mate, as if they already knew one another quite
well, though they really did not. One day they
would—and soon, she hoped—but until then it
hurt no one to think of him that way.

He invaded her thoughts constantly. And her
dreams. He would suddenly appear, that big
strong body, the seriousness of his expression,
his occasional flash of humor that seemed to

surprise even himself, the way he strode across a room, owning the space.

She loved how he could change his demeanor from stern and commanding to wry and gentle in a heartbeat. Somewhere inside Caine, Grace suspected there was a well of good humor waiting to be fully tapped. Vestiges of it escaped now and again and she longed to have him reveal it completely, to hear him laugh with abandon and let go of his demons.

The thing that appealed to Grace most about Caine was that he appeared to care what happened to her. That made him the only one in the world who did and certainly dear to her because of it.

She loved his face, scars and all. He would never credit that, so she might as well not tell him. Grace was mightily afraid that, on all counts, she was hopelessly infatuated with the man.

Mrs. Oliver fussed over her constantly, yet treated her quite differently than she had before the incident on the road. Now she asked instead of telling. She deferred instead of demanding. Amazingly, the other servants followed her lead implicitly. Grace found herself completely in charge for the first time in her life and took full advantage.

"Mr. Harrell?" She looked up from the writing desk in the study as Hadley's factor appeared in the doorway. She feared he had been neglecting his estate duties of late to concentrate on her protection. Thus far there had been no threats apparent. "Is there a problem, sir?"

"There are two riders approaching along the main road, ma'am. I thought you should know." He pursed his lips and raised his bushy gray eyebrows as he awaited her response.

She tensed, heart in her throat. Surely it wasn't her uncle or men he was sending to collect her. He would not dare such a thing. Would he? "I doubt anyone bent upon mischief would ride in at midmorning."

Even as she said it, she could not erase from her mind the memory of the times, twice before, that she had been found by her uncle's minions and returned to him.

Chapter Seven

Mr. Harrell rushed to reassure Grace, "Oh no, ma'am, the visitors are not anyone you should fear. One of the riders appears to be the captain, judging by the mount he's on."

Grace jumped up from the desk and flew past him on the way out of the room. "Notify Cook. We'll need something special prepared to feed them," she ordered over her shoulder. "I will receive in the drawing room."

She hurried there to wait. After a few calming breaths, she pinched her cheeks for a bit of color and brushed back an errant strand of hair that had escaped the confines of her morning cap. Then, on second thought, removed the foolish cap and stuffed it under a cushion.

It was too late to change her gown, but there was little choice to be had in that direction anyway. Most of her new clothing, the morning gowns in particular, were still in pieces awaiting construction. The borrowed gray would have to suffice.

Grace had to laugh a little at herself. That she should want to look pleasing to the captain surprised her. He had chosen her when she was at her very worst and his expectations today would doubtless be quite low in any case.

She heard the commotion outside when he arrived and arranged herself on a divan to wait for him.

"Captain Morleigh and Lord Trent, ma'am," Judd, the butler, announced in a somber tone.

Grace rose and smiled as the two men entered. "Welcome!" she said, and held out her hands to Caine. He looked so fine, even in his travel dust. Rather rakish, in fact.

He raised her fingers to his lips. "I trust you've recovered from your misfortune on the road?" He seemed to take in every detail of her appearance as he asked.

"I have indeed." Grace withdrew her hand and offered it to Trent. He reacted less familiarly, merely bowing over it. "It was good of you both to come, but not at all necessary. Would you join me, or have you other business to conduct?"

Trent cleared his throat. "If you would excuse me, I will leave you two to speak privately."

Grace nodded. "Please consider yourself at home here, Lord Trent. We shan't be long."

"Why thank you, ma'am. I shall do that," Trent replied, and promptly left with Judd.

Caine smiled. "I see you've assumed command." He gestured for her to sit, then joined her on the divan. "Does Wildenhurst agree with you then?"

She brightened. "Oh, yes! I knew I would love it here and I do. Everyone has been very agreeable and we're getting on quite well. I can hardly wait to meet the neighboring families and perhaps entertain a bit. But I suppose that will have to wait awhile."

"Oh. You would enjoy company? Parties and the like?"

"Yes, of course!" She gestured around the drawing room. "This is a perfect size for dancing, isn't it? Please don't judge my social abilities by my dislike of the ball where we met," she said, laughing at his concern. "Even though I never had a London season, I attended all our local events and helped my parents host a few. All of that was curtailed by mourning, of course. Wardfelton's evenings were rather dark events with few ladies in attendance. I've quite missed the dancing and gaity."

"I see. Yes, I suppose you would," he said, apparently still troubled by something.

She leaned toward him, hands clasped in her

lap. "And how have *you* been? And Lord and
Lady Hadley, how do they do?"

"Well enough, thank you," he said, a frown
still marring his strong features. "I've come to
let you know Trent and I have discovered the
identity of the brigand who accosted you. His
name does us little good, however, since we have
not yet been able to connect him with anyone
of means who might have hired him to do the
deed." He sighed. "Do you think it was Wardfelton, Grace?"

She nodded. "He came immediately to mind."

"To me, as well," Caine admitted. "However,
I am at a loss when figuring his motive. Any
ideas?"

"None at all. When I first came to him, we
got on rather well. After that first year, things
changed abruptly. He acquired a sudden dislike
of me, a hatred, really."

Morleigh shifted to face her fully. "Do you
know *why?*"

Grace shook her head and shrugged. "No.
He never declared it outright, but I began to feel
very strongly that he wished I would cease to
exist."

He placed a hand over the one she rested on
the cushion beside her. "Was he very cruel to
you, Grace?"

"Not to my person," she admitted. "All his
threats were implied."

She noted a hardening of his expression as he spoke. "Well, you won't have to endure that again, I assure you."

Grace hesitated a moment before venturing a notion that had occurred to her well after the attack. "Perhaps my uncle is not the culprit. Is there anyone you know who might wish *you* to remain unmarried?"

"It is possible that my cousin, next in line for the title, might want to prevent it. He will be my heir if I don't marry and produce an heir. However that seems rather far-fetched, the more I consider it. Doesn't it seem more likely he would simply try to eliminate *me?*"

"Well, I wouldn't dismiss him out of hand. The assassin did ask for Morleigh's woman instead of using my name as my uncle might have done."

She hated to mention the other possibility. This one, he would not like. "What of your friend Trent? I felt from the outset that he does not approve of me in the least."

Instead of anger, he offered an indulgent smile. "You may strike Trent off your list of suspects, Grace. He has been my best friend since we were lads and has saved my life twice."

She pursed her lips, but could not hold back the words. "Perhaps he believed he was saving it yet again. Or at least protecting your future."

"No, Grace. It most definitely is not Trent.

He would not need to have you killed to prevent our marriage. All he would need do is seriously object and give me valid reasons for it. The worst he has done is to tease me, which he has always done about everything under the sun. Please trust me on this."

He patted her hand again. "Now, I want you to stop worrying. You will be perfectly safe here. I will go back to London, find whoever is responsible and take care of the matter."

Grace turned her hand palm up to grip his. The move seemed to surprise him.

"I do trust you," she said.

He looked taken aback, but finally spoke. "Thank you. I've given you precious little reason to do so as yet, but I appreciate that."

"Nonsense! You have given me every reason," she said, meaning every word.

Trent entered in something of a rush, stopping just inside the door. He looked from one to the other as he bit his bottom lip. Something had obviously upset or excited him.

Grace raised an eyebrow. "Is something amiss, Lord Trent?"

"Uh…no, not amiss exactly. I wonder if I might have a private word?"

"With me?" Grace asked, unable to resist testing his patience.

Trent shook his head and fastened a concerned gaze on Morleigh. Grace tugged her hand from Caine's clasp and rose. "It is a bit early in the day, but there's brandy in the cabinet there if you'd like a tot while you confide." She gave Trent a saucy grin as she swept out and left the men to their business.

Her hand still tingled with the warmth and comfort of the captain's touch. She cradled it beneath her breast, even as she warned herself not to read too much into his attentions.

She was of mixed feelings about his treatment of her today. While a part of her resented his superior "I shall handle everything for you" attitude, another part enjoyed his promise of security.

To be fair, the first impression he must have had of her was that of helpless female. She clearly saw now that she had let herself become a victim of her uncle's intimidation. It was as if Caine had awakened her somehow when she had been at her lowest point. And the unfortunate incident on the road had shaken her fully out of her former grief and apathy. No, she could not blame him for viewing her as weak and inept, but she could change his opinion and gain his respect in time.

He would never regret choosing her, she decided with a firm nod of her head. Never. She would see to that.

"You won't credit what Mrs. Oliver has told me!" Trent exclaimed as soon as they were alone.

Obviously agitated, he began pacing the plush turkey carpet and rubbing his forehead with his thumb and forefinger. "I still can't credit it."

Caine waited for him to relate whatever it was, his mind still on Grace's calm assertion of trust.

"It was *she!*" Trent said, stopping to offer a gesture of disbelief. "Grace herself disarmed that man! Can you believe it? Mrs. Oliver hit him, yes, but it was Grace who saved them both." He strode over and plopped down beside Caine. "She lifted her skirts, man. She enticed him on purpose. Then she kicked the stuffing out of his privates and brought him down!"

Caine stared wide-eyed at Trent. "What?"

Trent nodded, then shook his head. "Oliver finished him off with the pistol's butt. According to her account, Grace then helped her load the bodies, clambered atop the coach, saw to the coachman's wound, then drove them here herself!"

"Give over. The woman must be exaggerating."

"Not so! She swears it's all true." He shook a finger at Caine. "You have sorely underestimated this girl, Morleigh."

"*I? You* are the one who had her wilting in a faint." Belated fear rose in his chest at the mental image of Grace physically confronting a full-grown man. "Go. Find her and send her to me."

Trent threw up his hands as he stood. "Find her yourself, man. I'm still coming to terms with this." He resumed pacing and scratched his head. "I cannot believe I have so *misjudged* anyone, especially a woman. It's not like me at all."

Caine huffed. "This is not about you, Trent." He strode out to locate Grace, intent on giving her a real dressing-down for risking her life that way.

He ran into her in the vestibule, literally. She backed away laughing and rubbed her nose. It had collided with his chest.

"What were you thinking to do such a thing?" he demanded.

"Sorry, I didn't see you in time to stop."

"Not that, wigeon! The brigand. Oliver told Trent it was you!"

"Oh, that. Well, Mrs. Oliver actually did him in. I told you that."

Caine rolled his eyes. "Yes, but it was you who lifted your skirts. Do you have any idea what might have happened if—"

"Well, he was reloading and meant to kill us, so I redirected his thoughts to something less fatal."

Morleigh grasped her upper arms and shook her once. "Did you consider what might have happened if you hadn't had enough strength to—"

"Unman him?" She laughed nervously. "But I did."

"What if you had missed your mark, Grace? What if he had—"

She shook off his hands and raised her chin. "You're more worried about his defiling my person than shooting me dead as he did Madame?"

"Well, no, of course not, but—"

"Then stop treating me like an idiot! It was our only chance and I took it! If he had thrown me to the ground to have his way, I trust Mrs. Oliver still would have had sense enough to take advantage of his lust and bash in his head."

She exhaled a gust of anger while a moment of silence ensued. But apparently she wasn't finished asserting herself. "Do my actions offend your male sensibilities?"

He stood back, took a deep breath and inclined his head. "Somewhat, but I will rethink it. I beg your—"

"Indulgence? Forgiveness? And if you say *attention,* I shall hurt you!"

He smiled, all anger erased. "Come now, Grace, what you did merely shocked me, that's all. I'm relieved you were so quick-minded. And happy you weren't hurt or worse. In fact, I'm rather proud—"

"Very well then. So long as we have an understanding. You are wrongheaded, as most of your gender usually is, and I am—"

"Absolutely rude for completing almost every thought I put into words."

She looked to be hiding a smile herself. "If I promise to cease my rudeness, what shall you concede?" she demanded, arms crossed and foot tapping with pretended impatience.

"To hear you out before going on the attack," he promised.

"So be it."

She sparred really well, Caine thought, proud of her spirit.

"Are you hungry?" she asked. "I'm famished. I was coming to tell you the meal is ready."

"Thank God," Trent piped up. He had been listening, propped in the doorway. "I thought we were about to be put on the road back to town."

He strode forward and tucked one of Grace's hands through the crook of his arm. "Never contradict this woman, Morleigh. She scares me to death and I'm staying firmly on her good side."

"One wise man on the premises," Grace said with a wry laugh. "Come along, Captain," she said over her shoulder. "Food usually improves a man's temper."

"A woman's, as well, one would hope," he replied, taking her other hand. They walked three abreast to the dining room for the noon repast.

Caine was still too shocked to say much, but his mind whirled with varying emotions. He alternately felt a great need to spank or salute her.

One thing he was certain of, life with Grace would never be boring. However, he was not certain if that was a good thing or bad at this point.

"You could remain here for a while," Trent suggested to Caine after they had finished eating. "There's nothing you could do in London that I can't do for you. Would you leave a lady alone after such a scare?"

"I'm not frightened in the least, but I would welcome your company," Grace said with a smile. "Please stay if you like."

Caine knew he had no right to stay at Wildenhurst, that he should return to London forthwith and dedicate himself to discovering their enemy. However, Trent could continue the investigation and Caine supposed he really should remain for at least a few days. "Very well, if you're sure."

Trent was right that Grace should not be left alone. Heaven knew she had fended for herself for too long as it was.

They bade Trent farewell and stood together out front, watching him canter down the long drive. "I know I promised you solitude for three weeks. Are you certain you won't mind my intrusion?" he asked her.

She shook her head and answered firmly, "It is your home, after all, and this would give us the chance to become better acquainted."

Caine made his decision. "Then I shall stay,

of course." He knew he might regret the hasty choice if he thought about it for too long. But regret was not something he entertained often and he made up his mind he would not in this instance. Grace wanted him to remain, so he would.

They met at breakfast the next morning. Caine had no idea what to do with her now that he was to keep her company. As if she read his thoughts, she asked, "What shall we do today?"

He looked out the window at the rolling meadows beyond the lawn. "We could ride if you like. You do ride?"

Her little bounce of excitement answered before she did. "Oh, yes! And I've missed it so much," she said, eyes bright with anticipation. "I dared not do it without your leave. I thought it might not be safe."

"I'm glad you didn't go out without me." Caine admired her sense of caution and prudence, noting that this was the first he had seen of those qualities. "However, we should be fine if we stay on open ground and well away from the wood. There is no access to the back acres, except through the river."

She pulled away and lifted her skirts to take the steps. "I'll run up and change!"

"You're fine as you are. We'll not see a soul who would question your attire."

"I haven't a habit yet anyway, but I need my borrowed boots!" she said, holding up a slipper-clad foot.

Caine noted the smallness of it. How dainty she was all over and how thin. He could scarcely believe she'd had enough strength in that tiny foot to unman a killer. "Meet you at the stables then," he said as she hurried inside.

When she arrived, he had the horses saddled and ready, his own gelding and the gentlest mare for her. Grace still wore the serviceable gray gown, but had topped it with a bright scarlet spencer. "Most becoming," he commented, delighted to see her in bright color for a change. "Puts roses in your cheeks."

"Thank you, kind sir! My one completed garment from the materials you purchased. As for the pink face, I but needed the fresh air and sunshine your garden has supplied. It is such a gorgeous day, isn't it?" She handed him a small cloth bag with a strap. "Hang this over your shoulder, if you please."

He took it. "What's in it?"

She grinned, helped him adjust the strap. "Bread, cheese and wine. My contribution to the outing."

"Brilliant." He grasped her waist and lifted her onto the worn sidesaddle no one had used for years. "I'll order you a new saddle when I get back to Town," he said.

She laughed. "I'd rather have that than the curricle you offered. See how frugal I can be?"

He mounted his gelding. "Aha, then perhaps a young mare instead of the matched team?"

"Definitely preferable! However, I've grown quite fond of Betsy here. I have spoiled her with apples already, haven't I, old girl? Yes, I brought you one for later!" She patted the mare's neck and was rewarded with a loud neigh.

Caine laughed with her at Betsy's unexpected response and felt a release of tension he hadn't realized was there. They would get on well, he thought with relief. They both loved horses, riding and the country air. He might look forward to future visits. If he found he had the time to spare.

They set out across the meadow at a gallop. She sat a horse as though born to it and didn't appear to suffer at all from lack of practice. With the wind tearing at her hair and her face alight with joy, Grace looked incredibly young and almost beautiful.

Her small-breasted, thin-waisted, narrow-hipped figure appeared that of an adolescent only just crossing the threshold into womanhood. She wore no cosmetics to enhance her features and her silky hair flew freely, undone by the wind and set free of hairpins.

Caine wished for boyhood again and the chance to have known her in early youth before grief and war had turned their lives grim. Perhaps, just for today, he could dismiss all worry and pretend it was so.

"Race you to the water's edge!" he called out.

With a shout of laughter, she urged Betsy to full speed. Caine held back a bit in order to let her win.

He had not felt so happy in years. Surely the fabric of his life would hold together if he abandoned responsibility and stole a few days of pleasure for himself. He looked at Grace, a vision of total abandonment, and envied her precious ability to live in the moment. Perhaps she could show him how to do that, if only for today.

Chapter Eight

Caine dismounted at river's edge and went to assist Grace. He reached up and grasped her waist. She felt so slender and so soft. The fact that she wore no corset registered immediately. Both her hands rested on his shoulders as he lifted her. He couldn't seem to help holding her entirely too close, sliding her down his front until her feet rested on the grass.

He told himself it was just to see what she would do, how she would react to his nearness. She never once protested or braced herself away. Instead, her direct blue gaze never left his.

She didn't smile, but neither did she frown. Her lips were slightly open and her expression was…well, the best he could describe it was inquisitive.

Caine had to remind himself to release her,

and only then did she step back. And smile up at him, a knowing smile, as if she was fully aware that he suddenly saw her not as a girl, but a woman.

"I like this," she said in a breathless voice. Then she looked around and pointed. "There is the perfect place." Without a pause, she scampered over to sit on a large flat stone, removed her boots and stockings and dangled her feet in the water. "Come on," she urged, patting the space beside her. "It feels wonderful!"

She was right. Neither even mentioned the impropriety of exposing bare feet and ankles. Hers were narrow, dainty and rather pretty. She lifted them out of the water and wiggled her toes when she saw he had noticed. Caine laughed at her childlike impulse, doubting there was another in the world as unaffected and natural as Grace.

"Tell me about your parents," she said, idly watching as she swirled her feet in the lapping waves, accidentally brushing his foot now and then. Or perhaps she meant to, as a small gesture of comfort or something. "Did they die when you were very young?"

The topic was painful, but Grace certainly had a right to ask questions about his family. "Mother contracted scarlet fever when I was ten. It weakened her heart and she died soon after. My father, as well as my older brother, were

still living when I bought my commission six
years ago."

"What happened to them? Do you mind my
asking?" Her gaze fastened on him then, rife
with apology or concern. Caine realized it felt
good to have someone really care how he felt.

"No, of course I don't mind. You have every
right to ask." What woman wouldn't want to
know? For all she knew now, they might have
succumbed to some inherited malady that her
children could fall victim to in future. "They
were caught in a sudden storm as they were sailing off the coast, a pastime they shared often."
He looked out over the river.

"But you have no love of that, do you?" she
guessed.

He smiled. "No sea legs and no stomach for
it. Getting from here to the Continent with my
company proved a problem. Trent's ever-present
flask was a godsend, I can tell you."

She laughed softly. "We all have our embar-
rassments. What of your friend Trent? What
does he do now that he's no longer your lieutenant?"

Caine wondered whether her interest in Trent
could be personal. His best friend was rather
handsome and the thought stirred a small worry
that Grace had noticed that. "Oh, well, Trent
does a bit of everything and next to nothing
since he sold his commission. His father, the

marquis, kicked up quite a fuss when Trent followed my lead into the army. Trent's an only child."

"Ah, the heir," Grace said with a nod. "So one day both you and he will sit together in the Lords, all pompous and stodgy in your wigs and robes."

"Now, there's a picture." Though it would more than likely happen, it was hard to imagine. "The pair of us, as we were at our schools and on our belated grand tour with the army."

"Aha, Bonaparte's wars kept you from the usual acquiring of continental polish, so you two joined the fight to pay him back!"

"That, plus an equal part of rebellion against our fathers' expectations. Then there were the uniforms, of course." He turned and winked at Grace. "Drew the ladies like lodestones." Speaking of those times now, even considering how his engagement turned out, he decided the years hadn't been a total waste.

"Dashing comrades-at-arms," she said with a chuckle.

"We really were comrades, y'know. Still are that. He's been more of a brother to me than my own ever was." Caine looked up at the clouds, lost in the past. "In fact, I hardly knew Trevor at all. He was already away at school when I was born and on his visits home, he and my father were usually out sailing or busy in Town."

"Poor little left-behind," she said. "At least you had your boon companion. Denied that grand tour to sow your oats, you and he must have set London on its ear when you came of age." She cut him a sly glance and grinned. "Didn't you?"

"We certainly tried." Caine appreciated her way of lightening a conversation. "Sorry, but I refuse to bore you with details of my misspent youth."

"And I have no business asking," she said. "It's only that my past is so boring. I thought to live vicariously in hearing of yours."

"Boring?" he asked, curious to know what her life had been like. "You assisted your father, which must have proved exciting at times. And you met someone dashing to love very early on. Were you happy before your great losses and these past two years?"

She looked off into the distance. "Yes," she said simply with no further explanation of what might have made her so.

After a few moments lost in her thoughts, she looked at him and smiled. "I am happy at this moment and I believe one should relish that where one finds it, however small the measure." She nudged his elbow with hers. "Now you are meant to say how profound you find that observation and declare that you agree completely. Go on…"

"I do agree and it was profound." Caine noticed that she liked to touch and was in no way reticent about it. That nudge, for instance, an occasional hand on his sleeve or the soft bat of her palm on his hand, the touch of her foot. It seemed so natural, as if she were totally unaware she was doing it. He was unused to touches that were not deliberate and a means to an end.

"You're very unusual," he said. "And that is a compliment, by the way."

"What a kind way of putting it. I suppose I must thank you."

Only moments later, in the silence that ensued, did it occur to him that Grace might have thought he meant her appearance unusual. And he didn't know how to explain what he had said without making it sound worse.

"Ah, this is heaven," she crooned, leaning back, propped on her hands, her face lifted to the sun. She turned to him and opened one eye. "Tell me, do you fish?"

So she had forgiven him. "Not for a long time. Have you ever?"

"Of course! Many were the days I provided dinner." She sighed theatrically and faked a sad frown. "Life was hard for a poor doctor's family, you see. I was forced to fish for variety in the diet. Father was paid with chickens so many times, I thought I should grow up clucking!"

Caine threw back his head and laughed.

"Bring me fishing tomorrow!" she exclaimed, pressing her hand on his. "Please, please?"

"We have a holding pond behind the gardens, Grace. Full of fish, unless Harrell's a slackard."

"Not the same," she declared, giving his hand a slap and resuming her position of soaking up the sunshine. "Nothing tastes better than a trout that made you work for him. You'll see."

"So I shall. Maybe Harrell can scare up poles and hooks."

"In the back of the tack room," she said immediately. "Along with flies and a bucket for worms."

"Which you will dig yourself, no doubt," he said with a chuckle. "This I must see."

"Oh, you will see and assist me, too. I shan't be the only one with grubby fingernails and dirty knees. Your soft life is over, Morleigh."

So, of course, the next day found them at water's edge again. Her patience with fishing surprised him a little, as did her willingness to bait her own hook. There were moments when he suspected the activity brought back memories she had hidden away for a while. Perhaps she had sat on a bank before in this same way with another.

He wondered if she had been very much in love with young Barkley and if she missed and mourned him still. What would it be like to lose to death someone you greatly loved? He had suffered over the loss of Belinda, of course, but that was not the same thing at all. The woman he had loved was still very much alive and he'd had pride and anger to sustain him while recovering from losing her. The love he had felt for Belinda must not have been very deep and it had certainly been misplaced. His recovery felt quite complete now. He wondered if Grace's was.

Caine hesitated to broach the subject, but he so wanted to know. "Grace, are you still in love with young Barkley?"

She sighed and inclined her head. "Well, I loved him but I'm not certain I was ever *in love* with him, if you know what I mean. We were childhood friends. He was great fun, quite the clown as a boy." Her eyes took on a dreamy look. "Then when he came home from school at last and was commissioned, he looked very dashing." She laughed. "I was sixteen, mad for the uniform, fascinated that he actually had grown side whiskers."

Caine smiled. "In love with love, then?"

"Oh, most assuredly. I confess I was curious, too. He proposed because I let him kiss me, you see," she admitted with a grin.

"Were you…intimate?" Caine asked before he could catch back the question.

She gave an elegant little snort. "Not quite *that* curious!"

Caine had to laugh, both at her words and

with surprise that she had taken no offense at his asking.

She set down her fishing pole. "And what of you?" she demanded, tossing a stick into the water. "Did that Thoren-Snipes girl entrap you as shamelessly I did my beau?"

"No such excuse," he answered. "She seemed…well, more than she actually was and I asked for her hand with all the eagerness of green youth and wild expectations."

"You fell in love with her."

"With the girl I thought she was, yes. Her brother objected, so there was a challenge for me, as well. Belinda promised to wait for me until the war was over. And so she did. You have heard the rest, I'm certain."

"To parrot your question to me, do you love her still?" Grace asked him, head cocked to one side in that probing way she had that made one feel compelled to answer.

Caine pursed his lips for a moment as he put his cane pole down and tossed a rock in the water where her stick now floated. He looked directly into Grace's questioning eyes and answered truthfully, "No. Absolutely not."

She grinned. "Older and wiser now, are you? But you should know, sir, no one of our gender is precisely what she seems. Ever." Her face contorted and her fingers formed into claws as she pretended to threaten him. "So best beware!"

Caine huffed a laugh. "An admitted shrew, I believe I can handle. Taming her with food should work! Are you hungry?"

"Famished!" she exclaimed, scrambling to her feet and brushing off her skirts. "Let's eat."

She helped him spread the blanket and arrange their small feast. "This is a lovely way to spend a day, isn't it!"

"Even if the fish aren't biting," he replied.

For some reason, he became obsessed with giving Grace more than a few days of well-deserved happiness if he could. He knew that, in doing so, he would find more than a little joy himself. He already had.

And so it went. Three lovely days of nothing but sport and sweetness, laughter and lolling about. By some unspoken agreement, neither of them mentioned Wardfelton, the attack on the road or their future as man and wife.

There were so many times he felt fascinated by her mobile lips, the way they pursed in that little moue when she was puzzled, or how they could stretch into a wide gleeful smile in an instant, lighting her whole face from within.

He thought about kissing her more than once, but it was too soon. It might make her think he was one of those men who had nothing else on his mind when he was around a woman. She might also believe he did it only because she had admitted kissing Barkley and withdraw from him completely. So he refrained. It would only have been a test anyway, he told himself, and she deserved more than that when he did kiss her.

The day would come when he would, of course. He would be her husband. But for now, for these few days, he simply wanted to be Grace's friend. To know her as a person. She had warned him that no woman was precisely what she seemed to be. But Grace was so open and honest, how could she not be?

Caine would always think of the time as the halcyon days, surpassing any other he had ever known, even as a boy. Grace had restored something in his soul that he had lost and forgotten. He only hoped he could hold on to it.

Reality intruded on the morning of the fourth day when Trent returned and Grace prepared herself for Caine's departure to London.

After the three of them shared the midday meal, Caine asked Grace to accompany him through the garden to the stables so that they could speak privately.

Trent had said his farewell and gone on ahead to have the horses saddled for their ride.

"This has been a poor attempt at courting," Caine said.

"No, no, it was wonderful, if far too brief," she said.

"I wish I had a longer time to visit, but I did

promise you your time alone to adjust." He looked down at her, directly into her eyes, as if searching for something.

She was first to look away. "So you did." Now she wished she had never asked for that.

Their lovely time out of time was over and he seemed to regret that as much as she did. That was some consolation.

All the matters they had forgone discussing for the duration should be addressed at some point. Grace decided to begin with what was most important to her. "Tell me, will we bide here after the wedding or return to Town?" She reached out and plucked a dead head off a rose-bush, watching the last of the petals drift to the ground.

"You may do as you like, of course. I promised you could. But I must remain with my uncle as often as possible. He believes his time is near and he has affairs that should be put in order."

"Will he not come for the wedding then?"

Caine shook his head, though his answer was positive. "He plans to attend. Insists on it, in fact. We can make him comfortable in the carriage, bring his physician and take the journey slowly. Unless his condition worsens between now and then, he'll be all right, I think."

She smiled up at him. "You care for him a great deal, don't you." It was not a question.

"I love the old fellow, even when his demands

drive me mad," Caine admitted. "He and my aunt were always like parents to me, even when mine were alive."

"You're a good man, Caine," she said.

He cocked an eyebrow. "If not so good to look at."

"I would never say that, nor would anyone with two good eyes." Then she realized the *faux pas* and covered her mouth with her hand. "Oh, I'm so sorry. I wasn't thinking."

"Not to worry. I was just teasing you. And thank you for the compliment, however undeserved."

"But it's not undeserved! You have to stop seeing yourself as that stupid girl described you." She reached up and touched his eye patch. "Take it off."

He backed away, glaring at her, his lips drawn into a firm line.

She braced her fists on her hips. "If I'm to run from you, wouldn't you want me to do it now before you're shackled to me for life? How can you bear wedding a woman you cannot trust to stay? Take it off and test me."

"You're a demanding little tyrant, aren't you?"

She nodded. "At times, but this is all I've asked you for and really meant it. Do it, Caine. I dare you."

To her surprise, he reached up slowly and removed the eye patch. She gasped with surprise. "You have your *eye!*"

He glanced away, obviously embarrassed.

"It moves with the other! Can you see out of it, Caine?"

One shoulder lifted in a shrug and he nodded once.

She threw up her hands in dismay. "I'd just begun to think you a sensible man! Why on earth would you cover your eye and give up half your sight for vanity's sake? If you place so much value on appearance, why take an ugly wife? Will you put a patch over *me?*"

"You are *not* ugly!" he replied. "Are you attempting to destroy our bargain with a fight?"

"Do you want it destroyed?" she demanded. "Have you second thoughts?"

"None! If anything, I am more resolved!"

"Why?"

He turned away, then back to face her. "Because I *like* you, damn it!" he exclaimed. "I need to protect you and I *care*. Make of that what you will!"

"I shall make the most of it then," she snapped, and crossed her arms over her chest. "So, goodbye, Captain."

"Goodbye, Grace," he said.

She marched right up to him, snatched the eye patch out of his hand and stalked back to the house alone.

Inwardly, she was bursting with happiness. *He could see!* How bloody marvelous was that! And his scars didn't signify at all. They were not pretty, she admitted, but they were not what she would deem disfiguring, either.

And he *liked* her.

She glanced over her shoulder as she reached the door. He still stood there, such an imposing figure, one hand on his hip, watching her.

Grace couldn't resist. She shot him a defiant grin and raised a hand in farewell before ducking inside.

Did she imagine she heard his laughter?

Caine's step felt light as he walked on to the stables. Mr. Harrell awaited him there, along with Trent and the saddled mounts.

"I did not wish to speak of this in front of Lady Grace, Mr. Harrell. Now that I'm leaving, you should assemble every able-bodied man on the estate and have them armed. Not only the few I've seen patrolling, but *all* of them," Caine ordered.

"Oh, that was done at the outset, sir, even before you came," Harrell assured him. "Many are stationed well out of sight so you or anyone approaching wouldn't notice. All are mindful of any traffic upon the roads leading in and guards are posted at every entrance to the house itself, night and day."

"Yes, I saw those few every day." Caine was impressed. He had been so preoccupied with Grace's company and so sure he could protect her himself, he hadn't thought to question the number of guards.

"The earl will be happy to hear of your initiative, as am I. In fact, I plan to suggest that you be properly rewarded for the effort that goes beyond your official duties."

"Thank you, sir." Harrell's chest puffed out. "I reckoned the need immediate when Lady Grace arrived."

Caine smiled and nodded. "Carry on, Mr. Harrell, and send word if you need anything. You have enough weapons?"

"Loaded and well manned, sir. There's more powder and shot on order. If it turns out we don't need that now, there's always the fall hunt."

Fall hunt? They had not had one since his father and Trevor died. Was Grace already planning one or was this Harrell's idea? In either event, it was not a good idea, but he would take that up later.

Caine mounted up. "We shall return soon," he told Harrell. "Keep a sharp eye."

He and Trent rode out, pacing their horses for the long ride to London. Trent's thoughtful look prompted Caine to ask, "Do you still think I'm mad to marry her?"

"I think you're mad if you don't," Trent replied. "How was your visit with her?"

"Enlightening," Caine replied, thinking that was the understatement of the century. He had come to like Grace enormously and fully appreciate her originality. Unless he was badly mistaken, she liked him, as well.

Her independence certainly suited their situation. He knew she would be fine by herself when he was occupied with business. And on occasion, when he was not, she would welcome his company. A perfect arrangement for both.

If there was a detraction from that perfection, Caine admitted it was his burgeoning desire for Grace as a woman. She managed to stir his senses even though he could not precisely explain it. Her *joie de vivre,* perhaps. She did embrace life with an energy he envied. The more he was with her, the more he wanted a taste of that, a taste of *her.*

Trent nodded his approval. "Well, I must tell you, Mrs. Oliver informed mc last time I was here that Grace ordered armed guards the moment they arrived. Harrell merely followed her directions. You shouldn't give him the credit."

Caine smiled to himself. He had figured as much.

Trent continued, "True, Grace is no beauty and she could cut you to ribbons with that saucy tongue of hers, but she's amazingly resourceful and…well, quite interesting," Trent observed.

"Mmm-hmm."

Trent gestured, palm up. "You must admit, the girl's no henwit. Took a cartload of courage to do what she did to that highwayman."

"Daring."

Trent continued, his mood thoughtful. "And she has this way about her, y'know? A way of moving with a purpose. Not jerking about or anything like that, but efficient, I guess you might say."

"I noticed."

"Can't see how one could help but do that. However, she eats an enormous amount of food, did you see that? Last time I was here and this time, too. She'll beggar you at the market." Trent released a harsh sigh. "She could run to fat. Three helpings of pudding." He shook his head. "I would never mention that to *her,* you understand. But I expect she'll realize it herself before it comes to that, smart as she is."

Caine inclined his head in agreement. "I daresay."

Trent sounded half in love with Grace himself, obviously taken with her boldness and courage, if not her face and figure. He had obviously given it much thought in the past three days. As had Caine, in a much more personal way. Grace was perfectly charming and he was happy that Trent could see it, too.

Her appearance had changed, though Caine had trouble pinpointing precisely how. Her features were the same, so that wasn't it.

She still wore her hair, straight as a rapier, scraped back into a tight little chignon unless the wind destroyed its severity. He loved when it did that. With outdoor exposure, it did look lighter, streaked with sun and with more shine to it. Like silk. Several times he had touched it briefly just to feel its texture.

Perhaps the difference he saw was due to the hair and the color of her complexion. She looked healthier, pinker. She had clear, beautiful skin, flawless, in fact, though it had looked deathly pale before. Country air obviously agreed with her.

Her vivacity and outspoken manner, something he had admired from the very beginning, certainly overrode any plainness. In truth, she no longer looked plain to him at all. He had been perfectly honest with her as far as his own perception went. She was not ugly.

She had an increased air of confidence that he certainly approved. Her humor enchanted him more than he could say. The girl could make him laugh out loud. Who would have thought?

And didn't she seem quite within her element running the Wildenhurst household! He hoped she would accept that there would be little opportunity to entertain as a couple after they were married. He hated to deny her that, but needs must.

She loved his old home. He looked back at the house that would belong to him when he became earl and then to his son if he ever had one. The impending death of his uncle, the event necessary to inheriting, saddened him.

"You're frowning. Was your parting with her unfriendly?" Trent asked, showing sincere concern. "You didn't quarrel again, did you?"

"Didn't you notice? She stole my eye patch," Caine said, turning back to view the road ahead.

"By God, she's precocious! I've wanted to do that for weeks! If you ask me, I always thought the thing looked a bit theatrical." He leaned toward Caine and squinted at his scars. "Not as red as they were, are they? Did she remark?"

"Only to exclaim that I still had my eye. She expected an empty socket. I suppose my having the eye mitigated the scars."

"You won't wear the damn patch again, will you?"

Caine shook his head. "The only person whose opinion matters to me doesn't seem put off, except by my vanity. I trust you now believe I chose that person wisely?"

Trent met his gaze squarely. "I think you picked up what appeared to be a rather ordinary rock and discovered a solid gold nugget. But I don't see how you could have known her value at first glance. How did you?"

"It was her eyes," Caine replied readily, surprising himself with a truth he hadn't fully realized until now. "I looked into her eyes and they hid nothing."

Chapter Nine

⁓⦾⦿⦾⁓

The next week provided little in the way of solving the riddle of who had hired the assassin, despite the leads Trent had amassed. Those came to nothing. In fact, his and Trent's questioning in all quarters only served to reveal publicly the fact that the attempt on Grace's life had failed. Word was out in Town. Now Caine had to worry that another attempt might be made.

On the Friday, he walked down Fleet to Rundell and Bridge Jewelers at Ludmore Hill, intent on purchasing a wedding ring for Grace, as well as a bride gift.

"Something with diamonds. White stones. Nothing ostentatious," he specified when Mr. Rundell asked his preference. "The lady is quite dainty and her taste, modest."

Once he had decided on a simple gem-studded

band of gold, he asked to see something worthy of a morning gift, perhaps with blue stones. Rundell nodded with satisfaction. "I have just the thing, a versatile parure fit for a royal. Understated and elegant and absolutely exquisite."

Caine lifted and examined a delicate necklace of fine blue sapphires, the exact color of Grace's eyes. He touched the matching combs and imagined how they would look in her hair. "Excellent! These are perfect," he commented as he returned the set to Rundell to have it properly boxed and wrapped.

"Captain?" asked a soft voice just behind him. He felt a hand on his back, a light touch.

He turned abruptly. Belinda stood there, radiant in a bright paisley shawl and white day gown that exposed far too much of her generous bosom. The lovely mounds heaved as she took a deep breath and smiled, focusing on his chin.

So she still could not look at his face. Caine sketched a perfunctory bow. "Miss Thoren-Snipes."

She looked away and gestured nervously toward the front window. "I saw you enter and finally summoned courage to follow."

"I commend your bravery." He turned back to the counter to await his purchases, hoping she would go away.

"Aren't you happy to see me?" she asked in a near whisper.

"No happier than you were the last time you saw me," he said without turning.

"How dare you!" she exclaimed. Did he imagine she stamped her foot? "I've come in here to explain why I ran from you. I was in a state of shock when I saw your wounds. Any woman of delicate constitution would have run!"

He turned and cocked his head. "And any woman of breeding would not have broadcast her reaction and unfairly labeled me a cold, unfeeling monster to anyone who would listen, would she?" He again faced the counter. Surely she would leave now.

The white-haired Rundell winced and busily adjusted his cravat.

"So now you would give me the cut direct?" Belinda whined.

"I am a direct sort. You would be wise to mark it."

"Oh, don't be mean, Caine! I heard that you are to be married to someone else. Surely a wicked rumor," she simpered, "since you are still betrothed to *me*. A gentleman never goes back on his word. He *cannot*."

Caine took a deep breath, trying to control his temper. "When you declared to one and all how you were so fortunate to escape such a gruesome match, I took that as a very public cancellation."

"I never cried off it to *you!* I know you do this to shame me. And you pretended to choose another in my stead, declaring *love* for her, proposing at an assembly?"

"Yes, at Cavanaugh's. No pretense about it. I am engaged."

"You cannot be! She is plain as a peasant and worth less than nothing! *Everyone* told me so!" She issued a patently fake sob. "You've made me a laughingstock among my friends!"

"You will recover. I did."

She uttered a cry of disbelief. "You are horrible! I have never known you to be so cruel!"

What more could he say to be quit of her? "You have no patent on that quality. If you wish forgiveness for all you have said of me, then I give it. If you think this tantrum will rekindle what is now a defunct attachment, I must disappoint."

She uttered a pitifully loud moan and ran weeping noisily from the shop. He could swear he heard her mutter a curse just before the door slammed behind her.

Mr. Rundell winced again and cleared his throat. "Lucky escape, indeed, if I may say so, sir."

"You may, this once." Caine opened his money folder and peeled off the notes to pay for the jewels, adding a generous gratuity. "A bit extra for your future discretion," he explained. "I should not like this incident repeated. Anywhere."

"Of course not, sir." Rundell inclined his head. "Unless you require my repetition of it… for legal reasons, you may consider it completely forgotten."

Caine himself would not forget it. The exchange with Belinda only served to reinforce his opinion of her vain and childish nature. Either she could not bear to be replaced by another in Caine's affections even though she had been the one to reject him, or she had reconsidered the benefits of attaching herself to him now that he was slated to become titled.

Neither reason spoke well of her. He understood her shocked reaction at seeing his scars for the first time, but he could not forget how she had branded him a monstrous sight to all of society. Adding, ostensibly to excuse her own behavior, that he had gone cold and ruthless in the bargain. That had not been necessary or in any way kind. Marriage to her would have proved a disaster and he knew he was well out of it.

He met Trent at the club as arranged, but recounted none of the Belinda episode. No need to upset a friend, when it would serve no purpose.

"We shall have to step up efforts," Trent remarked as Caine joined him in the reading room. "I've checked the papers daily to see whether an account of the incident has been officially reported. See here. No details, but what it does say is factual."

Trent read aloud, his voice barely audible. "'An attack on the carriage bearing Lady Grace Renfair, betrothed of Captain Lord Morleigh, was thwarted last week on the road south of the city. Unfortunately, her modiste, Madame Avril Latrice, was killed. The perpetrator was dispatched, as well, and is no longer a threat to travelers. Additional guards have since been posted to police that road. One must wonder why there was then a scarcity of protection that allowed such a vicious attack.'"

"Word of mouth probably preceded this by at least a day or two," Caine remarked.

"Undoubtedly." Trent folded the paper and laid it aside. "How soon do you think there will be another attempt now that the one who was responsible has been alerted of the failure?"

"Who knows? I suppose that depends on who wanted it done and why, what sort of resources he has and so forth. At least Grace is well protected where she is. Let's go again this afternoon and see whether we can locate Wardfelton's solicitor at his home address. It seems a strange coincidence that he should be away for—"

"Excuse me, Caine Morleigh?" a deep voice demanded.

Caine stood and faced the questioner. "I am."

"By God, it *is* you!" The man slapped Caine on the shoulder and laughed. "Caine! It's Devil Neville, man! Don't you know me, coz?"

Caine stared at the stranger. And that he was. He bore no resemblance at all to the skinny lad Caine recalled from his youth. But the wavy black hair and dark-fringed eyes looked familiar. "Neville?"

"So you made it home from the wars! I heard, but I've been away from Town since you came back. Are you well? I was told you sustained a frightful wound." He peered sympathetically at Caine's scars.

"I do well enough," Caine declared. He turned to Trent. "I present Neville Morleigh, my cousin. Neville, my good friend, Lord Trent." He watched as they shook hands and exchanged greetings. Then he asked, "What are you doing in London?"

"Can't a fellow settle down? I live here now." His smile faded. "I was so sad to learn of the deaths of Trevor and your father. Such heavy loss at once, and you were away at the time."

"I was," Caine returned, nodding, "And thank you."

"So now you are heir to Hadley," Neville said with a sigh. "The responsibility must be trying. I know I shouldn't like it myself."

"Neither of us was born with the expectation," Caine admitted wryly, "but I believe I shall manage, as I'm certain you would do if the opportunity ever arose."

Neville regarded him with a canny expression. "You must not think I envy you, Caine. I do not. You're infinitely more suited to the job than I would ever hope to be."

"How comforting to hear it."

"But you don't believe me, I can see, and think I can guess why. I read of your fiancée's trial on the road from London last week. Everyone with the slightest reason to have sought her death must be suspect. Even myself."

Caine said nothing to that, knowing that his silence would provoke Neville to explain himself more fully.

"I need nothing that you will gain, cousin. My own business ventures have been successful and I promise you the title would only hamper me in pursuit of those."

"What sort of business ventures? Gambling?"

Neville grinned. "Ah, thinking of those card games we used to play, eh? You know I never won. That taught me never to rely on chance and especially not on my limited skills at gaming. I'm in shipping, properly insured and closely monitored. But I'm not so busy that I wouldn't be happy to add my efforts to yours in determining who instigated this menace against your lady."

"Why?"

His cousin's shoulders shrugged with impatient resignation. "Word has it you're looking for the culprit. And because she is your betrothed and will soon be one of our family, but I see you are still cautious. So be it." He reached into his pocket and handed Caine a card. "This is my direction here in Town. Do come by if I can be of any assistance."

Caine tucked the card away without looking at it. "If family is so important, why have you not visited since we were boys?"

"I have done. It is you who were away, first at university, then at war. As for me, I went abroad and sought my fortune. Business has brought me to London at least thrice each year and I always make time for Uncle and Aunt while I am here." He smiled again. "So you see, I've not been remiss, except to keep correspondence with you." He shrugged. "I fear I am not a great letter writer, but I have asked after your welfare whenever I had the opportunity. Have you done likewise?"

"I have," Caine said. "The reports were not favorable."

Neville looked confused. "No? Whom did you ask?"

"The earl, of course. He posed you as a ne'er-do-well, a gambler, drinker and waster of funds."

Caine saw the instant hurt in his cousin's expression and it looked genuine. Perhaps it was an act, but if it was, Neville had missed his calling and should be on stage.

"Well, then," Neville said in a quiet voice. "I

should go. Nice to have met you, Lord Trent. Good to see you again, cousin." He turned abruptly and left.

"What do you think of him?" Caine asked Trent.

"That he was sorely troubled by the earl's assessment," Trent remarked. "What will you do?"

"Speak to my uncle, of course. I begin to suspect there might have been devious machinations afoot on his part to get me wed."

"So you won't comply with his condition if the earl has lied about Neville?"

Caine cast Trent a look of surprise. "Not marry Grace? I pledged myself to her and it cannot be undone unless she decides otherwise."

Trent pursed his lips. "Can't risk another breach-of-promise suit, eh?"

Caine had told Trent of Thoren-Snipes's threat of that, and would discuss it no further. He dismissed the topic altogether. "This distraction has cost us time. Come, we must find that solicitor and see how Wardfelton's affairs stand."

Grace stitched for a week until her fingers were sore, wondering all the while where she would ever wear so many gowns. Four new ones for morning wear hung in her wardrobe, already finished. Two ball dresses were complete and her wedding gown lacked but the hemming and attaching the lace. She, Mrs. Oliver, Mrs.

Bowden, Jane and two women from the village worked as constantly as they could.

"There!" she exclaimed to Mrs. Oliver as she held up the short jacket. "This riding habit has all the button holes bound. If you will trim it with the grosgrain edging, Jane can apply the buttons and it will be done!"

"You have the blouse yet to do," Mrs. Oliver reminded her.

Mr. Judd appeared at the doorway to the morning room. "A young lady to see you, madam. I put her in the drawing room."

"Thank you, Mr. Judd." She laid aside the garment in her hand, happy for any excuse to leave the sewing to the other women. "Who is our visitor?" she asked the butler.

"A Miss Thoren-Snipes, ma'am. Should I send for tea?"

"No. I believe this will prove a rather brief visit," Grace told him. She did not intend to offer that chit so much as a stale biscuit. However, Grace figured it might do well to hear whatever she had to say.

Grace patted her hair and smoothed down an errant strand that had escaped her chignon. She regretted not wearing one of her new frocks today, but she was saving them for Caine's arrival. The old gray one she had on would have to do.

"Miss Thoren-Snipes. To what do I owe the

honor of your unexpected visit?" Grace said by way of greeting as she entered the drawing room. She did not invite the woman to sit. "Have you ridden all the way from London?"

"No, I am visiting friends at Hollander House, but three miles distant. I felt I had to come and speak with you."

"Concerning…?"

"Morleigh, of course," the woman said, frowning at Grace. "Apparently, knowing him is *all* that we have in common. I did not think you'd be quite so…"

"Quite so what?" Grace asked, forcing a smile as she appraised the beauty of Caine's former fiancée. Diminutive and dainty, dressed in a lovely riding costume of deep rose, Belinda Thoren-Snipes epitomized the English ideal of womanhood. She had perfect features, an hourglass figure, pale blond curls, dimpled cheeks and a girlish air. Any man would fall at her feet and worship her. Caine had been no exception.

"Forgive me, but you hardly seem the sort Captain Morleigh would ever choose to marry." The girl's comment was so sweetly made.

"Not *your* sort, you mean?" Grace kept her smile in place. "Well, I must suppose he decided against repeating past mistakes."

The woman sniffed as she dismissed Grace's words with a flick of her hand. "I came to warn you, not to suffer insults."

Miss Thoren-Snipes had an interesting pout as she fiddled nervously with her gloves. Grace noted that her breathing was rather rapid. No doubt she would like to say what she'd come to say and be gone. Fine with Grace.

"Warn me of what?"

Belinda's rosebud mouth took on an ugly twist, her lips barely moving as she spoke. "Caine Morleigh is a dangerous man, Miss Renfair. Not a proper candidate for marriage to anyone."

Grace pursed her own lips and raised her eyebrows as she digested that. "I have heard your opinion of the good captain repeated in Town. However your current version sounds considerably worse. Before he was only so ghastly looking you could not abide his presence. And cold, I believe you said. Now he's become dangerous, as well? How so?"

"He…he… He attacked me! With vicious words and in a public place in front of people! He's a horrible man with no tender feelings. None!"

Indeed, the woman appeared upset. It was entirely possible that Caine had said something to her if approached, but Grace could not believe he had sought her out to do so.

"So you believe that, on your word alone, I should cancel my wedding?" Grace asked.

"Yes! You must! I had to come and tell you. To

warn you!" She crossed the room hurriedly and stood directly before Grace. Her tone was vehement. "The man has killed people, you know, and it has unhinged his mind. You should have heard the things he said to me! So cold and forbidding! He is a crazed ruffian tricked out like a gentleman, but do *not* let yourself be fooled. He will do you harm one day if you are unwise enough to marry him. Why, I do not doubt he was the one who hired someone to assault you on the road, probably to *kill* you because he suddenly realized his mistake in proposing. Speculation about that is all over Town, you know."

Grace had heard quite enough. "If this is the new tale you're spinning for society's consumption, you go too far. Continue spreading these lies and I will encourage him in every way possible to sue you for defamation of his character."

"He would not dare sue me!" she cried.

Grace inclined her head as if thinking about that. "Perhaps not. He might simply *kill* you and prove you right."

"Ooh, you are a shameless, fortune-seeking hussy! Even worse than he! I hope you are miserable together, do you hear? *Miserable!* I hope you *die!*"

She stomped out of the drawing room and down the vestibule, the heels of her riding boots clacking rapidly on the tiles.

Grace stood at the drawing-room entrance

and watched as Judd opened the front door for her exit.

She had an enemy in that one. Then a darker thought dawned. The jealous Belinda was dead set against the wedding and had gone to quite uncomfortable lengths to persuade Grace not to carry through. Could Caine's former fiancée have hired the highwayman? Those parting words made Grace wonder.

Chapter Ten

Over a week had passed and Caine still had found no answer. He had written and reassured Grace that Belinda was incapable of arranging a bowl of flowers by herself, let alone a murder. The very idea was laughable. Her visit to Grace was nothing more than a vitriolic attempt to ruin his life because he had scorned her at the jewelers.

The investigation was proving futile in most regards, but at least Neville was less of a suspect now. It seemed he really was financially secure, had recently married and either owned or managed a shipping company. The details of his business remained a puzzle.

Today, Caine and Trent called upon him again, hoping to get answers and put the pieces of that puzzle together.

Neville's address had been the initial surprise, a town house right in Mayfair, his wife's inheritance from Lord Ludmore. Caine vaguely remembered the old man. Apparently, Neville had appropriated the very rich widow.

Caine and Trent were guided to an exquisitely furnished drawing room and announced. Neville was already there, along with a stunning young woman.

"Greetings!" Neville said with a welcoming smile as he stood. "My dear, I should like to present my cousin, Captain Caine Morleigh and his friend, Lord Trent. Gentlemen, my wife, Miranda."

Caine and Trent bowed over her hand in turn. "It is so good to meet you both," she said. "Congratulations on your impending marriage, Captain. And, Lord Trent, we are happy that our cousin has your kind support in the enquiry of the unfortunate attack on his betrothed. Will you stay for a light supper with us?"

"No, thank you. Kind of you to offer, ma'am, but not tonight," Caine said. "We are expected elsewhere."

"Another time, perhaps."

Neville smiled his approval of his wife's niceties and raised a brow in some unspoken suggestion. She gave an almost imperceptible nod to it, then addressed Caine and Trent. "If you will excuse me, sirs, I shall absent myself and leave you to your visit. I do hope we will meet again soon in happier circumstances."

"I'm certain we will," Caine replied politely.

They watched her leave and close the door behind her, a graceful exit. "She is charming and very beautiful," Caine told Neville.

"Titled and wealthy, too," Neville agreed with a grin. "So you see I can have no designs on the earl's largesse." He sighed. "I am content beyond imagining." He gestured to a grouping of chairs. "Please, do sit down."

"Thank you," Caine said.

"About this wealth and contentment of yours. Uncle knows, does he?" Caine asked, allowing his suspicion to show.

Neville's smile faltered. "I thought he did. After you told me the things he said to you about me, I went to question him, but he would not receive me when I called. Perhaps he was thinking of my father and confused the two of us in his mind. I regret the misunderstanding. His opinion matters a great deal to me, Caine. So does yours."

"Duly noted," Caine replied. "You could easily right things if you would agree to spill a few secrets about your business activities and recent whereabouts."

"Perhaps, but unfortunately I am unable to lay everything bare. My business affairs are my own and must remain so. My whereabouts these past few weeks consisted of traveling with my wife. Our wedding trip, you see. However, I take no offense at your asking and my offer to aid you still holds. Anything I can do, you have but to ask."

"Thank you," Caine said. "I will let you know." He rose to leave. "Come along, Trent. We should see the solicitor if we can find him."

"Wardfelton's man?" Neville asked as he followed them out of the drawing room into the foyer. His question revealed that he had already done a bit of detective work without being asked.

"Yes. Do you know him?" Caine asked.

"I know *of* him. Elusive, is he? Look, I have this friend, an enquiry agent of sorts," Neville declared. "He has worked for me on several occasions in my business doings and has an amazing way of locating people and ferreting out private information."

Caine wondered if the fellow might ferret out some of Neville's for a proper price.

Neville continued. "You think Wardfelton's solicitor is the one? Why would he be after Grace?"

"We haven't been able to find the man to ask," Trent declared. "Caine has done everything we know to locate him."

"My Mr. Cockerel will find him," Neville said. "Meanwhile, shouldn't you be readying for your wedding? It is…what? Only a week away now."

"Not to worry. I'll be ready," Caine assured him.

"Aunt asked if Miranda and I would attend. Would you mind if we came?" Neville asked. "I would appreciate the opportunity to square things with Uncle and also, Miranda and I would love to be there to meet your bride and help celebrate your marriage."

"Yes, of course you may come," Caine said. He would not feel at all comfortable with having Neville anywhere near Wildenhurst and Grace if there was a chance he could be the one responsible for the recent attack. But Caine felt he could hardly retract his aunt's invitation on a slight suspicion. In fact, he did not really want to believe Neville was guilty. "Why not plan to travel with the family? Six days from today, at first light."

"Excellent idea. But six days, when the wedding is in seven, Caine? Your lady must be wondering if you even remember she's there waiting."

They were at the front door now and Caine was past ready to leave, still uneasy about discussing plans in front of Neville, not ready to trust him fully. But the man stood between him and the door, obviously reluctant to end the conversation. Caine had to wonder if his cousin was that delighted to reestablish the familial connection or if he was busy formulating plans for the next assault.

"I will go to the country earlier than the others," Caine said, unwilling to reveal his exact itinerary to one whom he didn't fully trust.

"And I'll be with you," Trent announced. "There might be arrangements that require assistance!" He obviously realized Caine's attempt at misdirection. "I could attend to errands, all things a groomsman should do, eh?"

"Such as?" Caine asked, forgetting Neville altogether when faced with the idea of Trent hanging about Grace when he obviously liked her so much. Trent had hardly passed a day since their last visit to Wildenhurst without mentioning how marvelous Grace was.

"Oh, I don't know. I'll think of something," Trent said, winking at Neville. "Our lad here is somewhat green-eyed with jealousy, y'see."

Neville smiled fondly at Caine. "This bride of yours must be quite a beauty."

Caine merely shrugged. What could he say without disparaging Grace's looks. And yet, he thought perhaps Neville should be set right about what to expect. He might, by surprised word or expression, offend Grace when he did meet her.

"Grace is lovely in her own quiet way," Caine said at last, adding, "Quite unique."

"She is that," Trent agreed with a nod. "Well, we should be off."

"I'll send word when I learn anything from Mr. Cockerel," Neville told Caine. He stepped aside and opened the door for them and offered a firm handshake to both. "Godspeed, cousin. And to you, Lord Trent."

When they were settled in the carriage, Caine asked Trent what he thought of their second meeting with Neville.

"He seems sincere as the day is long," Trent said, "But he still holds secrets that even my sources can't unearth."

"Yes, and I have to wonder why," Caine muttered.

"So, will you actually go to Wildenhurst earlier than planned?" Trent asked.

"I don't know yet." Now that the idea of it had arisen, Caine began to feel an eagerness to see Grace again, to reassure her, even to argue with her. That anticipation boded well, didn't it? He thought of the future with Grace and how knowing her had already kindled a certain excitement.

Whatever life had in store for him, he had the distinct feeling that it would never be dull and complacent with her for a wife.

Her apparent fragility had proved deceptive, and though he had not been particularly drawn to her physically at first glance, that had changed. What he felt was not a burning urge to possess her body, but to hold her, to comfort and protect. It was a subtle desire, an inner need, he decided, and something that would last much longer than the hot flame of passion.

Yes, he liked that idea. It made perfect sense and would make marriage a less consuming effort. More comfortable, certainly.

The carriage bumped along in the gathering darkness as Caine and Trent headed back to Hadley House. Fog had settled over the city and lent a decided chill to the air.

Trent seemed content with the silence between them. Caine wondered if perhaps he had reacted too strongly to Trent's admiration of Grace. He didn't want his best friend to think his loyalty was in question. He also didn't like being labeled jealous.

"Would you do one of your portraits for me when you have time?" he asked, certain that a compliment to Trent's talent would mend fences. "I'd like a picture of Grace."

Trent sniffed. "I can recommend a good miniaturist. Does watercolor on ivory."

Caine sighed. "I don't want that. One of yours would mean something. You know Grace."

"Well, if you really want me to," Trent said, sounding somewhat mollified. "Perhaps she'd like one of you, too."

"Settled then. Those would make an excellent wedding gift. You'll stay for supper, won't you?" Caine asked. "You might as well stay the night. That way we could be off to Wildenhurst at first light. I've decided to go."

"Of course, if you're certain you want me to come," Trent said.

Caine grinned. "A week in the country will save you a fortune in gaming losses. And you can do the pictures then. What else have you got going on?"

"The investigation," Trent reminded him.

"Neville will carry on. He said he would. We can continue it after the wedding, since I'll have to come back to London anyway. Grace will come with me, of course. If she wants to."

"What do you mean *if she wants to?*" Trent demanded. "Why wouldn't she?"

"I promised her she could do as she prefers. She's had no freedom in years, Trent. I decided it was a fair term to offer."

"Damned fool!" Trent muttered under his breath. But Caine heard. And agreed.

When they arrived at Hadley House, Trent exited the carriage first. Shattering glass and a loud report greeted Caine as he followed. Both men instinctively dropped to the street as a second shot rang out.

"There!" Trent cried, scrambling to his feet at the sound of boots pounding the cobbles. Caine spied a figure dashing down the street at top speed. He jumped up and broke into a run.

"Caine, wait!" Trent called from a few steps behind. "Caine, you've been hit, man. Stop!"

Trent's hand grasped his arm and pulled him to a halt. "You're bleeding!"

Caine felt no pain, only red-hot rage. He yanked out of Trent's grip. "He's getting away!"

"Leave it, Caine! Look to your shoulder!"

Two of the Hadley footmen had caught up to them now, puffing with exertion. They looked at Caine with concern, as did Trent.

Then Caine felt the burn and looked down at his lapel where a round hole marred the wool. "Damn," he cursed with a cough of disbelief.

"There's an exit wound. Went straight through. Let's get you to the house. You there, find his lordship's doctor," Trent ordered as he and the remaining footman tried to assist Caine.

"I can walk, damn you!" Caine insisted, and did so.

Only when the burst of outrage and excitement faded and he faced the stairs inside Hadley House did faintness threaten to overtake him. He staggered down the hall to the library and collapsed in a leather armchair. "Who was he? Did you see?"

"Another hireling, I'd guess. No, I didn't see his face."

"This changes things," Caine gasped. "It's not only Grace they're after."

"Brilliant observation," Trent muttered as he

began helping Caine remove his morning coat. "Bring linen, man. And hot water," he ordered in an aside to the hovering footman. "Move!"

Caine allowed Trent to tend him until the physician arrived. Then he was helped upstairs to his room, undressed by his uncle's valet and put to bed.

All the while, he ignored the increasing pain and focused on the possible reasons behind the shooting. His and Grace's attacks were connected, of course. Who would want one or *both* of them dead?

"Preventing the marriage has to be the goal," he said to Trent.

"Again, marks for the obvious," Trent replied. "Now, leave off speculating and take the laudanum, Caine."

There would be no trip to Wildenhurst for him come morning. That was Caine's most worrisome thought as he felt the pain-numbing drug take effect. "Go on without me. Please keep her safe," he ordered Trent. "And don't like her… quite so much."

"I shall camp outside her door," Trent promised.

"Yes…*outside,*" Caine muttered, knowing he must trust.

The next morning when he awoke, Trent was still there by his bedside. Caine pushed up, wincing at the sharp, pulsing ache in his bandaged shoulder. "Why are you still here?" he demanded.

Trent stood and walked over to the bed. "I'll be leaving as soon as I know you're recovering. In the meantime, I've recruited three more able guards and they're on their way."

"Hurry after them!" Caine snapped. "How do you know they can be trusted?"

"Because we served with them, Caine. Smythe, Vickers and Tombs. Found them at the Whistlefish down on the docks last night after you slept. They're loyal men, damn good shots and need the work."

"Oh. Well, that's good then," Caine said, clenching his eyes shut, relieved that Trent had taken charge. "I still wish you'd go now."

"Soon enough, but Grace will want to know how you are when I get there and I thought I would wait and see. So how are you?"

"Well ventilated. Where is Ackers? Did he say how soon can I travel?" Caine barked.

"He agreed to five days if you rally and show no sign of infection. Can you use the arm? He was worried about damage to the nerves, but I told him you seemed to move it naturally enough immediately after the shooting."

Caine flexed his fist and gingerly moved his arm side to side. "Hurts like the devil."

"There was that good half hour of digging

out threads of fabric and another of stitching you up, but he says you should mend quickly if you could move it and if it doesn't fester. How do you feel otherwise?"

"Groggy. It's that vile dose. I won't take any more."

"Then lie back and go to sleep." Trent reached for a tasseled cord and draped the tail of it over the head of the bed. "Here's the bell pull if you need anything. There's nothing you can do at present but heal and rest."

Caine worried that someone would make another try at Grace, since they had failed to kill him. Of course, he could still die, he knew very well. Even in war, blood poisoning killed more soldiers than did actual wounds. "Gavin…if I don't survive for whatever reason, promise you will look after Grace?"

Trent smiled down at him. "Ah. You only use my Christian name when you're desperate for me to act like one. So I will. I promise if you die, old boy, I shall marry her myself."

Caine shot him a go-to-hell look, even as he realized that was only Trent's way of ensuring a speedy recovery.

Caine had to get to Wildenhurst soon, but he didn't think he could make it today. Besides, he did not want Grace to see him in his current condition. Despite Trent's teasing and his own unreasonable jealousy, Caine knew he could trust his best friend.

The day passed in a feverish haze of uneasy slumber and the interruption of it by periodic bloodletting and the application of stinking poultices. His shoulder ached abominably. He finally agreed to another very small dose of laudanum that would allow some relief.

A scratch on the door awakened him. Sun streamed through the east window. This must be his breakfast. He had little hunger for it.

A maid entered without waiting for his leave to do so. And she carried no tray. That was curious. Caine pushed himself to a sitting position with some effort.

The woman curtsied, head bowed so he could hardly see her face beneath the ruffle of her mobcap. "A posset, sir. From the doctor. Says you should drink it all to speed your wellness."

Caine noted her attire, dark brown fustian half covered by a dingy white apron, its bib clumsily pinned to her bodice. The lowliest kitchen maids in Hadley House dressed better. He eyed the porringer she held out. Pewter. Not the silver always used to serve one of the family or guests. Suspicion shook him to full awareness.

"You brewed this yourself?" he asked conversationally.

"As the doctor directed," she answered, sounding a bit breathless. Her posture, dress and attitude were all wrong for whom she professed to be.

"In the kitchens *here?*"

She nodded.

He doubted Cook would allow such a creature near her implements. He took the small bowl with two handles when she held it out. "Have I met you before?"

"No, sir. I don't work here. I've come from the doctor."

"Ah, I see. So Dr. *Quentin* sent you? You work for *him*."

"Yes, sir. Could you drink it now so I can be returning?"

There was no Dr. *Quentin*. Caine reached for the bell pull that Trent had arranged so that he could call for assistance and gave it a sharp tug.

The maid edged toward the door.

"Stay here," Caine ordered.

She turned and ran. Right into Trent, who grasped her upper arms.

"Bring her back in," Caine said. "I think she was attempting to poison me."

Trent turned her around and forced her back to the bedside while she struggled, shook her head and loudly proclaimed innocence.

Caine held out the porringer. "Fine. Then *you* drink it."

She began to weep and thrash wildly against Trent's grip on her.

Caine sighed and lay back, exhausted. "Take her below and confine her. Have someone locate a rat catcher and test the mixture on vermin. If it is poisoned, send for the authorities." He looked meaningfully at Trent. "Question her before you turn her over and find out who sent her."

When they had gone below, Caine made a decision. He would go to Wildenhurst and he would go today. If the would-be killer were this determined, there would be another attempt on either his life or Grace's. They could better defend against that on one front as opposed to two.

He yanked on the cord again, and when a familiar maid came this time, he asked for Hadley's valet to help him dress and pack.

The pain was nothing compared to his worry about arriving too late to save Grace if someone had already gone after her. Her guards there might never suspect a woman like the one who had tried to finish him off.

Chapter Eleven

Grace sat curled on the chaise beside the window in her bedchamber and hurriedly stitched the final inches of hem on the rose silk pelisse. She snipped the last thread. There.

They were behind schedule on her wardrobe and she feared they might have to seek more assistance if they were to complete her new wardrobe before the ceremony.

She laid the pelisse aside and looked up as the maid entered. "Yes, what is it, Jane?"

"Mr. Neville Morleigh awaits your pleasure in the morning room, ma'am," the maid announced.

Caine's cousin, the one next in line for the title and Morleigh fortune! The man had no reason to be here now unless it was to get rid of her.

She could not risk a confrontation, so she made a quick decision. "Hurry, Jane, summon Mr. Harrell. Tell him to have several of the strongest men apprehend and lock Mr. Morleigh away until we can notify Captain Morleigh that he's here."

Jane's eyes rounded. "But, my lady, Mr. Neville is—"

"I know very well who he is, Jane! Do as I say and make haste!" She watched Jane bob a curtsy and rush to obey.

Grace went immediately to her writing desk and dashed off a quick missive to Caine, informing him of his cousin's presence.

Perhaps this would end all the worry. If the ne'er-do-well cousin were the culprit and had come here himself to kill her, Caine would know what to do with him. If he had come for another reason—though, she could not imagine what that would be—then there would be no harm done other than to the man's dignity.

Hurriedly, she took the back stairs and ran to the stables herself. "Josh?" she gasped, approaching one of the grooms.

"Aye, ma'am. You'd be wanting to ride out again? Not sure that's safe without—"

"No. I need a messenger to hie to London straightaway and give this letter to Captain Morleigh."

She waited until he summoned a man for the task and handed him the letter. "Go armed and with all speed and if the captain decides to come here, stay and accompany him. Keep a close watch out."

That accomplished, Grace returned to the house. Mr. Harrell met her as she entered. "Mr. Morleigh is secured, ma'am. We locked him in the root cellar and posted a guard. I think you're right he came to cause mischief. He was a wild one as a boy and still is. Took three of us to subdue him."

Grace nodded. "I couldn't think why else he would come. The captain did tell me he was suspect in arranging the attack, so I thought caution the most prudent course. I've sent a messenger to London. So you spoke with Mr. Morleigh as he was locked away?"

"He was right heated up, ma'am, fighting, threatening me and my men and blathering on about how he'd come to offer you protection. Said someone shot the captain last evening."

"Shot him?"

When Grace gasped in fear, he shook his head. "Had suchlike happened, ma'am, the captain or his lordship would have sent for you without delay, or at the very least let you know. This cousin likely made up the tale so we'd let him near you. We should wait for the captain's orders. No doubt, he'll come post haste and take care of matters."

"Thank you, Mr. Harrell. That will be all," Grace muttered, distracted by the possibility that this Neville person spoke the truth. But neither the earl nor Trent would have sent *him* to break such news to her. Caine had told her of his uncle's low opinion of Neville Morleigh.

In any event, she would soon know one way or the other after her message reached London. All she could do at present was wait. And sew. And hope the cousin lied and there would be a wedding after all.

As the day wore on, she grew more fearful that something had happened to Caine. She almost had Jane pack her valise so that she could head for Town, but convinced herself finally that she should not risk it. Perhaps the cousin intended to have her do precisely that in response to his tale of Caine's being wounded. He could have someone waiting to accost her on the road.

Just as she sat down to tea that afternoon, Mr. Harrell appeared. "Ma'am, his lordship's carriage is coming down the road at breakneck speed!"

"It's too soon for an answer from the captain! Our rider would have only just arrived there!"

She hurried past the steward to the front entrance to await the approaching conveyance. The weather was fair, a perfect day for riding. Caine would have come by horseback as he had before. The sense of forboding that had increased since Neville Morleigh's arrival hit her full force. Something terrible had happened. She could feel it in her bones.

The carriage halted and Trent bolted out. Two footmen joined him at the carriage door and Grace saw them half lift Caine from the interior. She ran forward. "Is it true? Was he shot?"

Trent nodded, his gaze still on Caine as the men carried him. "He wouldn't stay abed as Ackers ordered. The ride was too much. Now he's fevered and weak."

"Bring him upstairs," she ordered, running ahead of them to prepare. "Mrs. Bowden, Mrs. Oliver! Come quickly! Bring the medicines!" she shouted from the vestibule. Now was no time for decorum. Her captain needed care.

Late into the night Grace tended Caine, bathing his face, arms and chest with cold cloths and dosing him with feverfew and willow-bark tea. He was out of his head with fever.

The men had undressed him and covered him decently before leaving him in her care. Grace had ordered them out, along with Mrs. Oliver, ignoring the woman's protests that an unmarried lady should not attend a grown man's sickbed.

Doing so was in no way proper and Grace knew it, but she was to be the man's wife, after all. She had more knowledge of tending the ill than all of them together. And she was, given Caine's present inability to give orders, the ranking member of the household.

She held his head as he drank the willow-bark tea Mrs. Oliver brought up. "We will need more," Grace told her. "Prepare yarrow, as well. The receipt is in the medicine book. I will ring for you when I need it."

When the woman left, Grace removed the sheet that covered Caine. She recalled everything her father had recommended for a fever resulting from a wound, and all that she had read about it in his books.

The fever was natural, occurring with almost every injury of any consequence, but she could not let it grow so hot as to do damage of its own. He would not die from this, she thought, unless left untended. She silently thanked her father for all those valuable lessons and the freedom he had given her curiosity.

She determined to remain detached from the feelings generated by her first sight of Caine's unclothed form. There were scars he had never mentioned that few people would ever see but her. Those were probably nothing compared to the ugly ones imposed on his soul by things he must have seen in the war.

Every comment since, every look askance at the evidence of his last battle must dredge up the pain of it all. This man had suffered too much. "Poor lamb," she whispered as she bathed his body to cool it.

He was a well-made man, strong and vital.

She knew he would recover. And he would be hers. Eventually she would lie with him, feel the strength and warmth of his embrace. The very thought created a fever inside her that nearly rivaled his. Could she make him want her as she wanted him?

She shook off the salacious thoughts and sighed at her foolishness. He would be mortified if he knew of it and so would she if he woke up and found her looking at him.

For hours, Grace tended him diligently, then finally he began to sweat. When he groaned and shivered with cold, she wrapped him again in the sheet, added blankets and sat beside him as he slept.

Trent knocked and entered the room around midnight. "Let me sit with him awhile, Grace. You look done in."

"No," she said absently. "I'm well enough."

"Harrell spoke to me about your *guest* and I released Neville from your makeshift jail."

"Was that wise?" Grace asked.

"It's all right. He's returning to London in something of a snit. Neville's no longer a suspect. He has been helping us and insisted on coming immediately when he heard that Caine had been wounded and was unable to protect you. Said it was his duty as family to stand in for his cousin."

"So you and Caine do not believe he could

be involved in the attempts?" Grace turned to see Trent shake his head. "Well, he will get no apology from me until I know for certain he's innocent!"

Trent stood at the foot of the bed, his gaze fastened on Caine. "Is he improving?"

"The fever has broken, but he's exhausted by it and his sleep is deep. I must keep him cool."

"Here, let me." He took the cloth from her, dipped and wrung it out, then placed it on Caine's brow. "I owe him my life, Grace. Trust me to tend him awhile." He shot her a crooked smile. "Sorry, I realize you never offered me the privilege of dropping the courtesy. Do you mind?"

She sighed, flapped a hand and sat down heavily in the armchair by the window. "You might as well. I suppose we are to be constantly in each other's company."

"You don't like me, do you, Grace?"

She leaned her head back and closed her eyes. She did not want to have a conversation at all and certainly not about this, but unless she left the room, it could hardly be avoided. "I like you very well, Lord Trent."

"Just Trent, please. And yes, I daresay we will see much of one another in future. I hope to be your friend, as well as Caine's."

"Then answer me this, *friend*. You have never

approved of my marriage to him," Grace said. "Why is that?"

Trent met her gaze steadfastly. "I objected to his choosing you on impulse, almost without thought, so I believed. But since? Well, I now believe you are perfect for him in every way."

Grace wasn't sure he was sincere, but at the moment, hardly cared one way or the other, she was so tired. "Fine then. See if you can get him to drink more of that tea, will you?"

"What's in it?" Trent asked as he raised Caine's head and lifted the cup to his lips.

"Yarrow," she explained, too fashed to feel much other than impatience. "It rids a body of impurities and helps to fight off a return of the fever."

He gave a little grunt of a laugh. "I read once that yarrow's a witch's brew, used as a love charm."

"Ask him how loving he feels when he wakes and is calling for the chamber pot ever quarter hour," she retorted. An indelicate statement, she knew, but did not care in the least. She was exhausted and in no mood to be teased. "I'll leave him to *you* then."

"As well you should."

They settled into an uncomfortable silence for some minutes. Then he turned to her, keeping his voice low as he spoke. "Grace, do you know Wardfelton's factor?"

She was not surprised he had changed the topic from bodily functions. Though she would have preferred not to talk at all, she answered. "His solicitor? Yes. Mr. Sorenson. I met him a number of times. He was often at the house the first year I came. Less later on, I think, but I hadn't the run of the place then, so I'm not certain. Why? Do you suspect him of conspiring with my uncle in some way?"

Trent busied himself with the cloth, wringing it out and laying it again on Caine's brow. "I wonder if this Sorenson might have embezzled your inheritance and feared he'd be found out when the marriage settlement was arranged. That's the only motive he would have for getting rid of either of you. Of course, that could be Wardfelton's reason, as well. Could be either of them or they could be in collusion."

Grace sat up straighter and tried to clear her head. "My uncle told me often that I had no funds left to me. He could be right. I doubt my father had much personal wealth when he died, since he was a country doctor and hadn't many well-to-do patients. Whatever he had after he inherited was probably allied with the title and property that went next to my uncle."

"We shall see," Trent told her. "Meanwhile, you needn't worry. This place is proof against any threat at the moment and we will see it stays so until you and Caine are married. Then he will

have the authority to sort out anything that has
to do with your inheritance."

Grace thought about that. "Morleigh will own
me then," she muttered to herself. "But he has
promised me a certain freedom."

Trent laughed softly. "Straining at the bit already? What sort of wife will you be, I wonder."

"Perhaps an absent or an invisible one, a name
on the marriage lines to satisfy his lordship's
decree. That is what Caine was after when he
chose me, was it not?" That sounded bitter to her
own ears, and was in fact how she felt.

"Ah, but if I know you, you will never settle
for that," Trent said.

Grace frowned and crossed her arms over her
chest and closed her eyes, dismissing the topic
and Trent. No, she would not settle for it. She
wanted the captain and she would have him.

"He doesn't want to see you," Trent said as he
met Grace in the corridor outside the sickroom
the next morning. He had finally convinced her
to go to bed and rest and now she was returning after a few hours of sleep. Then he clarified,
"Rather, he doesn't want *you* to see *him*."

"But that's absurd! I spent most of the night
in there. I've already seen him." More of him
than anyone realized, Grace thought with a huff.
"How am I to tend him if he won't let me in?"

Trent pointed to the stairs. "He had me send

for the village doctor. That's probably him coming up now." His voice dropped to a whisper. "With his lancet and bowl, no doubt. Or leeches."

"No!" She knew the man. He had been summoned by Mr. Harrell after John Coachman was shot. He was an apothecary, as well as a surgeon, and seemed competent enough for one of that ilk, but he was no physician. She trusted Caine's treatment to no one but herself.

Grace tried to push past Trent, but he held her back. She had the irresistible urge to stamp on his foot. "I will not let Caine be bled!"

"Simmer down," he insisted. "I won't allow it, I promise. The wound needs to be looked at, Grace. So go, have your breakfast and leave him to the doctor and me. Caine's surly now that he's lucid and you don't want to go in there."

"But I have to—"

"Grace?" Trent patted her shoulders as his hands rested there. "Humor me, please. Caine's somewhat indisposed and a female attending him would not be the thing at all."

"Oh." She felt her face heat. It was one thing to bandy about indelicate matters at midnight in a sickroom when feeling too exhausted for propriety, quite another to speak openly of them in the bright light of day.

The village doctor reached the top of the stairs and gave them a nod as he approached.

"Well, then…" She backed out of Trent's grasp and straightened her skirts with a nervous gesture. "Call me if I am needed."

"On the instant, trust me."

She watched uneasily as he ushered the doctor into Caine's bedchamber and closed the door behind them. For a few moments, she stood there listening, heard the muffled sound of Caine's angry protests and smiled. He sounded strong enough to fend off lancets and leeches on his own.

Filled with a sense of satisfaction that she had done the best she could for him, Grace went downstairs to see how the household had been faring without her direction.

For two days, she kept busy with the duties she had assumed, she sewed on her trousseau, she collected herbs and flowers from the gardens. And periodically, she attempted to gain access to the patient.

Caine was having none of it. He obviously did not want her to see him as he was, just as Trent declared. She wondered if he realized that she had seen him in a much more vulnerable state and felt embarrassed to face her.

She admitted that if the situation were reversed, she would probably feel the same. Still, she could not resist pushing, always unsuccessfully, for a brief visit. She quite missed Caine and was somewhat miffed that he was not missing her.

On the afternoon of his third day at Wildenhurst, Grace was just coming down for tea when the butler met her at the foot of the stairs. "An unfamiliar coach and four approaches, my lady," Mr. Judd informed her. "Mr. Harrell and the lads are at the ready."

Grace nodded. "If the visitors offer no threat, show them to the drawing room. I will be there directly."

She hurried back upstairs and went straight to Caine's room to fetch Trent. When she knocked, he opened the door immediately and blocked her view of the interior.

His dishabille surprised her. Trent was usually dressed to the nines wherever she saw him. Today, he appeared exhausted and unkempt in rolled-up sleeves and his shirt gaping open at the neck. "Sorry, his nibs still won't see you, Grace. Perhaps later in the day."

"It's you I wanted. Someone's coming to visit, in a coach and four, no less. Will you greet them with me? I fear it might be my uncle."

Caine piped up, ostensibly from the bed. "Trent! Send one of the lads to help me dress."

"You stay exactly where you are!" Trent ordered over his shoulder. "Give me a moment," he said to Grace. "Do not go down without me."

She agreed. He had to don his neckcloth, coat and, she hoped, a loaded pistol.

Her stomach tightened with a knot of apprehension. It would be very like Wardfelton to barge in unannounced, demanding she return with him, especially if he thought Caine was still in London. Or if he knew Caine was wounded. That would mean that he…

A sudden commotion and voices in the vestibule downstairs demanded attention. Grace peeked over the railing.

"How is he, I say? Someone get that gel here with answers! Judd, step lively, man. Go find her!"

Trent ran down the corridor and took Grace's arm. "Come, that's his lordship's bellow. Hurry down before he bursts a vein. What the hell is the old rascal doing here, I wonder?"

"Apparently he's come to see after Caine! We should have sent word."

"God, yes. I forgot," Trent whispered. "He'll be furious we haven't." They reached the curve in the stairs and saw the earl glaring up at them. "Rest easy, milord. Your heir is alive and well."

"You there," he said with a curt nod to Grace. "Is my nephew abed then?"

She dropped a curtsy. "He is, sir, but recovering nicely. Your rooms are ready for you, as usual. You must be exhausted after such a long journey."

"Yes, yes. Damned annoying," he admitted gruffly, leaning heavily on his countess's arm. "Not at all the thing, is it, Bewley? Haring about like we used to."

"No, dear," Lady Hadley murmured. She smiled rather vacantly at Grace. "We came early for the wedding. There is still to be one?"

Grace wasn't altogether certain there would be, but she nodded. "I believe so, ma'am. Would you like to go up to your rooms now? I'll send someone to lay a fire."

"Nonsense!" barked the earl. "Not cold enough to waste wood."

"A fire would take the chill off, Haddie," the countess said. "A nice pot of tea, too. And biscuits."

Trent had gone forward to assist the earl. "Mr. Judd and I will help you up, sir."

"Hmmph. Damned nuisance this. Used to bound up steps like a leaping buck. I could still do it if I took the notion." He issued a rumbling cough and slung one arm around Trent's neck. Judd took the other, relieving the countess, and they lifted his legs to carry him.

Grace watched their awkward ascent, then looked to Lady Hadley. "Is the earl getting on better these days?"

"Yes, it seems so," the countess said with a heavy sigh. "Dr. Ackers is to follow later today."

"Good news. He can see to the captain's wound when he comes."

Lady Hadley didn't remark any further.

"Come, take my arm," Grace offered. "We'll go up together and I'll send Jane down for your tea while Mr. Judd lays a fire for you."

"You're a sweet girl, Belinda," the lady said.

Grace smiled. "It's Grace, ma'am. Remember? Belinda...declined."

"Oh, yes, of course. Declined." A soft chuckle. "The pretty one."

"Yes, ma'am." Grace sighed and held the countess's arm as they slowly climbed up the stairs. "She was the pretty one."

"Aunt Hadley!"

Grace looked up. Caine stood beside the newel post at the first-floor landing, frowning at his aunt. He was barefoot, wearing a belted banyan over a wrinkled linen shirt and dark trousers. His hair was sleep tousled and he badly needed a shave. She felt the maddest urge to hug him.

"It's all right, Caine," she said with a slight shake of her head. "We have everything in hand. You should go back to bed."

"Darling boy!" his aunt cooed, "You look a fright! We so hoped to find you well of your ague! Are you fevered?"

He sighed and accepted the woman's embrace when she gained the landing and reached out.

"No fever, Aunt Hadley. I'm feeling fine." He peered at Grace over the woman's shoulder and mouthed the words, "I'm so sorry."

"Her ladyship is probably tired." Grace smiled at him as she passed by them, unable to resist touching his sleeve. "See her to her chamber, then, if you're up to it. I'll find Jane to tend her."

She wondered if anyone had told the Hadleys the truth about Caine's having been shot. More likely, the countess only imagined he had the ague rather than believe anyone would fire a gun at her nephew.

Grace wished to heaven the wedding were over and everyone but Caine would leave for London. Perhaps she was more like the countess than she realized in trying to deny unpleasantness.

Chapter Twelve

The afternoon had taken its toll on Grace. The Hadleys' arrival had further stirred the household, already in a state of flurry and worry due to Caine's wounded presence. Then Dr. Ackers had come from London to tend the earl, eager to have a private conversation with Grace about her father's patients and Withering's research.

In addition to that, Mr. Harrell interrupted her day several times with concerns over providing two newly hired men with weapons and temporary lodging. Mrs. Bowden and Mr. Judd had almost come to blows over discipline of a footman and tweenie who had formed a liaison. And so it had gone, one thing after another.

Late that evening, after everyone was settled, Grace sat down with a cup of tea in the library. It had become her favorite place of refuge. Here, she could escape the bustle of the household. Everyone usually assumed she was reading or going over accounts and left her alone. Yet this evening, Trent did intrude.

"Caine asked me to come down and see how you are. He's very upset about his aunt."

Grace set down her cup, rubbing her brow to banish the ache that had formed there. "Why so?" She motioned idly to a chair, a reluctant invitation for him to sit.

Trent hesitated for a moment, then sat down. "You know, what she said to you. Sometimes she doesn't think."

"Oh, the mistake in identity?" She dismissed that with a sigh. "I took no offense at that. The poor lady was weary and confused."

He sat back in his chair, apparently content to stay for a while. "No, about her other comment."

"That Belinda is the pretty one? Well, Trent, you can't fault her for honesty. Belinda *is* pretty."

"I didn't realize you knew her," Trent said, suddenly alert and leaning forward.

"A recent acquaintance. She came here to warn me not to marry her captain." Grace tossed her head and pulled a face, aping Belinda's haughty attitude. "He is *so* dangerous! Beware the captain!"

"She warned you off?" Trent's brow lined with concern as he sat forward. "Why didn't you tell us she had been here? When was this?"

"Before Caine was shot. I wrote to him about it and he answered immediately that she was only posturing. That it wasn't significant and we should ignore it."

"I can't believe she dared."

"You don't think she's the one who—"

Trent raised his shoulders in a shrug. "She hasn't the brains, but that brother of hers… I should speak to Caine about that." He pushed out of the chair. "Excuse me."

Grace jumped up and grabbed his arm to stop him. "Please don't put that in his mind, Trent! He might want to do something about it and he's not well enough. Let it go for now, please."

He turned and took her hands in his. "You're right, of course." He searched her face for a long minute. "May I make an observation? You won't misconstrue it?"

"Of course I wouldn't," she said, looking down at his grip on her fingers and back to his serious expression. "What?"

"Prettiness goes no deeper than the surface, but beauty shines out of the soul. You glow with it, Grace. I just wanted you to know that."

Speechless with shock, she just stood there as he released her hands, turned abruptly and left the library.

Caine remained in his room that evening, as did Trent, Lord and Lady Hadley. Grace dined alone, as usual, and spent another restless night.

Trent joined her for breakfast the next morning. "You look refreshed," she commented, toying with her spoon instead of facing him directly. "Sleeping better now that our patient is improving?"

"He's sleeping through the night without laudanum. Grace, about what I said—"

"So when will he emerge from his cave again, do you think?" She interrupted him because she had determined to forget his remark to her last evening and never speak of it again. Either he had made it out of pity, or worse, was developing some sort of tendre for her, which definitely wouldn't do.

He nodded and smiled. She hoped he understood the matter was finished.

"Caine will see you this evening. He apologizes for appearing in such a state yesterday and says he will make himself presentable and come down for supper."

"It is about time!"

"The man is vain past forgiving," he said with a shake of his head. "Doesn't want anyone to view him in any light but the best."

"No," she argued. "Not *vain* precisely. He simply has a low opinion of the female gender and believes all of us are that much taken with how a man looks."

"And you disagree with that, of course."

Grace shrugged. "Some of us obviously *are* that way, given his past experience."

"Ah, but not Saint Grace of the beautiful soul! Do you forgive me for yesterday's flirt? I can't seem to help myself."

She laughed. He wouldn't let her forget it. "You are an intolerable tease, Trent. How is Caine really doing this morning?"

"Bearlike, if you must know, but I've seen him in worse temper. You'll have your work cut out for you in future, jollying him out of those moods of his…" He let the sentence drift as he shook his head and rolled his eyes heavenward.

"Yes, dear old Belinda also warned me he was dangerous. So you'd both have me cry off and leave the poor man at the altar?"

"Of course. Then I would have a clear shot at you myself."

"There you go again! Restrain yourself till you get back to Town, will you?" She got up and paced to the window, hiding her smile, determined to give as good as she got. "If you use up all your good lines on me, what shall you have to offer the London belles?"

"Practice, love, practice! I'm only half serious at the best of times. Caine's a lucky man, but I would never tamper with the best match ever made. You will be incredibly good for him, y'know." Trent rose as he spoke. "I'm going for a short ride and dispense with some pent-up energy if you will excuse me."

She grinned. "Too right I will. Go and devil a horse."

The butler appeared in the doorway before Trent reached it.

"A letter for you from Mr. Neville Morleigh, sir." He handed it to Trent on a silver salver.

Grace approached as Trent tore open the missive, both knowing it must concern the investigation.

Trent read it quickly, then refolded it. "Come. We'll brave the bear's den together. Caine should hear this now. Trust me, he's well enough."

"Knock first," she said, huffing from exertion as they topped the stairs. "He might not be dressed."

Trent chuckled and shot her a sly grin. "Never tell me you spent half a night with the man and didn't peek under the covers once. Have you no natural curiosity?"

She felt her face heat with color. "Have you no natural shame?"

"No, and that would make two of us," he admitted as he rapped on the door. He raised his voice. "Make yourself decent, Captain! Female in the barracks!"

She heard Caine curse.

Trent opened the door without waiting for

leave. Grace couldn't resist entering right behind him.

Caine stood before the washstand, straight razor suspended and his face half covered with lather. He was bare, save for the bandage on his shoulder and buckskin breeches with the front flap only half buttoned.

She stared, again fascinated with the way his chest hair narrowed down his midsection to the indentation of his navel. He looked quite different standing up and nearly naked. Madly muscled and rather delicious, in fact. She couldn't quite stifle a smile of pure appreciation.

"Damn you, Trent!" Caine exclaimed, tossing the razor in the bowl and reaching for the drying cloth. He wiped his face and ran a hand through his hair. "Good morning, Grace."

She reluctantly lowered her gaze to the floor. "Good morning, Caine. You're looking *well*." She feared she had sort of sighed that last word.

Trent snickered, then must have remembered why they were there. He held out the letter. "Message from your esteemed cousin. Seems Wardfelton's solicitor has vanished along with his account books. Neville's man traced him to the docks and found he took passage yesterday for the Continent on one of the trade vessels. Sounds as if we've discovered the culprit, eh?"

"Indeed. What about Wardfelton's involvement?" Caine asked even as he scanned the letter. "Ah, I see Neville has put a watch on him."

Trent nodded. "The solicitor was probably working alone. Wardfelton would be gone, as well, if it was he who played false with Grace's inheritance."

"I told you there might have been no inheritance," she reminded Trent.

"I think that's highly unlikely, but we shall find out," Caine said as he laid the letter on the washstand. "You realize Wardfelton could not simply disappear? He is an earl, after all, and I believe he would brave it out and challenge any accusation rather than abandon his title and everything that entails."

When he turned back to them, he looked Grace over as if he had never seen her before. For a long moment, he said nothing. Then he turned away again. "If you two would give me a few moments to finish here and dress, I'll meet you downstairs."

"In the morning room," Grace said. "Trent and I just ate. The food's still warm. No one else is up yet."

"Coffee will do," Caine muttered.

"I'll do my utmost to entertain her until you interfere," Trent said.

They left and Trent closed the door behind them.

"You are a horrible man," Grace said in a

gruff whisper. "Downright perverse to tease him that way."

"I know," he said with a sigh. When they were on the stairs, he stopped and touched her arm. "Grace, he's going to want to leave today, so be prepared for that. He might even want to delay the wedding."

"He said nothing about—"

"He will. I know that look. I've known him for so long I can usually tell what he's thinking." He took her arm and continued their descent. "Did you see the way he looked at you just now, once the surprise of our intrusion was over?"

Grace certainly did recall. "Yes, and did you think he seemed more disappointed than usual in the way I look?" Jane had put up her hair in what Grace believed was a flattering style. Her morning gown was new, a bright shade of blue just the color of her eyes. And with regular meals, she had lost the gauntness of face and body. "I thought I might appear a bit better than when he was here before, but perhaps not."

She hated to admit, even to herself, that the countess's comment on Belinda's prettiness and Trent's touting her *inner* beauty had anything to do with her effort to improve her outer looks. She had made a real effort.

Trent huffed a sigh. "Ah, Grace. Ill as he's been, and not having really looked at you for over two weeks, Caine wouldn't have noticed the difference until just now."

"It might be blue he dislikes!" She shook her head. "You know, how he hates yellow. Or perhaps it's my hair." These curls were not natural to her, a vanity perhaps not as flattering as she had thought. "I knew I should have worn a cap, lace or something to properly cover it."

Trent turned her to him and stared into her eyes. "It's neither. You look beautiful. You bloom with health and confidence now. The problem is that you're no longer the wretched little wraith left on the vine for him to pick and tuck away, Grace."

"Why should he mind that?"

"Wait and see for yourself. I will lay odds he puts off your marriage, probably to give you a way out of it. When the matter is settled, I expect you'll have money, enough to marry where you please. Caine will see to that, one way or another."

"What? You can't possibly know if there ever was any inheritance and I will certainly never accept charity! Anyway, why would I want out of the marriage? I'm well content, even eager to have it done. What do you think of that, Lord Trent?" she demanded.

"Eager, Grace?" he asked with a touch of sarcasm. "Well, what I think is that you will have to convince Caine you really mean it, my dear, and that will be no easy task."

Caine finished shaving and dressed for riding. He intended to leave for London as soon as possible. His shoulder was healing well enough, though it still pained him. That pain was nothing to that which he expected to feel when he set Grace free of their engagement. He had to do it, because it was only right.

He had worried about it almost constantly since those wonderful three days they spent together at the outset. Seeing her yesterday and especially this morning had convinced him that he was not right for her.

Grace was so full of life, so appealing and now, exceptionally lovely, as well.

She was not the woman he had thought her to be now that she was herself again. Fear of Wardfelton had almost ruined her health. The man had damaged her spirit, too, but that had healed very quickly, in the space of days. Now, weeks later, she was a beautiful young woman with everything to recommend her except a fortune. He would have to be shameless and with no honor at all to take advantage of a betrothal she'd agreed to only to save her own life.

It might have been a marriage of convenience he had planned for them, but it had been a marriage of survival for her. She had been desperate. How could he hold her to such a promise?

She would have a dowry, too, if he could recover it for her from that damned solicitor. If not, he would see her well fixed so she could make her own choice of husbands. He knew in his heart that her choice would not be a battle-worn cynic, who was more prone to argue than entice.

He had done little to encourage her to like him, much less want to be shackled to him forever. He had promised her freedom and she should have the ability to freely choose.

Grace had observed close-hand what she would be getting if she married him. She'd seen him at his very worst, bloodied and sweating, probably worse than that while he was out of his mind with fever. Damn, he hated thinking of it.

He made his way down the stairs to the morning room, dreading what must be done. Grace and Trent sat nursing their coffee as he entered. She quickly hopped up and poured him a cup.

Caine watched her, noting anew how lovely she was now, how the roses in her cheeks blushed the pearled sheen of her complexion and how even her lips seemed plumped to perfection. The striking blue of her eyes looked more intense with the color she was wearing. Her hair seemed even lighter than the last time, swept up into a crown of curls, interlaced with a blue ribbon.

"How beautiful you are." The words slipped out before he could catch them.

She lay a hand on his good shoulder, set down his cup and offered a merry grin. "Pure artifice, I assure you. My maid is a wonder with a curling iron and face paint."

He cleared his throat and shot Trent a look of dismissal. It did not take. Trent merely raised an eyebrow and stayed right where he was. On second thought, perhaps it was just as well the conversation did not go private.

"Now that the solicitor has left the country, there should be little danger of another attack. No point to it, really. So I believe I should go to London today and question Wardfelton about the matter. It's time we got to the bottom of this."

Grace's smile faltered. "The wedding is in three days. Why not wait until after?"

Caine sipped his coffee before answering. "As to that, it would be best, I think, if we postponed the ceremony until we've cleared everything completely. Then we shall see." Somehow, he couldn't utter the words that could end things between them. Not yet.

Trent raised both brows then as he turned to Grace and pulled a comical frown. Caine could have boxed his ears.

She took her chair, propped her elbows on the table, rested her chin on her hands and looked directly into Caine's eyes. "No," she said simply.

"I am going to London," he declared. "I have to go."

"Fine. Go," she said. "But be back in two days."

Caine turned to Trent. "Please leave us."

Trent pushed back his chair, raised his hands in surrender and walked out. He shot Grace a smile over his shoulder, but she paid no attention. Her eyes were on Caine.

When they were alone, Caine started to state his case, but she interrupted before he could. "No," she repeated. "We will not delay, nor will we cancel the wedding, Caine. Everything is planned. Jilting me will be worse than anything my uncle ever did to me, you see."

She abandoned her recalcitrant pose and got up, going to the window to look out so that her back was to him. Caine suspected she was hiding tears. He'd had no intention of hurting her. He rose and followed, cupping her shoulders with his hands and turning her around to face him. "Grace, things have changed…."

"I know, but my mind has not." She grasped his face with her hands, raised to her toes and pressed her lips to his. When he would have pulled back, she held him, increasing the intensity of the kiss.

He couldn't resist her moan of encouragement. Damn, she tasted so sweet, so determined, as her tongue touched his.

He abandoned himself to the kiss, embracing her fully and holding her body as close as he could. How soft and giving, insistent, enticing. He wanted, needed... Until her hand accidentally brushed his wound and he jerked in pain. She jumped back, alarmed.

They stared at each other in shocked silence. The kiss was more than either of them expected, he reasoned. Grace didn't appear to have been quite that thoroughly kissed before and Caine wondered if he had, either.

He knew he'd never felt quite that out of control during a mere kiss. Huh. There was nothing remotely *mere* about it. He was aroused, breathing rapidly. He saw that she was, too.

"One week," he said finally, and added, "Please."

She sighed and nodded, looking rather helpless.

He kissed her again, keeping this one quick and perfunctory with no body contact. He could not afford to linger or there would be no waiting, even for a week. Perhaps distance would help solidify his thoughts on the marriage. Right now they were rather liquid. And hot. "Keep well," he whispered as he released her lips.

He left before she could recover and speak. Heaven only knew what she would say or how he would respond.

Trent was waiting in the vestibule with his

coat and hat. "Let's go then," he said. "Unless you'd like me to stay."

Caine didn't even bother to reply to that idiotic suggestion.

Trent insisted they take the carriage and Caine didn't protest. He knew he was not up to an all-day ride, and it did look as though it might rain.

Once on the road, Trent began his inevitable questions. "So is the wedding still on? I warn you, if you cast her off, I plan to—"

"Stop there. I have no intention of casting Grace off. She insists we carry through and, as you well know, I am honor bound. Only *she* can end this farce and is apparently unwilling to do so." *Thank God.* He leaned back against the squabs and closed his eyes. "Though I cannot for the life of me, think why she wouldn't. I promised her protection and couldn't even protect myself."

"She loves you," Trent said with a grin.

"You're a bigger fool than I thought if that's what you think. She's only grateful and feels obliged."

"So you no longer want her?" Trent prodded.

"I want her, all right. What man wouldn't want her? It's just that she's not the same she was before."

"Ah, I see, not what you bargained for," Trent

said, nodding sagely. "Now she's become the very sort you wanted to avoid, another Belinda."

"She's not a whit like that little she-devil, and you know it. But now she'll require a great deal of attention. Managing. Entertaining," he added. "She admitted as much when I was here before. She loves parties, balls and such. How can I be dancing attendance on a woman and fulfilling all my duties at once? Damn it, I have to figure a way."

"Oh, I'll gladly dance with her," Trent offered. "And I daresay, there'll be a crowd of admirers willing to do the same."

"Just so," Caine agreed with a sad shake of his head. "How long do you suppose it would take her to realize her mistake in tying herself to me? How could I compete with men who haven't a care in the world past what color waistcoat to wear?"

"You have a rather low opinion of her, Caine. She's not so shallow as that. Grace cares about you a great deal. Looks like love to me, or at least, the promise of it."

"No, it's only gratitude. Not an auspicious emotion on which to base a marriage."

"Neither is convenience, your motive for choosing her in the first place," Trent reminded him. He had gone serious now, all teasing aside. "Were I you, I would look again and see if I could find better reason. You might possibly love her, too."

Caine was afraid to look any deeper. He already knew he wanted Grace. He might find that he did love her.

Losing Belinda had nearly destroyed him, but at least that had been swiftly over and put behind him. He shuddered to think what it would be like to be married to a woman, truly loving her, and suffering *constant* rejection once she realized her mistake.

Chapter Thirteen

No matter what she did, Grace kept thinking about that kiss. That and the heat of his body pressed to hers had awakened a hunger she had not known was sleeping within her. She thought she had experienced desire before, but that chaste touch of lips and slight tingle she felt with Barkley had been nothing, a mere hint of the raging storm that Caine Morleigh's kiss could unleash.

Now she wished to heaven she had never read all those medical texts in Father's library when she was a girl. How had she ever thought herself worldly beyond her years merely because she knew how a man and woman fit together? Words on a page told nothing of the feelings that must accompany all of that. And she had only a brief taste of those feelings. All too brief.

Grace tried to dismiss the thoughts until they would be appropriate. It was all she could do, so she had to stay busy every minute with other things.

She was sick to death of sewing. The house was in order, menus all planned and there was nothing to do now but wait for the wedding. She hated waiting. So what next to do to keep Caine off her mind?

Maybe this was an ideal time to see for herself how the earl was progressing. He kept to his chamber, taking his meals there and she had hardly seen him since his arrival. All she had was Dr. Ackers's word that he was taking the concoction she had suggested and was much better. She wanted to see for herself.

Yesterday, they had spoken at length about her father, who had attended university the same years as Ackers, though they had known one another only in passing.

He assured her he had begun treating the earl, using Withering's writings as a guide. They discussed trusting apothecaries who furnished the substance and Grace convinced him that she could provide better quality from the plants growing wild in the wood. They talked of preparation and dosage.

He reminded her of her father in attitude if not appearance. He had the same intelligent eyes, but Ackers was a slight man with effeminate features, thickly pomaded hair and an overlarge mustache. Grace quite liked the doctor.

"I should like to speak with Lord Hadley," she told him as they met by chance at midmorning in the downstairs corridor. "Is he awake this time of day?"

"Always, unless he's very ill. Lady Hadley rises late, so he will probably be alone. Shall I accompany you?"

"That's not necessary. I won't be long and I promise not to tire him."

He agreed, so Grace went upstairs to the earl's chambers, knocked softly and entered without waiting for a reply. "Milord, I've come to see how you're feeling today."

"Eh? Well, come in, come in, gel. What is it, then?" He pushed up against the pillows and frowned at her. "Bad news?"

"No, sir, not at all! I thought I would keep you company for a little while, if you don't mind."

He squinted at her. "Looking pert today. Nice frock, that."

Grace curtsied, holding out the skirts of her new rose morning gown. "Thank you, milord! I see where Morleigh gets his way with the ladies." She put on her best smile and approached his bedside.

The earl chuckled. "Cozening his old uncle won't get you any more blunt, gel. He'll be getting it all soon anyway."

"I hadn't a single thought in that direction," she assured him, eager to get to the point of her visit. "Could we speak about your condition, sir?"

He appeared amused. "Heart's giving out. Shouldn't take long. You can wait, can't you?"

"It's nothing to do with me, or with your nephew inheriting. Dr. Ackers says that he told you my father was a physician and treated quite a few gentlemen with heart afflictions."

The earl nodded. "Gave 'em that stuff Ackers gives me."

"Yes, sir, what do you think of it? Do you feel any stronger?"

"I do." He cocked his head. "But it won't last, y'see."

She reached for his hand. "May I study your pulse for a moment?" When he shrugged and indicated he would let her, she pressed her fingertips to his wrist. After feeling the uneven pattern, she risked a further presumption. "Could I listen to your heartbeat?" He nodded and Grace leaned forward, laying her ear against his chest.

"Still fluttery," she remarked as she straightened again. "But I suppose you know that even better than I. We could make it steadier and stronger, but, as I'm certain the doctor told you, increasing the dosage carries risk."

He laughed, a rusty grunt of sound that ended in a cough. "Ackers is an old woman, more scared than I ever was that I'll die. I am his only patient, y'see, so he's overcautious."

"Not without cause, sir. There's a chance that increasing what he's given you might make you sicker than you are." She let out a sigh. "Or worse."

"Too much could kill me," he said, nodding. "Why should you prolong my old life when I'm worth more to you and Caine dead than alive?"

"Caine loves you, sir, and your living longer will make him happy. If he is happy, then surely I shall be."

She saw a sheen of tears in the weak old eyes. "Loves me, does he? Ha. Well, then calm Ackers's fears if you can and let's see what happens."

Grace conversed with him a few minutes longer, turning the subject to country life and happier things. Then she bade him good morning and left, eager to find the doctor again, glad to have a purpose that would occupy her mind.

The next few days crawled by for Grace. The nights were worse.

The only unusual occurrence was the arrival of a letter addressed to her. Mr. Judd had brought it to her that morning, along with several invitations to various events nearby. She had thought little of it at first, except to wonder who might be writing to her now that Dr. Ackers was here.

Then she read it and wondered whether she should send for Caine immediately. But she was safe as could be here, wasn't she? Caine would be back soon anyway and there was nothing he could do about it even if he were here.

So upset she could not sleep, she had donned a robe in the middle of the night and come down to the library to fetch something boring to read.

Certainly not that letter, she thought with a grimace as she glared at it. The horrible thing had arrived in the post and still lay open on the desk. She was unable to touch it, even to throw it away. In spite of her resolve, it drew her to it yet again. Perhaps she had overlooked some clue as to who had posted it.

This time, she tried to suppress her outrage and examine it objectively, as one who was un-involved in the message.

It was addressed without title, simply to Grace Renfair. There was no greeting inside, only the one paragraph and, of course, no signature.

Ask yourself why he would propose marriage to someone of your sort. It was because you looked fit to die and he hoped you would. He has to wed, yet wants no wife. Cry off and run if you wish to live. Beware his tricks. Beware his friends. Save yourself.

Her first thought was that Belinda Thoren-Snipes had sent it. But Grace had made it quite clear to the woman that her warning held no credence. Why would Belinda bother with a second of the same nature? Surely the woman's pride would hardly allow that.

Grace tapped a finger against her lips as she studied the hand. The graceful penmanship indicated someone with much practice at it, one who had perhaps studied calligraphy.

Wardfelton's handwriting was spidery and backslanted. She had seen it on his outgoing correspondence that first year when he had treated her with civility. Trent's writing was entirely different, too, for she had a sample of that. Caine's was a bold hand with few curves and no flourishes.

Judging by the comparison of this to the writing of her uncle, Trent and Caine, Grace felt fairly certain none of them had written it.

It made no sense that Caine would write anything so self-incriminating anyway. He certainly couldn't be guilty of attempting to have her murdered. Someone had tried to kill him, too. She had come to trust Trent as a true friend. Despite his constant flirting, she knew he wanted her to wed Caine.

Perhaps part of the message might be true, however. She had looked *fit to die,* as the letter said. Wait! Whoever wrote that must have been there at the ball to see her the night Caine proposed. How else would the writer know how she had looked? Trent and her uncle had attended, among countless others. Belinda had not, but she had friends who were there.

Grace was eager to have Caine return and see this. She quickly laid a book over it, determined to leave it covered there until he came.

Trent had posted a brief missive to her the day before, stating that Caine was feeling amazingly well and the matter of the solicitor was *progressing,* whatever that might mean. Had they caught the man or not? Would Caine return as planned or delay the wedding further?

Her greatest fear was that he would postpone it forever. She knew he did not trust that she would make a good wife. The only way she could disabuse him of that notion was to actually *become* his wife and show him.

It angered her that her confidence in that ability waned with every hour that passed. Suppose he was right, she thought whenever her defenses were low. What if the feelings she had for him were, as he must think, only surface emotions guided merely by the desire to thank him for choosing her? To reward him. And herself, too, she admitted. She really wanted him.

Only when she was with him did she know for certain that the instant infatuation she had experienced that first night they met had deepened into something more lasting and undeniable. At least on her part, she was sure it had.

Suppose he really felt nothing for her? She had felt his desire when they kissed and he'd held her against him, but he might feel that, have that response, for almost any woman who virtually threw herself at him. She had been too forward. Scandalously forward and she should be ashamed.

However, she was not sorry at all and would kiss him again, given half a chance. Given a ring and vows, she would do a great deal more than that.

She hoped that she had at least shown him that he was not horribly disfigured, as Belinda Thoren-Snipes had declared. That stupid little idiot needed her hair yanked out by the roots.

Grace unfisted her hands and folded them sedately against her waist, determined to regain her composure and settle her thoughts enough to go back to bed and to sleep.

The arrival of Trent and Neville Morleigh the next morning surprised and disheartened her. Caine was not with them.

"We have news for you!" Trent announced as he entered the morning room, where she received them.

Grace gestured for them to sit down. "Good news, I hope."

Trent nodded. "The solicitor has been found. He was responsible for everything and is no longer a threat."

"Where is Morleigh?" Grace asked, more interested now in the absence of her bridegroom than in the apprehension of their suspect.

"Coming along in the morning by carriage. We rode, you see, and he still wasn't up to jouncing along on a horse for hours," Neville explained. "We came on early, thinking you would be relieved to know the man who tried to have you done in is dead himself."

"Dead?" she asked.

"Fished out of the Thames last evening. Been there several days at least. Must have jumped in soon after his boat disembarked. Unfortunately, the account books were nowhere to be found aboard the vessel. Probably at the bottom of the Thames."

Grace sat down heavily and pressed her fingers to her temples. The relief was so great, she could hardly believe it. "You're certain he was the one?"

"Must have been," Trent assured her. "His pockets contained a waterlogged announcement of your betrothal and the names and directions of three people. One man named was the one who murdered Madame Latrice and would have killed you. The other hired man, the one who shot Caine, will be found soon since we have his name. The woman has already been arrested for entering Hadley House with the intention of poisoning Caine soon after he was shot."

"What! Why did no one tell me of that?" Grace demanded.

Trent soothed her with a placating gesture. "Because you had enough to deal with tending Caine. The woman was never anywhere near successful in the endeavor."

Grace groaned, burying her face in her hands for a moment, fully realizing the horrid determination of the one who wished them dead. She fought to calm herself. They were saying this man was dead now. Drowned. Surely it was over.

"Well, I suppose those names are proof enough for anyone," she said, turning to Neville, whom she had quite ignored until now. "And you are innocent, sir. I am so glad of it."

"You had me taken up so quickly when I arrived here, you nearly convinced *me* of my guilt," Neville replied with a grin.

Trent came over to sit beside Grace and took her hand. "Now all you have to worry about is the wedding. Anything we can do to help with preparations? I am, after all, the best man."

Neville groaned. "Or so he would have you believe. All I've heard the entire ride is how lucky Caine is and how he doesn't deserve you."

Grace laughed. "He's a wretch! And I do apologize for my mistake in thinking you were the villain of the piece. I was too overset by Caine's wound to give you my regrets after you were freed. I suppose I should have listened to what you had to say instead of having you tossed into the root cellar."

He grimaced. "Not a pleasant place to languish, I admit, but at least I wouldn't have starved. My wife might take longer to forgive you, though. She was quite upset that you didn't recognize me as the upstanding fellow she believes me to be."

"You are married, sir? Would I know her?"

"Perhaps as Miranda Williams when she was a girl, or later as Lady Ludmore. She was Baron Ludmore's widow. We were wed a bit over month ago in a very quiet ceremony, since it is her second marriage and she was hardly a year out of mourning."

"I don't believe I've met her, but congratulations to you, Mr. Morleigh," Grace said. "I do hope she can attend the wedding, too, and I will tender my apology to her in person for treating you so poorly. We should celebrate your nuptials, as well as ours, since your whole family will be here."

"Thank you for the thought, but the day should be yours and Caine's alone. May I offer my sincere best wishes, ma'am?"

"Please call me Grace, now that we are to be cousins," she offered.

"Of course, and I shall be Neville to you. I'm certain you and my Miranda will get on famously."

Grace could well understand his wife's anger. "I shall see she forgives me, then. And I must thank you profusely for your part in the investigation and finding someone to help."

"We have not uncovered all thus far," Trent said. "We still suspect that Wardfelton has done wrong by you and your inheritance. Without the account books, however, it will be difficult to prove."

Neville said, "He is still under investigation."

She waved her hand to dismiss the worry. "I am free of his wardship and that's the important thing to me."

Trent got up and helped himself to the bottle on the sideboard. He returned with a glass of brandy for both her and Neville. He went back and retrieved a glass for himself. "Shall we toast?"

Grace raised her glass. "To new friendships. My heartfelt thanks to you both."

She sipped, then set down her glass. "Now to get you two settled. Please make yourselves at home here and ring if there is anything you want." She pulled the bell cord and had Mrs. Bowden show them to their quarters.

They left her happier than she had been in days, just knowing the threat was over and that

Caine would be here tomorrow. Their wedding would commence the morning after.

Back in London, Caine dismissed Neville's enquiry agent and sent a footman to the Hadley stables to ready his mount. He was glad he'd sent Trent and Neville on ahead. Guards had probably been reassigned to other duties. Everyone at Wildenhurst would be unaware that danger to Grace still existed.

It was already late in the day and he should hurry. Though his favorite bay was a goer, Caine knew it was impossible to run at top speed for long, certainly not for eighteen miles on a dark road, risking injury to horse and rider.

Caine had to travel much slower than he wished and, even so, arrived exhausted late in the night. He approached the stables. No one rushed out to meet him, so he knew it was as he feared. The guard had relaxed, probably at Trent's suggestion.

Caine woke a stable lad and ordered him to care for the bay, then took a lantern and went to the back entrance of Wildenhurst. The door was not locked. He entered the kitchens, which were dark and deserted in the middle of the night.

He sat down on a bench to take off his muddy boots, then blew out his lantern and left it on the table. No point in rousing the entire household before he notified Trent, Neville and Grace of the still-existing threat—that Sorensen was not the culprit, or at least not the only one. Also interesting was the fact that Wardfelton had shaken surveillance.

Caine decided to go to Grace first so she wouldn't be frightened if she was awakened by the outdoor commotion of Mr. Harrell's getting the guards back on duty. More important than that, he had to make certain she was all right. It had been entirely too easy for him to enter the house without anyone the wiser.

He knew Wildenhurst so well he had no need of a light to find his way upstairs to the bedrooms. He also knew that Grace slept in the north end, in the room adjacent to the one in which he had recovered from the fever.

Caine treaded silently through the upper corridor until he arrived at her door. Then he paused. How should he wake her? Gently call her name from across the room or go in quietly and wake her with touch?

Touch, he decided, would be less likely to startle her. He opened the door, stepped inside and turned to close it.

The blow felled him immediately.

Chapter Fourteen

"Grace!"

She had raised the brass lamp to strike again when she heard him groan her name. Weak moonlight from the window revealed only shapes, but she recognized his voice immediately.

"Caine?" She dropped her makeshift weapon and knelt beside him, her hands on his shoulder. "What were you thinking, sneaking into my room? I almost killed you!"

Caine reached up to feel the damage to the back of his head. She could swear she heard him laugh.

"What is wrong with you?" she demanded. "Have I addled your wits?"

Caine slipped his arms around her and crushed her to him so that she was sprawled across his lap. "More than you know. We could have used you in battle against the French."

She brushed the back of his head with her hands. "Oh no, it's swelling. You'll have a goose egg. I'm so sorry!"

"Nonsense. You did precisely what you should have done. I was a fool to steal up here like a thief in the night, but I wanted to wake you first and explain—"

She kissed him. It began as a way to stop his words. He must have come to tell her he was delaying the wedding again. Why else would he seek her out in the middle of the night for private words?

Then as he responded and the kiss grew fierce, almost desperate, Grace saw her chance. She wanted him and she knew, at the moment at least, that he wanted her, too. With her fingers threaded through his hair, she renewed her assault. Her tongue battled with his. She loved the intimacy of it, the taste of him, the urgency of the need that swept through her.

She moved against him, sinuously inviting closer contact with that part of her needing him most. Slowly, as if in mindless surrender, he lay back on the floor.

Grace stretched above him, fitting her body to his as he embraced her. His eager hands clutched, caressed, explored and tangled in her nightdress. And then she felt his palms hot on her bare flesh, soothing, exciting, claiming.

Grace knew the instant his reason intruded. Caine's hands halted their delicious exploration and he tensed beneath her.

"What's wrong?" she gasped, her mouth only inches from his.

"This!" he hissed through his teeth. "*This* is wrong." He lifted her away from him, yanked her nightdress down over her body and smoothed it with a hand that trembled. He sat up.

She knelt beside him, not touching, sighed with resignation and wished she were capable of cursing out loud. So close, she thought, frustrated to the point of anger.

Nevertheless, in all fairness, she had to grant him credit for self-control. He did have her best interests at heart. It was simply that his idea of best interests and hers did not coincide at the moment. She should not be angry with him. But she was.

It piqued that she had not been able to overcome that iron control of his. "We certainly wouldn't want to make such a dreadful mistake," she snapped. "Anticipating vows that might never take place."

"I was thinking of you, Grace. You know—"

"I can *guess*. No point doing anything until it must be done," she finished, hating the bite in her voice even as she said it. Vanity was a terrible thing and she recognized it right away, though it had lain mostly dormant in her until tonight.

He turned to her, a mere shadow in the darkness of the room, but an ominous presence all the same. "You think I don't want you, Grace?" When she didn't answer, he added, "Well, I do."

"Nicely said, if not meant. So tell me why you've come here in the middle of the night and then leave."

He rose then and reached down to help her up. She pretended not to see his outstretched hand and got up on her own.

"This is not how we should begin, Grace. I never meant to... Well, I was carried away, but there's no excusing it. Are you all right?" He ran his hands up and down her arms as if searching for injuries.

She batted at his hands and turned to go and light the lamp beside her bed. Then she realized it was on the floor where she had dropped it after crashing it over his head. She smelled the bit of fuel that had spilled. Thank goodness it had been nearly empty and that she'd had the presence of mind to remove the glass globe. She found a candle, stuck it in the holder and lit it with a sulphur stick.

"I came to inform you the danger is not over, Grace."

"The solicitor isn't dead?" She whirled around to face him. "They said he was dead!"

"You need not worry about the details," he said gently. "You will be well protected. I'm telling you because I don't want you to be alarmed when you hear Harrell summoning the men to guard you more closely."

Grace hated the tone of his voice. "Tell me everything," she ordered in a firm voice. "I am an adult, Caine, if you will remember."

"I never treat you like a child, Grace."

"You *do!* As if I cannot process what you say or understand the onus of this threat! As if I'm completely without the sense to act on my own if need be!"

"I am trying to spare you worry, Grace." He threw up his hands and glanced heavenward as if for assistance. "You are just like the rest. All tantrums and fits."

"The *rest?*" she demanded, then lowered her voice, realizing this could become quite public if she roused the household. Besides, this *was* nearly a tantrum she was having and if she let it escalate, it would prove his point.

She took a deep breath, striving for calm. "The rest. Well, what sort of women do you frequent, Caine, and why cast their faults upon me? This is to do with that cork-brained Thoren-Snipes henwit, isn't it!"

He made a rude noise that sounded like a

curse. "Does any woman have the presence of mind to sustain a coherent conversation? They inevitably end in tears, recriminations, outrageous changes of topic. Or *sex!*" he exclaimed. "None of which solves a thing!"

Well. "And how many women do you know? Two?"

He huffed, threw up his hands again and shook his head. "I didn't come to you to argue! This is ridiculous."

She marched right up to him, shaking a finger under his nose. "You cannot, in your wildest imagination, credit me with overcoming a highwayman, can you? Or admit that I could have killed you tonight before you realized what was happening?"

She gestured wildly, so upset she feared she might strike him again if her hands weren't busy. "Some trick of fate, some stroke of luck, perhaps, but not Grace Renfair employing her wits and defensive means! Oh, nooo!"

He kissed her. Assuredly to shut her up and she knew it. She almost bit him, but refrained due to the practicality she had so recently boasted. He was bigger, stronger and perfectly able to do her harm. Not that he would, of course, but momentary surrender seemed the better part of valor. And she loved his kisses, even this sort. Especially this sort.

Her bones nearly melted along with her anger,

but she kept the anger cool by hanging on to a thread of pride. He released her mouth and she granted him his goal. She said nothing.

Small concession on her part, she could scarcely form a thought, let alone a word.

"Now then," he rasped, sounding as shaken as she felt. "Since you insist on the adult version of events, here it is. Wardfelton's solicitor was no suicide. He was murdered. I think Wardfelton killed him or had someone do it."

"What of the evidence found in his pockets?"

"Planted there by whoever killed him. He was strangled and there were bruises made there by strong hands. No water in his lungs, so he was dead before he entered the Thames. The coroner discovered this when he performed the autopsy. This was done only last evening."

"After Gavin and Neville left London?" Grace guessed.

"Yes. The enquiry agent, that fellow Neville hired, learned of it. He came and told me. He also said that your uncle has not been seen by the man set to surveil him since last evening. So there you have it, Grace. The whole sordid tale."

Grace nodded as she drew in a shuddering breath, determined to behave reasonably. As if her body was not on fire for Caine still. As if she had her self-touted wits under control.

His findings were serious and discussing them certainly deserved more urgency than solidifying their betrothal by seducing him. That seemed a lost cause anyway. Caine had a mind of his own.

She probably should thank him for full honesty, but she still resented the tardiness of it. "So it is my uncle's doing, all of it," she snapped, fisting her hands together in front of her to keep them still.

"I believe so. I reinstituted your guards as soon as I arrived. I had no problem gaining entrance tonight, to the house or to your room. If I had been the culprit and you had been sleeping..."

She went to the bed and sat down, patting the mattress beside her to show she was granting him a modicum of forgiveness. Her temper had cooled. The excitement of her terror, subsequent arousal and their confrontation were now dwindling. Grace felt rather hollow at the moment.

He sat, but left a good deal of space between them, indicating he would not repeat what he considered a great mistake. Fine. Now she must find a way to help evaluate the problem or he would continue to believe she was a featherbrain given to fits.

"All right. We know that my uncle is probably behind these attacks and obviously determined to prevent our marriage. Do you think he will give up once it is a fait accompli? If it ever becomes that?"

Caine sighed and she could imagine his expression of determined tolerance as he answered. "I think it is developing the marriage contract that he dreads. His solicitor is dead, the account books missing and probably at the bottom of the river. By all rights, he should feel safe now."

"But we cannot count on that," she guessed.

"Best not. My next logical step would be to approach your uncle again and demand terms this time. It is usually the bride's family that insists upon those, for her protection. I shall ask for your dower funds. If he refuses to produce your father's will or evidence that you have nothing, that indicates his guilt as far as I'm concerned."

"I've told you and he's told you that I have nothing to settle. That could well be true."

Caine shrugged. "Then what motive could he have to stop the wedding? He has to know that I will, as your husband, have the legal right to investigate your holdings at any time after the ceremony."

"You wish to delay it again," she guessed.

"What I am saying is that we cannot rely on the marriage itself to remove what he might see as the threat. In fact, it increases it. Yet, I find it hard to believe he would commit murder over several thousand pounds of misused funds. That, I can't figure."

"Assuming there were funds to misuse," she reminded him again.

"I believe there were. But if so, why did he not simply replace the money? The scandal would be minor, given the offense and he could easily lay blame at the solicitor's door, whether it was true or not." He got up and began to pace. "It makes so little sense!"

"He might be financially strapped and unable to make it right," she suggested.

"You think so? He owns the valuable town house and his country estate must contain treasures he could sell, even if the land and house are entailed."

Grace tried to recall what her uncle might possess that would be worth selling. "The paintings, statuary and much of the furniture were gone when I arrived. He said he planned to refurbish, that everything there had been old and outdated. Yet he bought nothing new to replace anything while I was there."

"Selling off. See, that's telling." Caine shook his finger as he paced and considered.

Grace racked her memory. "The books," she murmured, running a hand through her hair and twisting it into a coil. "Most of the books were gone, as well. There were some newer ones left, but not many. The old ones, some priceless first editions that Father had pointed out to me in the two years we lived there, were no longer in the library."

Caine had stopped pacing to listen. "But the town house is not entailed. He could have sold or mortgaged that to cover a theft."

Grace shrugged and shook her head. "We might be misreading his motive altogether. Perhaps it's simple hatred. He suddenly seemed determined to drive me to suicide long before I met you."

She watched Caine's face harden the moment she said that. He looked fierce enough to kill. "When was this?"

"Ever since his regard for me changed, he's been at it one way or another. For months after I came, we got on well. I think I told you that."

"Yes, go on. Every detail you can recall."

Grace shrugged a shoulder. "He was never affectionate or eager to have me there, but he acted cordial enough. He allowed me to supervise the household staff, to act as hostess whenever he entertained and occasionally asked my opinion on inconsequential matters. Then, overnight, he changed."

"How so? Did he…hurt you?" Caine demanded. "I want the truth, Grace."

"You believe I would lie to you about it?"

He stalked over and sat down heavily on her bed again, rubbing his face with his hand. "No, of course not. This upsets me, that's all. I want to throttle the man and he's not here. I never meant to direct any anger at you. So he didn't hurt you?"

"No. He confined me to the house, to my room for the most part. He only allowed walks in the garden. Supervised walks. And he seemed particularly concerned about halting any correspondence. I was cut off from the world. There were veiled threats of poison. I became afraid to eat."

Caine shifted restlessly. "You were so thin."

"I was required to join him for supper. Meager fare, that. I ate only what I saw him eat. He would glare at me down the table, sometimes add an evil smile and trail one finger along the edge of his knife. I suppose that was meant to interfere with my digestion."

"I'm sure it did," Caine said, his voice tight with fury. "Why on earth did you stay, Grace? Why not run?"

"I did, twice, even though I had nowhere to go and no means to get there if I had. He had me brought back and informed me yet again that he had the legal right to do as he would with me. Such is the law."

"And a bad one that needs to be remedied!" Caine exclaimed.

She confirmed that with a nod. "As it is now, a woman cannot go running off on her own unless she intends to take to the streets. I am reluctant to admit it, but I became desperate enough to do that." She paused. "Without proper training, references or recommendation for employment, none of which I had, acceptance or ruination are the only choices for a female. Unless she seeks the protection of another man, one with honorable intentions. Such as you," she added.

"I was your only means of escape. Small wonder you agreed so readily to marry a perfect stranger."

Grace couldn't deny it. "A *perfect* stranger, yes," she said with a smile. He either missed or ignored her small jest.

"I don't like the laws regarding women any more than you do and once I have a say in the House of Lords, my first order of business will be to take up this issue. But for now, I need a full understanding of your ordeal. So when the rumors went round that you might be dead, he produced you at that late season ball to prove you were not."

She made a face, thinking of her uncle's orders that evening. "Thank God he did. I was near the end of my patience with that man. I might have done *him* harm."

Caine laughed without humor. "I daresay you might." He reached over and took her hand. "I will resolve this." He sighed wearily. "But you should not have to marry to escape him, Grace.

Once this is over, you will be free. I'll see to that."

She snatched her hand from his. "You offer it so often, it must be *you* who wishes freedom. I have stated time and again and have shown you clearly how willing I am. Now I am losing patience with *you!*"

He reared back his head. "Should I be afraid?" She heard the smile in his voice.

"Perhaps you should. I never meant to embroil you in this sort of fix." Grace felt the sting of tears and looked away from him.

"We'll sort this out, I promise. The main thing is to keep you safe until we do."

He was so kind, she felt the need to weep. But she would not. He already saw her as a weakling, failing to stand up to her uncle and falling in a faint after the proposal. Little question as to why he felt he must coddle her as he did. And very likely why he wanted to set her aside.

"I am stronger than you think!" she declared as she lifted her chin and faced him squarely.

"Have you any idea how exquisite you are?"

Grace simply stared at him, wondering what had prompted that.

"I'll wake Trent and my cousin now," he said. "Where are they?"

"The green and blue rooms just down the hall," she murmured, holding his gaze.

"I will see you in the morning. Try to sleep

again." He rose, walked over and picked up the lamp, replacing it on the table beside its glass globe.

The candle beside it flickered. The flame caused shadows to dance on his rugged features, highlighting the scars, giving him a saturnine appearance.

"Devilishly lucky for me you didn't bring the highwayman's pistol to bed with you," he said.

She swallowed hard, imagining what might have happened if she had.

He turned as he reached the door and opened it. "I promise never to underestimate you again, Grace. And I admire you more than you will ever know."

She stared at the door as it closed behind him. *He thought her exquisite? He admired her? Well, then.*

Chapter Fifteen

Caine felt so proud of Grace. What a resilient spirit she had, what a practical nature and inner strength. He remembered the waif of the ugly yellow dress and how she had sparred with him even then. And now she could add beauty and good health to that self-confident nature. She was damned amazing and full of fire.

If she had intrigued him that first night, he now found himself absolutely fascinated. He was either in love or in lust with her, perhaps both, and he certainly had never bargained for either.

Trent and Neville joined him in the library, interrupting his ruminations. He had wakened them a good deal more carefully than he had done with Grace.

Gingerly, he touched the aching knot on the back of his head. If one small woman could inflict that much damage with a lamp, he could only imagine how those two would have reacted to their doors opening quietly in the middle of the night.

"You have a headache?" Trent asked as he flopped down in a chair beside the grate. He had thrown on his clothes, shirt open at the neck, not having bothered with either neckcloth or coat at such an hour.

"Nothing significant," Caine replied. Damned if he would relate what Grace had done to him. He would never hear the end of it.

Neville wore a dressing gown over his trousers, quite the fashion plate. He raked Caine with an assessing gaze. "There's blood on his shirt-front," he remarked to Trent. "Been fighting, coz?"

"A small accident. Now to the purpose of my coming," Caine said, determined to change the topic. He immediately began relating what he knew of the solicitor's death in much the same brief fashion that he had with Grace. He included his own conclusions as well as hers.

"So you've already spoken with Grace tonight," Trent said.

"He has," Grace announced, sweeping into the room. "I hope you gentlemen won't mind if I join you."

They all stood immediately. Trent straightened his shirt and ran a hand through his tousled hair. Neville smiled and bowed.

She, too, wore a dressing gown, one of dark green silk trimmed with gold gimp. She had pinned up her hair in a casual way that flattered her features enormously.

Caine tried without success to banish the candlelit vision of her earlier, hair mussed, slumberous blue eyes at half-mast, her breath coming in fits and starts after he kissed her. His hands tingled with the memory of the silken pliancy of her body beneath that modest nightrail. Even the subtle scent of her stirred him so he could hardly think straight.

He shook his head to clear it. The woman played havoc with his senses without even trying. Now was not the time to have his faculties disturbed. Lives were at stake. Did she know what a distraction she was?

"You should be abed," he told her, but tried to couch it in the form of a suggestion instead of a command.

"So should we all, but circumstances demand we settle on a plan, don't you think?" She went to the carved oak cabinet, opened it and removed a decanter of brandy and four glasses. "Shall we?"

Trent went to assist. "You see? This is why I love your lady, Caine. She keeps spirits in every room! And best of all, she's so eager to share. Allow me to pour, Sweeting."

"My, my," Neville said with a lighthearted chuckle. "You do like to live dangerously, Trent." He accepted the glass, swirled his brandy and took a sip. "I recall from childhood how jealous Caine was of his toys."

Grace raised her chin and looked down her small, straight nose at Neville. "A greater danger is to those who consider me a *toy,* sir."

Caine smiled and held his tongue. No reason to upbraid Trent for flirting. The man would cut his own throat before betraying a friend. And there was certainly no need to chastise Neville. Grace had taken care of that.

"So, what shall we do about Wardfelton?" Trent asked.

Caine set down his glass. "The men are assembling and remanning their posts. If Wardfelton comes here or sends anyone, they will be apprehended and dealt with."

Neville gave a wordless sound of approval. "I'll leave for Town tomorrow. It's time to approach the banks, twist a few arms and dig more deeply into Wardfelton's finances. This business of Sorensen's murder leaves little doubt the earl is our man. We must find him."

Caine agreed. "Trent, will you be going, too?"

"I'll stay. There's still the wedding," he said. "Or do you intend to postpone it yet again?"

Grace preempted quickly before Caine could answer. "Yes, we must delay it, perhaps indefinitely. Caine believes it will do nothing to change my uncle's plans to be rid of one or the other of us."

"Indefinitely?" Caine asked.

Her nod was defiant. And resolute. Her expression was pensive as she regarded the three of them in turn, settling last on Caine.

Obviously she had been rethinking their earlier conversation about freedom, Caine decided. Though he had suggested it himself, her belated agreement struck him like another bullet. With this strike, there was no delay in the pain.

His heart sank as he thought of not having her. Ever. And knowing he had caused this himself made it worse. Could she really have changed her mind so completely in less than an hour? He picked up his glass, tossed back the brandy in one draught and winced at the burn.

"Well, I'm off to bed," Neville said with another slight bow to Grace. He left in haste.

Grace followed him out of the library without another word. Caine watched through the open doorway as she glided to the stairs and started up.

"Rather downcast, isn't she?" Trent remarked. "She has to be worried Wardfelton will strike again soon." He poured himself another shot of brandy. "As we all are. Or is it further delay on the marriage that bothers her?"

"I honestly don't know," Caine admitted. "This has become so much more complicated than I expected. She's more complicated, too. Certainly not the same girl I proposed to at the ball."

"Not biddable, not retiring and definitely not weak-minded," Trent agreed. "Not ugly, either, though she never really filled that requirement."

Caine shook his head. "No, yet her appearance has changed so drastically, it stuns me every time I look at her. She's so lovely now her health has improved, she could have her choice of men."

"So why stick with you, eh?"

Caine scoffed. "I'm not the man I used to be, my friend. I only wish I had known her then."

"Ah well, truth to tell, you weren't all that pretty before the scars, old friend. You only thought you were. Women are attracted to confidence, y'see. You did, and still do, have that in abundance."

"Grace has never minded my scars, not even at first. They are not the problem. I simply believe she should have a say in her future and not have to accept me as a husband just because she promised in order to save herself."

Trent glanced at the doorway as if he could still see Grace. "She has nothing but her good looks at present. Perhaps with a dowry, she'd have excellent prospects, but whatever her uncle had of hers is likely gone. As it stands now, you are probably her best bet. Were I you, I'd close this deal while you have the chance. You'll never do better."

Caine laughed wryly. "Trust you to lift my self-esteem."

"You want her. You know you do," Trent said.

"As I said, I'd like to be fair to her. Conscience demands I *must* be fair."

"Fair? Life's never *fair,* Caine." Trent sighed. "Not being a widow of means, she must belong to some man. Better you than the man who wants her dead, or some other man we don't know."

"Yes, but I wonder how we would get on once she realizes I have no intention of doing the social whirl each season with house parties interspersed? She has missed that, losing her fiancé when she was so young, being companion to his mother in their grief, then suffering virtual imprisonment by Wardfelton. She has had hardly any social life and she'll surely want that now."

"Only natural she should, and she deserves it," Trent agreed.

"I know that. I just wonder how am I to provide that if I'm to do the earldom justice? I have more work than I can handle and haven't even inherited yet. Imagine how that will increase once I must sit in the Lords and help govern. You and I have talked of this before. There seems no solution, so we might as well let it be."

Even as he said the words, Caine realized that other nobles managed to juggle duty and social obligations well enough. He would not be righting all the wrongs in government by himself. And who would he be governing for anyway if not the people of Britain, the families, his own included? Grace in particular.

"Best call off the wedding, then," Trent said with a smile. "Shall I take her off your hands?"

"Oh, stop." Caine glared at him. "You push me too far, Trent. Why do you do that?"

He toasted Caine with his empty glass. "Just driving home a point. You want her. You don't want anyone else to have her. So do her justice, for your sake and hers."

"I never thought to do otherwise, however this goes."

Trent set down the glass with a thunk. "Remember that your cousin is not the wastrel your uncle painted him. Don't marry Grace and Neville can be responsible for the earl's wealth and investments. All you'd have then is the title, the entailed manse and the Lords to contend with. Tons of free time to do your *duty* to the country. And to miss what you might have had with Grace." He looked unusually serious. "But if you do give her up, I will step in. That, my friend, is no joke. Jilt her and, I swear, it will happen."

"Jilting her never occurred to me and you know it. Go to bed," Caine ordered, impatient to end the discussion. "And stop coveting Grace. Unless she throws me over of her own accord, she will be mine."

He wasn't really angry with Trent and they both knew it. The man did have a way of resetting Caine's priorities and that was his sole intention. Wasn't it? He had not been smiling with that last warning.

The very idea of Trent wooing Grace for real disturbed him to the core, even though he was certain that would never happen. Fairly certain.

Trent might not stoop to that, but some man would step in sooner or later if she broke the betrothal. Grace would be obliged to find a husband quickly to avoid her former situation with Wardfelton. Unless they found evidence against him, she would have to go back to her uncle or marry someone.

Was she considering crying off after all? Perhaps the argument they'd had convinced her she should. She hadn't seemed to mind the delay of the wedding just now and, in fact, had agreed to it all too readily.

The word *indefinitely* disturbed him no end. He had to know exactly what she meant by that, and there was no way to find out unless he asked her to explain it. Now he could demand that explanation in private.

Caine hurried to the stairs, hoping she hadn't fallen asleep yet.

This time, he knocked.

Grace heard the rap on her door and knew it had to be Caine again. "Come," she said just loudly enough for him to hear. She was sitting in the chair beside her window, looking out at the moon-shadowed stables. Figures came and went as she watched.

"The men are assembling and arming to return to their guard posts," she said as Caine joined her. "There are so many, seeing them all at once."

"Every one that we and Harrell could muster."

"I've been thinking." She looked up at him. "You must be wishing you had never spoken to me that night at Cavanaugh's."

He blinked as if she had surprised him. "You can't believe that, surely. Is this why you seemed so eager for another postponement when Trent asked about it?"

She looked back out the window. "I don't believe this marriage will ever happen, Caine. Perhaps it shouldn't."

"So you've thought about what I said earlier, about your having a choice."

She stood and faced him. "No, it's because I

have made my feelings for you all too clear and still you draw away. I am not what you want."

When he would have spoken, she silenced him with a gesture. "Please make no declarations of concern for me, of your duty or keeping to your word as a gentleman. That insults me, Caine. You are honorable and we both know that. But I am not what you want in a wife."

"You are *all* that I want!" he protested, his words soft, yet adamant.

"No. Your voices carried and I stopped to listen, Caine. You were right in what you said to Trent. It's true I would require more of you than you could ever give."

"I would give you everything I have," he declared.

"Except your constant presence in my life, eventually your love and children." She wrapped her arms around her middle to still the trembling. "You must think me an ingrate to want so much after all you've already done on my behalf. I'm not, Caine. I feel enormously grateful to you."

He ran a hand through his hair and began to pace. "Gratitude is not what I want from you, Grace. That is the problem!"

"Your offer of marriage is what brought us together and gave me relief from a situation I could not control. How could I not thank you with all my heart? Because of all that I owe you in that regard, I have to let you go. You must find someone who suits you better."

"*You* suit me," he argued, moving closer. "No one else."

Grace put out her palms and backed away. "Please leave my room, Caine. Enough has been said."

If he came any nearer, she knew she could not resist throwing herself into his arms and pleading for him to care. He did not and never would. "Please go," she added, turning away.

Grace stood very still long after she heard the door close. A numbness had come over her, as if all life had drained away and left only a shell. Though she stared out the window, she saw nothing through the haze of tears.

"I don't want to leave," he said in a harsh whisper. "Not with you thinking as you do, that I don't care for you or want to marry you. I know what I said, but I was only trying to be fair." She heard his groan of frustration. "I *do* want you. But can't you understand what guilt I would carry, how miserable we *both* would be if you went through with this only because I was your only alternative? I don't want to be that, for you to see me that way, as a relief from danger. I would always be that for you, marriage or no. Just do not choose me for that reason!"

She whirled around and saw him standing, back against the door. His look of distress moved her more than a declaration of love might have done. A long silence drew out as they regarded one another.

Finally, she broke it. "I know there is desire between us. You could stay tonight for that alone and I wouldn't deny you. But you would see that as my repaying you for protection."

He said nothing, which was an answer in itself.

Grace sighed and pressed her fingers to her forehead, wishing she could rub away the memory of his embrace, that last heated kiss, his words to Trent, and think clearly.

"Anything I give to you at the moment, you will take as gratitude, Caine. And whatever you offer me, I would see as your way to keep me under your protection because you feel obliged to do it. Maybe both of us would be right."

"No, you would be very wrong," he said softly.

Her need to believe him was so fierce it frightened her. Yet he had not asked if he would be wrong in thinking her merely grateful. No matter what she said now, there was no way she could convince him of what she really felt for him.

"Could…could you leave me to think about it?" she asked. "Please, just for the rest of the night. We can settle things in the morning, one way or the other."

"Just for the night, then," he agreed finally. He crossed the room, took her hands and held them to his lips. His gaze held hers as he said, "Duty and fairness be damned, Grace. No matter what I've said, I do want to marry you if you want it, too."

He slowly released her hands, bowed ever so slightly and left as she had asked.

Exhausted as she was, sleep was out of the question. She tried for over an hour to shut out the worries, but Caine's final words echoed in her head and would not leave her alone. He did want to marry her despite what he'd said earlier. Could he mean it?

Grace left the bed and donned her wrapper. Perhaps a glass of milk with honey would help, she thought. With that in mind, she lit a candle, exited her room as quietly as possible and started downstairs.

The house was incredibly silent after the night's activities, all the servants long abed. She noted the comfortable, somewhat faded grandeur of the place. She loved every inch of it and hoped it would remain her home. Hers and Caine's. How could she ever make him see that she wanted him as a man, not a bulwark between her and disaster?

The cavernous kitchen was redolent of cinnamon, nutmeg and lingering wood smoke. She opened the cooling chest where perishables were kept and was about to lift out the container of milk when a noise alerted her. She paused, turning toward the back door. With the blast of night air, her candle had whooshed out. One of the guards, surely.

She waited. Perhaps whoever opened the door hadn't seen her. It wouldn't do to surprise him, armed as he surely was. But what if it was not a guard?

The room was totally dark and she sensed someone moving near the door. Prudence was the better part of valor. Grace sank in a crouch behind the cooling box and remained still. There were no further sounds.

She stayed where she was until her legs began to cramp from the uncomfortable position. Then she stood there in the dark, listening intently. Nothing.

The guard must have opened the door to check that all was well in the kitchen and then retreated, closing it again. She felt around until she found the candle, lighted it and looked around. Nothing appeared to have been disturbed. No one was in the room with her.

She abandoned the idea of having milk and hurried back upstairs. The incident, which was probably nothing significant, had shaken her more than she realized. Should she tell Caine?

The clock in the atrium bonged softly. Three o'clock. He would be asleep. Grace felt a strong compulsion to wake him. She admitted the sound in the kitchen only provided an excuse. Maybe she had imagined it for that very reason.

After all their arguing about the marriage, she could not deny how much she wanted to marry Caine. Somehow, even given the doubts he had, she would make things work.

When she reached his room, she didn't stop to knock. She entered in a swirl of silk wrapper and shut the door behind her. "Caine!" she exclaimed softly. He had already rolled from the bed, weapon in hand to meet an intruder.

"Grace?" He lowered the pistol. Moonlight haloed his form as he stood between her and his window. "What is it?"

"Morning's too far away," she whispered as she rushed to him and threw herself into his arms.

He closed around her, enveloping her with his strength and maleness, banishing any doubts she had about what she was doing. He was naked! Grace ran her hands over his back, loving the smoothness of his skin, the way his muscles hardened and flexed beneath her fingers. She drew in a deep breath, reveling in the compelling scent unique to him with its hints of bay rum, leather and Caine himself.

"This is your *yes!* At last, thank God." He groaned as he took her mouth in a wild and wondrous kiss. Grace answered his passion, so stirred by his obvious relief, she could hardly think. He wanted her here, he really did.

His hand slid between them, working loose the tie of her wrapper. She moved a handbreadth to allow that as she sought another angle and renewed the kiss. It went on and on, mouths seeking, finding, increasing hunger and answering demand.

Seconds later, she felt his naked warmth with only the sheer fabric of thin nightrail between their bodies. A moment more, and he had raked it up above her breasts and they were skin to skin. She moved against him, fitting closer, seeking.

He cupped her hips and lifted her. Grace locked her legs around him as he carried her to his bed and followed her down. His hands were everywhere at once, caressing, fondling, clutching and soothing. Yet not soothing at all. Inciting.

She heard encouraging sounds emerge from her own throat with no prompting from her mind, eager sounds that matched his own wordless entreaties.

His mouth found her breast and she almost cried out with pleasure. He murmured something, his words lost, their sounds and the whisper of his breath vibrating through her as he turned attention to the other. Sensations she had never felt rushed through her body, a liquid heat searing her veins.

He rose above her and entered her without a pause, a swift, determined exclamation to the sentence of her determined assault. The momentary glance of pain gave way to a heavenly invasion of pure pleasure.

He stilled inside her, his breath audible and unsteady. "Grace, I—"

"Love me," she whispered. A demand. A desperate wish. A prayer.

Bracing on his elbows, their lower bodies joined, he peered down at her. She wished she could see his eyes, his expression in the darkness, but he remained a silent, featureless silhouette above her. Her conqueror and her conquered. Grace closed her eyes and uttered a deep groan of encouragement.

He sighed once, a ragged exhalation, and then began to move. The exquisite friction, igniting something new within her, began to ebb and flow. She matched his rhythm, glorying in every thrust she met. Her senses ruled, eclipsing thought and reason and possible consequence. This, this was everything. This, now.

He lowered himself onto her fully and she welcomed the weight. Strong fingers spread beneath her hips and held her fast as he rose and thrust time and again in an escalating cadence she tried to equal and exceed. Reaching for something…

She gasped his name, breathed in his essence, clutched at the strength in his hard muscled arms, his back and lower still.

"Give!" he ground out in a harsh whisper. She gave and took, surrendered herself and claimed him at once and forever. The feelings were so overpowering, she cried out, reaching a pinnacle she had never dreamed existed.

He groaned again as he thrust harder, filling her completely. His body seemed to melt into her, as if they were one. When they stilled, exhausted and sated, Grace released a soul-deep sigh.

She did not want to move ever again, just wanted to lie and savor the euphoria. Never had she known this exquisite feeling was possible. Never would she give him up.

His lips brushed her cheek as he moved to her side. "Oh, Grace," he whispered, his words almost inaudible. "What have I done?"

"Whatever it was," she whispered breathlessly, "I hope you can do it again."

She felt the lazy rumble of what might have been a laugh, but emerged as another groan. A wry sound. No mistaking that.

"You deserved more care, but I was carried away, still half asleep," he muttered. "I am sorry, Grace."

It was her turn to laugh, weakly but with true amusement. "You are *not* sorry." With a concerted effort, she reached up to her neck and raked her nightdress down over her nakedness. "And neither am I."

"Are you all right?" he asked, brushing her tumbled hair off her shoulder and dropping a kiss there. "How do you feel?"

"Better than I can ever remember," she replied softly and sincerely. "And you?"

"Delirious. This settles it, you know," he said, sounding rather smug. And rather satisfied. "We will marry in the morning. No delay, indefinite or otherwise."

"No, Caine. We cannot."

Chapter Sixteen

Grace leaned into him, loving the way his strong arms surrounded her and held her close, as if she were precious to him. She turned her lips to his chest, just to taste him, to inhale his scent more keenly, to brand him as hers. "We can't marry tomorrow. Cook will need to rally her staff and work half a night to prepare a wedding breakfast."

"Hang Cook." He slid a hand to her breast and caressed her through the silk.

"It is early morning now and tomorrow is too soon. The day after, then," Grace suggested. "Will that suit?"

"And waste two perfectly good nights of married life?" he asked, continuing the caresses, becoming more determined.

Grace grinned and trailed the backs of her

nails down his arm, a languid gesture, a loving touch. "So this will be a nightly thing, you think?"

"Unless you bar your door and even then, I think so." His palm traveled to her hip as he pushed her back on the bed. "Perhaps an *hourly* thing."

"My, my," Grace said with a happy laugh. "How greed becomes you!"

He kissed the tip of her nose as his hand soothed her comfortingly. "It was your first time. You should rest and recover."

Grace ran a finger down the side of his face and smiled into the darkness. "If I did as I *should,* I would never have come here in the first place."

"You chose me freely, didn't you, Grace?" he asked, a hint of worry lingering in his voice. "I hope you're certain you want this marriage… that you want *me?*"

Grace blew out a gust of frustration and rolled her eyes. "If you think *this* was merely a gesture of thanks, perhaps not."

He rolled away from her and locked his hands behind his head. "Even if it was, there's no retreat possible for you now."

"Or for *you,* either!" Grace climbed off his bed and swept up her discarded wrapper. She tugged it on and tied the sash with a determined tug.

"Grace!" he exclaimed as he sat up. "Come back here!"

"You are the most *pigheaded* man! It's a wonder I love you at all!" She yanked open the door. "Do not come after me, you hear?" The slam probably woke the house.

And he did not come. She had halfway hoped he would. Fitfully, she passed the remainder of the night, wondering what the morning would bring. And, more crucial to their future, all of the mornings after that.

The next day dawned with a deluge. The pouring rain would force everyone to remain indoors, Caine thought as he dressed. He was filled with both anticipation and trepidation at seeing Grace. Would she still be angry?

The thought he had clung to all night was that Grace actually said she loved him. She'd not uttered it in the context he would have chosen to hear, instead coupling it with his being pigheaded, but she'd said it all the same.

He had to smile every time he thought of that. The words had slipped out in the midst of her fury, which made them all the more believable. He admitted he might not have taken her admission as truth if she had declared it in the midst of passion.

And what passion it had been. How eagerly she had welcomed his kisses, his hands exploring her body, making her his own at last. The memory of her smooth, creamy skin and the taste of her, her little cries of delight aroused him even now.

He tucked the sapphire parure in his coat pocket. Jewels should go well with an apology. He had planned the set as a morning gift anyway. This particular morning would probably seem more significant to her than the one after their wedding night. It certainly was significant to him.

"Where might I find my little lady?" he asked Mrs. Oliver as he stopped her on the stairs.

"In the morning room with his lordship," she said, eyeing him keenly as if she knew he had taken Grace's innocence in the early-morning hours.

His own guilt made him imagine that, he decided. "Lord Trent is up?" Surprising. It was not yet nine and Trent was a late sleeper.

"No, sir, Lord Hadley. He's up and about. Much improved! See for yourself."

Caine took the stairs two at a time. When he entered the morning room, his uncle sat on the divan. Grace had her ear to his chest. "What's this?" he asked, curious as to how they had gotten so close that his uncle would offer her a comforting embrace. And a greater question was why she might need one.

Grace sat up, beaming. "His heart! Come and listen! The foxglove has worked its magic!"

Caine approached them and stood, hands on his hips. "Foxglove? What are you talking about?"

"Gracie cured me, that's what!" his uncle exclaimed. He tapped his chest. "Sound as a sovereign!"

Caine frowned. "Foxglove, Grace? That's poison!"

"Not in a small tincture," she informed him. "It regulates the heartbeat. Too fast, it slows it, and too sluggish, speeds it. It has a steadying and strengthening effect either way." She smiled at Hadley. "Dr. Ackers has been taking great care, though, according to Dr. Withering's writings. A week on and a week off in dosing."

His uncle laughed. "She and Ackers have done you out of a quick fortune, boy. I ain't all that ready to cock up my toes now!"

"Glad to hear it," Caine muttered, distracted by the very sight of his uncle. His color looked as near normal as could be, his eyes much clearer. Except for his arrival at Wildenhurst, this was the first time since returning from the war that Caine had seen the man in other than nightgown and banyan. Dressed in trousers and morning coat, he was every inch the earl. "You look… splendid, sir."

"Neckcloth's not right, but I feel like a new

man." He lay a steady hand against Grace's face and gave it a fond pat. Then he got up. "Off to the kitchens. I'm not waiting for breakfast. Cook will have biscuits, won't she, Gracie? And coffee on the brew?"

"No coffee, mind," Grace warned. "Milk or weak tea, sir."

The earl knocked Caine on the shoulder playfully with his fist as he passed by.

Caine was too amazed to speak. He stared at Grace, who sat, one arm propped on the back of the divan. However did he manage to underestimate the woman when he strove not to with every breath he took? She kept adding dimensions he couldn't even begin to imagine.

"Come, sit," she offered, glancing at the cushion beside her that the earl had just vacated. "Immediately on arriving here, I wrote to Dr. Ackers about Father's patients and how well it worked for them. He and the earl agreed the risk was worth it."

"He's well! I can't believe it!"

"No, not precisely *well,*" Grace said, covering one of his hands with hers. "But he has more time with us now, I hope. Dr. Ackers says his heart is still damaged and will fail him eventually, but at least he will feel better in the time he has left."

"Ackers left for London today. I wonder if that was wise."

Grace squeezed his hands. "You mustn't worry. He had to see to his own family and promised to return in two days, three at most. I know exactly what must be done in his absence. I hope you trust me. Uncle Hadley does."

"Of course I do. And *Uncle Hadley,* is it?" Caine smiled, happy that they were getting on so well as that. "What of my aunt? Has she been well?" he asked.

Grace shrugged. "She always seems a bit sad, Caine, despite the earl's improvement. Do you think she misses city life already?"

He looked at Grace for a full minute without answering, unsure whether he should confide in her and, if so, how to begin. "She likes to shop. Uncle used to take her out daily and she would come home with some small thing or another."

"Every woman enjoys that."

"I suppose so." He smiled as he toyed absently with the ring he wore, twisting it round and round on his finger. "She'd want a pair of gloves or a few lengths of ribbon, such as that. Sometimes she would sit for the rest of the day, admiring whatever it was he bought for her. The next morning it would lie forgotten and she would ask to go out again."

Grace said nothing, just waited for him to go on.

"She's a child, Grace. No one ever told me why she's the way she is, whether it was a fever, an accident or simply the way she was born. Maybe no one knows. She was taught to write and read a bit somewhere along the way, but has trouble with numbers."

"Well, that's not so remarkable. Many women aren't taught that much," Grace said.

Caine went on. "She's quiet as a rule and her manners are usually so nice, people rarely notice how different she is or if they do, merely think her eccentric." He pursed his lips for a moment, then gave a nod. "But you noticed."

"Yes," she admitted. "Your uncle seems very fond of her and quite protective. One can see how much they care for each other in every exchange between them."

Caine nodded in total agreement. "He married her just as she is now over thirty-five years ago when she was twenty." He gave Grace a meaningful look. "They never had children."

Grace obviously grasped what he meant, that the Hadley marriage was and always had been platonic. He could see in her eyes that she understood.

"The earl must love her very much indeed," she said. "A remarkable man, that uncle of yours. I hope he lives forever."

"Yes, so does he. He worries dreadfully about what will happen to her when he's gone. I can't count the times I've had to promise him I would care for her as if she were my mother."

"Of course you will! I could shop with her," Grace offered eagerly. "We could go into the village today if she wants!"

"Not now," Caine said. "Even with guards along, it might not be safe. But I appreciate the generous offer, Grace, and so will Uncle Hadley when I tell him."

"I have years of experience as a lady's companion, so whenever she needs company to entertain her, I will do what I can. I've read to her from a novel I found here, but she doesn't appear to listen. All she does is embroider, hour upon hour. Is there anything else you can think of that I might do to make her happier than she is while they're here?"

He smiled and took her hand. "Just be who you are, Grace. I think that will suffice."

"I hope she realizes, at least in some small way, just how fortunate she is to have married your uncle."

"I hope so, too. There's no way to thank you enough for doing what you've already done for them."

"Some things are done with no thought of a return, Caine. But if you like, consider our debts to each other evenly paid. You saved me and I've saved the uncle you love. Now we can dispense with all talk of gratitude, can we not?"

Caine nodded as he took her hands and looked into her eyes. "I need to apologize, Grace. Forgive me for doubting your motive in coming to me last night. It was just so hard to believe you would actually…well…choose *me*."

"You still don't believe it," she said with a soft laugh. "But you will come to, I promise. Marry me, Caine, and try not to think too much."

He raised an eyebrow. "Because it makes me pigheaded?"

She nodded and made a face.

Caine reached into his pocket and drew out the jeweler's box. "Your morning gift."

Her eyes widened as he opened it for her and she saw the stones. "Oh, my! This comes a bit early!"

"So did the consummation," he reminded her in a whisper, grinning as she lifted the necklace and held it to the light.

"Oh, Caine, it's beautiful! How lovely this will look with my wedding gown!" She kissed him full on the lips. "Thank you so much!"

Caine had a sudden epiphany. "You know, Grace, we might have just discovered the secret to a happy union. You do something I can thank you for, I do something requiring your gratitude, on and on throughout life. Gratitude isn't a bad thing at all, is it! Perhaps that's the secret to a good marriage. What do you think?"

She shook her finger under his nose. "You're overthinking again. And talking too much, so hush and kiss me," she ordered.

He laughed out loud. "Thank you, Grace, I think I will!"

"Excuse me! I am interrupting."

Caine released Grace and shot Trent a quelling look. "You are, in fact."

"We're being married the day after tomorrow!" Grace announced, breathlessly.

"None too soon, I'll wager," Trent said, taking a chair without being invited to sit. "Hope the rain stops. *Happy is the bride the sun shines on.*"

Grace stood up and whirled around to peer out the window at the downpour. "It won't matter to me!" she declared. "No one could be happier, rain or shine!"

Caine thought she had never looked more beautiful, face flushed with excitement, modestly covered breasts rising and falling rapidly with arousal. She wore a rose-sprigged muslin gown, her hair pulled up into a braided knot tied with pink ribbons. Her childlike enthusiasm was contagious. He could hardly wait until she was truly his for all the world to know.

Neville joined them just then. "Greetings, all. Any further word from London in the morning post?"

"It hasn't arrived yet," Grace said, her happy mood suddenly diminishing. "By the way, I almost forgot. There was a letter." She fetched it and gave it to Caine. "I don't believe it was written by my uncle," she told him.

He examined it for a minute. "Belinda Thoren-Snipes. She's made some attempt to disguise her handwriting, but I recognize it from the few letters she sent to me. I could jolly well wring her neck for upsetting you, Grace." He tossed the letter down on the table.

Trent promptly picked it up. "At least you have grounds for libel if you can prove she wrote it."

"I know she wrote it, but it's not worth pursuing," Caine replied. He took Grace's hands in his and drew her to him.

"I'll handle the matter for you if you like," Neville offered.

"Forget it, please!" Grace insisted. "Let's not give it any consequence." Caine felt the chill in her hands and pressed them between his to warm them.

"Wise to dismiss it altogether," Trent agreed, frowning at Neville with a slight shake of his head. "Forget everything but having a wedding to anticipate, Grace."

"Quite right. Mr. Harrell will keep the guard up, so there's no need to worry, is there?" she said.

Her smile returned, but Caine thought it looked a bit forced. He wished he could get her alone and really reassure her that all would be well.

"Yes, everything seems well in hand," Trent said with assurance. "Besides, no self-respecting assassin would be lurking about in this down-pour anyway. Weather's fit only for ducks!"

Caine deftly changed the topic, regaling his friend and cousin with the news of Hadley's improvement, then assigning them tasks as his groomsmen.

Breakfast was announced later in the morning and the day crawled by with maddening slow-ness for Caine. He could not concentrate on cards or billiards or conversation. The thought of one more day like it wore on his nerves.

When they retired for the night and headed up the stairs, he caught Grace's arm and whis-pered in her ear. "My room or yours?"

"Neither!" she exclaimed. "We must wait."

"Why?" he demanded, frowning down at her.

"Just because," she whispered back with a teasing glint in her eyes. "So I might enjoy your impatience. It's very flattering."

"A streak of cruelty," he grumbled. "See, I *knew* you weren't perfect."

Her merry laughter assuaged his disappoint-ment, so he said good-night, kissed her soundly and left her at her door, hoping that kiss rendered her as frustrated as he felt. This night and one more. Then she would be his forever.

Later that night, Caine woke to a soft knock on his door. "What?" he muttered in a loud grunt. He opened one eye and squinted at the window. Still dark. Who would be waking him before dawn? Grace, of course, he thought as he came fully alert. She'd said no to him earlier, but she must have changed her mind. He rolled out of bed and grabbed his breeches, hoping he wouldn't need them for long.

He opened the door slowly, fully expecting to see her impish face grinning up at him. No one was there. His bare foot landed on a slick surface different from the plush turkey carpet. He bent down and picked up a folded paper that had been pushed under his door.

He lighted his lamp and opened the note. What was this, a dare?

"Meet me in the root cellar. There is something you need to see. Yours, G."

An odd place to meet. Surely she didn't mean to have a tryst there, the little minx, not when there were perfectly comfortable beds available.

He hurriedly dragged on a shirt and pushed his feet into his slippers. Whatever her reason for summoning him, why not simply wait until he answered her knock so they could go downstairs together if there really was something to see there?

What if someone else had left the note? He went over to the lamp and examined it again. He couldn't be certain, but the handwriting looked like Grace's, her feminine flowing hand that he had seen when she had written to him in London.

Someone could have forced her write it, but how in the world could anyone have gotten past the bevy of guards they had stationed around the property? Harrell had even added several more. The rain, of course, might have prevented them patrolling as they should. He listened, then glanced at the window. The rain had stopped.

Best be prepared for trickery. He checked his pistol's load and carried it with him.

Without lamp or candle to light the familiar route, Caine quickly made his way down to the kitchens. He followed the narrow stairway that tunneled from the very end of the ground-floor kitchens to the cellar's storage chamber beneath it.

The thick oak door stood half open and weak candlelight spilled from the interior. Softly, he approached the portal, listening for movement inside.

He peered in. A bundled form in the corner moved, and he heard her muffled shriek! "Grace!" He cocked his pistol and rushed in.

The last thing he heard as he fell was her tortured moan.

Chapter Seventeen

Grace wept as she watched Wardfelton bind Caine's motionless wrists and ankles with the same narrow, pliable rope he had used for hers. When he had finished, her uncle was breathing hard. "Perfect. Now to you again," he said, crouching beside her where she sat and reaching to remove the gag from her mouth. "If you scream, I will cut his throat," he promised.

"Wh-what do you want?" she rasped, terrified that he would kill them both. She glanced at Caine, but he had not moved.

"I want to know who else knows what you know."

"About what?" she asked, truly puzzled.

He scoffed. "You know very well what I mean! I'm sure you've told your future *husband* what you overheard. Who else?" he demanded.

"What I overheard *when?* Please tell me what you mean!"

"That night with Sorenson in my library, of course. What else would I mean?" He glared at her. "I saw you just outside the door that evening. You gave me that look of yours when we came out. You heard us and you meant to use it against me. I could see it in your greedy little eyes, planning blackmail. Well, I didn't give you a chance for that, did I!"

Grace struggled to breathe normally and make sense of it all. "For goodness' sake, Uncle, you were both speaking French! I don't know two words of the language, only its nasal sound! Did you forget I was never sent to school? Father taught me all I know. I only had Latin."

Wardfelton stared at her, wide-eyed with surprise. Then he narrowed his gaze. "That's impossible. All girls are taught French!"

"No, it's true!" she insisted. "As for the look you saw, I was upset that you ignored the summons to dinner twice! Everything had gone cold. When I came to see what was the matter, Sorenson was still there. You were always so furious with Cook when dinner was so much as a minute late!"

"Good God," her uncle groaned. He remained silent for several moments, apparently thinking about the situation. "Well, no matter now, even if what you say is true. This has gone too far."

"Please let us go. Neither of us knows anything damaging about you, Uncle. Please."

He glared at her. "You know I hired someone to kill you." He waggled his knife in Caine's direction. "And him. Bloody fools couldn't do the simplest of jobs I paid for. Now I have to..."

"But you don't need to do this, Uncle. You could just leave us here and go away." Again, she looked at Caine. He was moving a bit, coming to, she supposed, and almost hoped not.

Wardfelton scoffed, dragging her attention back to him. "Go away, Grace? Where?"

For a moment, he simply looked at her, much in the way he had before he had turned against her and treated her so bad. "It's unfortunate how matters have turned out if you really didn't know. I quite liked you at first." He made a wry face. "But I didn't mind disposing of James and your mother. Meddling fools brought it on themselves."

"Mother and Father?" Grace asked in a horrified whisper. "You *killed* them?" She shook her head, unable to believe it. "But it was cholera. Everyone said it was cholera!"

He nodded. "Convenient, that epidemic. No one examines a cholera victim all that closely, now do they? No, James found out, you see, and promised to expose me. And he had told that mother of yours."

Grace was weeping openly now, grieving for

her parents, as well as for Caine and herself. They had no chance of survival. He would cut their throats before she could get free to stop him. But he surprised her yet again as he stood up and went to the door.

She saw him glance up at the slit of a window. The thick, narrow panes, barely above ground, allowed a bit of light into the cellar in the daytime and provided ventilation when necessary. Unfortunately, she knew without looking that the window was ten feet up and too narrow to provide an avenue of escape even if it could be reached.

"Goodbye, Grace," he said, and stepped outside the door. She heard the key turn in the lock.

Caine's unexpected roll toward her surprised Grace. "You're conscious! Thank God!"

"We have to hurry, Grace," he muttered. "Your fingers are smaller to work the rope. Turn your back to mine and see if you can untie me. Not a minute to lose."

"Why hurry? He has locked us in." She began to work the bonds on her own wrists.

"No, but we can move that cache of gunpowder he intends to explode."

"What?" She looked up to see a hole in the glass with a narrow ropelike fuse running to a wooden cask that sat on a top shelf above the baskets of apples. Now she worked frantically at the ropes on her wrists and was free in less than a minute.

Caine still wrestled with his. She crawled over to him. "Be still, I'll do it."

He grunted in surprise. "How the hell did you get free?"

She worked at his bonds. "Childhood trick. Obviously, my uncle never played pirates with the local hellions the way I did. One quickly learns how to *let* someone tie them up! Clasp hands together, separate and expand the wrists as much as possible, wriggle around and cry a lot. Usually works, especially for girls."

He tossed the cords she'd untied and began working at the ones on his ankles. "Wonders never cease around you."

"Well, they might if we tarry." She rushed over and studied the shelving.

He jumped up and followed. "The sideboards are sturdy, but those slats won't support me. Besides none of these are bolted to the wall," Caine said, feeling the thickness of the slats. "And if *you* try, it could tumble forward. That keg's iron bands striking the flagstone could cause it to explode."

"What do we do?" she asked. "Wait, I know! Prop against the wall next to the shelves and crouch down. I'll climb your body."

He didn't argue, just did as she said. "Have a care you don't fall," he warned as she braced a foot on his leg and climbed until her feet were on his shoulders.

She held on to his head with one hand and balanced herself against the wall with the other as he straightened slowly. "Can your bad shoulder take my weight when I stand?" she asked, and felt him shift to aid the attempt.

"Go," he said, grasping her ankles.

"I'm going to stand now," she gasped. "If I can manage."

"Keep one hand on the wall, other on the shelves for balance, but don't pull on them."

She rose slowly and carefully. He felt the slight jerk as she yanked the fuse from the cask of powder and heaved a sigh of relief. "Done."

"Move the fuse well away from it," Caine said. "Are you steady up there?"

"So far. Are you steady down there?" she gasped.

"Did I mention that I love you?" he asked, tightening his grip on her ankles.

"Hush. You'll make my knees weak. Is this fuse far enough over?"

"I can't see a thing with your gown over my head. Ready to dismount?"

"How should we do this? Getting down might be harder than getting up, I think!"

"Walk your hands down the wall and lower yourself to a crouch if you can. There. Now, slide one foot at the time until you straddle my neck."

The skirt of her nightrail completely covered his head and her bare thighs surrounded his neck. "This feels rather wicked."

"Not a position I favor at the moment." Grunting with the effort, he squatted low so that she could reach the floor and helped her off. Then he whirled her around and grabbed her to him, raining desperate kisses all over her face until he settled on her mouth for a passionate kiss that seemed all too brief.

Breathless, he broke the kiss and groaned. "Is there anything you *cannot* do?"

She sighed, nuzzling his neck. "Well, I can't pick locks. When the powder doesn't explode soon after he lights the fuse, he might come back to finish us off."

"I'll be ready for him this time. I can take his knife," Caine assured her.

"Yes, but he has your pistol."

"Damn." He leaned against the wall under the window and drew her into a hug as he looked around the cellar. "We need to get out of here."

Grace thought about her uncle's actions. "You know, he could have cut our throats and had done with it. I thought he planned to, but he didn't. That would have been much more reliable than blowing us up, don't you think? I mean, suppose the powder was too damp or the fuse proved faulty? He hired others to do murder until they failed him. Maybe he lacks the fortitude for killing face-to-face."

"What of his strangling Sorensen?"

"Hired, I expect."

"Then there's your parents," Caine reminded her. "He confessed to that."

"Poison, most likely. No wounds visible. Again, he was probably removed from it."

Caine was not convinced. "Perhaps you're right, but if he leaves us alive, he knows we will talk. So he'll come back in—"

"Or set fire to the manor!" Grace guessed.

"Oh, God, it just occurred to me..." Caine's face changed, his expression one of horror. "Something quicker and more to the point than fire. If he brought in one cask of powder, there could be more. We have to get out of here *now.*"

Caine approached the shelves on the far end of the room away from the gunpowder shelf and rapidly began taking down the baskets and slatted boxes containing victuals. "Stack these against the wall over there so the floor's clear in front of the shelves," he ordered.

Grace obeyed without question, talking as she worked. "He could say it's our word against his. We have no proof. How do you think he got the gunpowder down here in the first place?" she asked, huffing with exertion as she hefted a box of turnips.

"Delivered it himself. Harrell would have thought nothing of it if Wardfelton arrived dressed as a deliveryman. Harrell had ordered some. Providing the guards with ammunition, as well as supplying it for the autumn hunt Harrell mentioned would require three or four casks of powder, the very reasons we need to vacate this room in a hurry."

"There's more powder?" Grace asked, glancing up at the one barrel on the shelf. "Out there? With him?"

"Very probably." He motioned for her to stand back against the far wall. "Shield the candle. I'm going to tip this and hope it falls apart with the crash. We need a battering ram. Stand clear."

He braced a foot against the wall, gave the shelving a tug and it fell. Grace winced at the clatter. She watched as he pried apart the boards. "There!" he said, lifting one of the long and sturdy side pieces. "The interior walls are not so thick, just partitions really. Mortar's old and crumbly."

"You hope," Grace muttered.

"I pray," he admitted. "Shield the candle." He gripped the board, backed against the outside wall and ran across the room. The board bounced and knocked him backward. Three times, he ran at it, striking the same place with the makeshift battering ram.

"I think it's giving way!" Grace exclaimed.

He hit it again and once more. One stone fell through to the other side. She cheered. Relentlessly, he banged the board at the surrounding stones. In moments, he had an opening a good two feet across and almost that high.

He paused for a few seconds and they heard a loud thump. Both looked up at the window. A barrel rested against it. *LMN WORKS* was stenciled on the side next to the pane, plainly visible in the steady candlelight.

"Go, Grace! Squeeze through to the wine room and go up the stairs. Get to the other end of the house and, for God's sake, hurry. Shout *fire* and wake everyone as you go. Get everyone to the far end and out through the conservatory. Count heads and make them stay together."

She grasped his arm as he lifted her through the hole. "But you—"

"Will be right behind you. A few more knocks and I can get through. Hurry now. Most of the men who sleep below will be out on guard but I'll check below stairs on my way to the stairs at the far end. Go on now. *Run!*"

Grace hit the floor of the wine cellar, felt her way to the stair there and ran through the pitch-dark kitchens. "Fire!" she screamed the instant she reached the vestibule. She lifted her gown and tore up to the first-floor bedrooms. "Wake up! Fire in the house! Everyone, go north side! Servants' stairs! Hurry!"

Neville emerged with a lamp just before she reached his door. "Fire?"

"Gunpowder! Root cellar! Wardfelton!" she gasped. "Help me get the others out the north end."

"Caine?"

"Waking those left in the cellar quarters." She hoped.

"Go on out," he said with a not-so-gentle shove. "Trent and I will clear the house."

The earl shuffled toward them, the countess huddled close. "Come!" Grace said, taking the earl's other arm. "We must hurry."

"Where are we going?" Lady Hadley demanded. "It's still dark."

"To the end of the hall and down the servants' stairs," Grace replied, trying to sound calm when she could hardly get her breath. "Mind you don't trip on your gown, Lord Hadley."

"I smell no smoke! Nose is as good as ever," the earl declared, lifting his head and sniffing loudly. "Where's this fire, gel?"

"In the cellar, sir. Let's move along now."

Several of the maids, including Jane, rushed by them. "To the conservatory and out!" Grace called to them. "Jane! Keep everyone together on the terrace!"

Judd approached at a trot, his nightcap askew, lamp in hand. The tweenies flew by, catching up to Jane and the others. "I let Mrs. Oliver and

Mrs. Bowden out through the library door," Judd informed her. He had Mrs. Bowden's large ring of household keys in his hand.

"Good. Anyone else on the ground floor?"

"No, my lady. Nor upstairs. Should we form up with buckets? I'll fetch Mr. Harrell and the lads."

"Leave it for now. Give me the keys and your light." They had reached the servants' stairs. "Go down with Lord and Lady Hadley. I'll be there directly."

Grace could not leave without knowing Caine was safely out of the root cellar. What if the other stones had not come loose? What if he were trapped there when her uncle blew it up? She turned and ran, the keys banging against her wrist.

She had just reached the kitchens when the world erupted.

"Where the devil is she?" Caine demanded, plowing through the crowd gathered on the terrace just as dawn was breaking. "Grace!"

He saw Judd. "Have you seen her? Did she come out earlier?"

"No, sir. She took the keys from me upstairs," Judd told him. "She went back down the main hall. Perhaps she went out the library door where Mrs. Oliver and Mrs. Bowden were. I told her they were there."

"Oh, God," Caine muttered, closing his eyes against what he already knew. She had gone back for him. The root cellar would be demolished, probably the entire southeast corner of the manor, including the kitchen.

He had been halfway through the lower level when it blew, relieved that he and the servants he'd awakened down there escaped injury and were only shaken. Now he might have lost her.

Might have lost Grace. He grabbed a lantern from one of the footmen, reentered the house and took the hallway at a run.

"Caine, wait!" he heard Neville shout behind him.

"Grace is still in here!" he shouted back.

"We're with you," Trent called.

"Go back outside!" he ordered. "The walls might not be stable at the other end."

But he knew they would not go back and they did not. He ran on. Dust still filled the air as he reached the back of the vestibule. The kitchen area was in ruin, windows shattered, debris everywhere. He saw her then, covered in dust, lying in a heap, nightdress up to her knees and her bare feet curled together like a sleeping child's.

"Oh, Grace," he whispered, kneeling beside her still form. He lifted her gently and held her against his chest.

Trent fell beside him. "Is she…"

"No!" Caine shouted, rising with Grace in his arms. "Trent, get the doctor!" He saw Neville standing there, mouth agape. "You! Find Wardfelton and bring him here. I mean to kill that son of a bitch!"

Neville and Trent ran out the maw that had once been the kitchen door and dashed to the stables.

Caine carried Grace out of the rubble and down the hallway to the stairs. There, he trudged up to her room, kicked open her door and laid her on the bed. She had not moved.

Mrs. Oliver appeared. "Is she…"

"She breathes, but God only knows for how long," he murmured, brushing the hair out of her eyes with a trembling and dust-stained finger. "Fetch water and cloths to bathe her. And a fresh gown. Trent's gone for the doctor."

"I'll see to it, sir," she said softly, and disappeared.

"Grace?" he whispered, leaning close to her ear. "Grace, can you hear me?"

Nothing. Not a twitch of an eyelid or any movement at all.

Caine took her limp hand in his and held it, two fingers on the pulse at her wrist. The vein was hard to locate and the beat seemed slow, almost not there at all. "Don't leave me," he whispered. "Please."

Chapter Eighteen

Mrs. Oliver nudged Caine's shoulder. "Jane's bringing water. Let's try a vinegarette, sir. That might bring her around."

He moved to let her closer. "Do it."

She waved the small bottle just beneath Grace's nose and gained a weak cough.

"Enough," Caine said, moving Oliver's arm to the side. "It might hurt her to cough if anything's broken."

"Or it could help clear her lungs if she's breathed in too much dust," Mrs. Oliver said. "Have you felt her head? Maybe she was just knocked out."

He ran a careful hand over Grace's head, examining it inch by inch with his fingers. "Nothing there that I can feel," he said. He continued, testing her shoulders and arms.

Mrs. Oliver stopped him when he reached her ribs. "Best allow me, sir," she said firmly, and took over.

Caine watched as the older woman did a hasty examination of Grace's form, right down to the toes.

"I don't believe anything's broken unless it's the neck or back," she told him.

"Oh, God," Caine groaned, covering his face with his hand.

"Now, now, sir. Not likely that's the case, is it? Hardly a mark on her, save a few scrapes. Not that we can see anyway. I need to undress her and be sure."

Caine shook his head, but he didn't know what damage the blast might have caused her. The only explosion he had ever witnessed was that of the shell that nearly blinded him. Not the same thing at all. Grace had no visible wounds other than abrasions on her arms, probably from climbing through that small hole in the root-cellar wall.

Jane arrived with a basin of water and the other things he'd asked for. She set them down and went to Grace's wardrobe for a gown.

"If you'd leave us to it now, sir, we'll see to her," Mrs. Oliver said. "We'll take every care," she added, laying a hand on his arm.

"No. I'll stay," he declared.

"Sir, we'll have to undress her. It's not proper,

your not being her husband yet and all." Her kind eyes met his. "Think of *her*."

He could not think of anything else. "Just outside the door, then," he said reluctantly. "If you find any hidden hurt she suffered, come and tell me."

"Straightaway. Without fail," Mrs. Oliver promised.

Caine leaned against the wall in the hallway, waiting. After a quarter hour, Mr. Harrell approached, hat in hand. "Sir, the search is on for Lord Wardfelton. Mr. Neville said we should fan out and take any strangers into custody, since none of us would recognize the man but him."

"Oh, you'll know him, I expect. No doubt he's the one who delivered the gunpowder."

Harrell's eyes widened. "That Mr. Trueblood? I thought it strange you would request a barrel put in the root cellar. He said you wanted it there for house use and it would be safe to do if it was kept well away from sparks. The rest he put in the outbuilding with the tools as usual."

Harrell covered his face with a hand and groaned. "Sir, he asked for work. Said he was home from the war. Said he needed something more steady than delivery work."

"So you hired him." Caine barely held his anger in check as Harrell nodded. "Well, it's done. We did need more guards and how could you know? So, did he actually work, other than bringing the powder?"

"He patrolled like the others."

"So I thought. And had the opportunity to roll all the barrels next to the house after we disabled his fuse on that one he had planted inside."

Harrell swallowed hard and ducked his head. "I'm sorry, sir. He had paperwork from LMN factory where we usually order."

"Where everyone in the south of England usually orders. Go, join the hunt and run him to ground, Harrell. I mean to kill him."

"Sir? Best haul him in to the London authorities, don't you think? He is a noble."

"Noble, hell. He's a blackguard who needs to die," Caine declared. "And I'll kill him even if I hang for it."

Harrell shrugged and offered a grim smile. "Aye, well, I doubt it'll come to that. Accidents happen all the time, don't they, sir. I'd swear to it."

"Go on, then. He'll be harder to track if he reaches the city."

Caine paced, impatience mounting, waiting to see Grace again, waiting for the doctor to come, waiting for Neville and the men to find Wardfelton. He should be *doing* something. But what?

Judd came up. "We've begun the cleanup, sir, now that it's light enough to see well. Perhaps you and the family will want to return to London until we've repaired what can be fixed."

Caine sighed. "Lady Grace shouldn't be moved, so of course I'll be staying."

"How is she, sir? Everyone will want to know." His concern touched Caine. Grace had made herself a part of Wildenhurst. The staff doted on her.

"As soon as I know myself, I will send word. In the meantime, have Lord and Lady Hadley's things readied and the carriage prepared for travel. They need to be away by midmorning."

"Right away, sir. What of Lord Trent and Mr. Neville? Shall I pack for them?"

"No. I expect they will stay, at least for today. Have someone bring food from the village until we can arrange a makeshift kitchen. Perhaps the fireplace in the drawing room will serve since it's the largest. Salvage what you can, but take care. The whole south end might collapse without its support."

"What of sleeping arrangements for the night, sir?"

"The master suite won't be safe, but that will be unoccupied anyway with the Hadleys gone. The upstairs maids will have to sleep elsewhere, too, perhaps the north end of the attic."

There was so much to do, so many things to see to, and all Caine could do was worry about Grace's survival. "You and Mrs. Bowden

take charge of the household. Arrange it anyway that's convenient for operation. Use your
own judgment and only come to me if there's
a crisis."

"Yes, sir. Not to worry."

Not to worry? When he could be losing all
that was dear to him? The woman he loved and
couldn't live without?

He began to pace again, running his fingers
through his hair, pressing his temples, trying
to banish the pounding ache in his head. Nothing could fix the ache in his heart except Grace
regaining consciousness and assuring him she
would be well.

How had he ever believed he could let her go?
Why had he ever thought she would be a drain
on his time and an impediment to his proper ser-
vice as earl? Now he doubted he would amount
to anything at all without her.

She had done more in organizing Wildenhurst
than anyone in his memory. She had saved his
uncle's life. And helped save Caine's and her
own in that cellar. She had restored his own faith
in women, surrendered her innocence without a
whimper and, most surprising of all, had made
him able to laugh again.

He felt the tears on his cheeks and dashed
them away. Hell, she made him cry, too. Made
him feel again, and dwell on something other

than his anger and vanity. Grace was all that her name implied.

"God save her," he whispered. "Please."

Trent came dashing down the hall from the main stairs. "The doctor's coming up. Hadley insisted on sending a rider to London for Dr. Ackers, as well. How is she?"

Caine shrugged. "Oliver and young Jane are seeing to her injuries where I may not." He swayed and Trent steadied him.

"Are you hurt, Caine?" he asked. "What's wrong?"

Caine shook his head and sniffed. "Fighting despair is all. She has to make it through this, Gavin, or I might not."

"Look at me, Caine!" Trent demanded. "Listen to me now. Grace is going to be all right. She's the strongest woman we've ever met and you know that."

"You love her, too," Caine guessed.

Trent slapped his shoulder. "Of course I love her, you idiot! Everyone loves her but that lunatic Wardfelton. Grace is my friend, same as you are."

Caine nodded. "Any sign of the lunatic? I look forward to choking the life out of him."

"No one has seen him, but he can't hide for long. Neville finally confided something to me today that you should probably know. He's worked for the War Office for several years.

Clandestine assignments, some abroad and some in England. He has suspicions concerning Wardfelton that have nothing to do with this."

Caine snapped to attention. "Perhaps they do have to do with it. Grace once overheard Wardfelton and Sorensen speaking together in French. He thought she understood them. That's why he wanted to kill her. And me, because he was afraid she'd confided in me, or would do after we were married. He must have been spying for the French."

"Neville thinks it's more likely he was a sympathizer or financier. He says Wardfelton's inheritance has dwindled to nothing and he has no acquisitions to show for it. Could be gambling, I suppose, but Neville doesn't think so."

"Grace told me he had sold off things of value from the country seat," Caine added.

"Yes, and he tried to sell the town house, too, but Neville's man has uncovered records showing that it was left to Grace by her father and he couldn't dispose of it."

Caine's eyes met Trent's as they came to the same conclusion. "Unless she was dead!" they exclaimed in unison.

"And still unmarried, so he would have it as her next of kin," Caine added. "This explains so much. The war's over and he's destitute with the possibility of being exposed for treason as long as she's alive."

Trent blew out a sigh. "God, speak of motive for murder!"

"He won't live to be tried for it. I mean to kill him," Caine said with cold determination.

"Not if I find him first," Trent said with a succinct nod. "And I'm off to do just that. Sorry you can't come, old boy. Give Grace my regards." He grinned as he backed a few steps down the hall. "And tell her I love her when she wakes, will you?"

"Go to hell," Caine said, but he smiled.

"Sir?" Jane said, standing in the doorway to Grace's room. "You may come in now."

Caine immediately dismissed Trent and Wardfelton from his mind and rushed to Grace's bedside. He swallowed a groan. She looked... lifeless. Pale and unmoving, laid out in a clean gown with her hands by her sides. Afraid to breathe, he picked up one of her hands and pressed his fingers to her wrist as he had done earlier. There! A slow, steady pulse.

The doctor arrived within the half hour, Dr. Samuels, the same fellow who had treated Caine's gunshot wound here at Wildenhurst. Caine did not dislike the man, but nor did he trust him completely. His smile was too obsequious and his manner annoying.

"Good day, Captain," he said by way of greeting as he set down his bag.

"Not thus far," Caine replied. "Thank you for

coming." He stood. "The women have examined her and there are no open wounds. Her knees, one shoulder and one hip are bruised, probably as she fell. The scratches on her arms were acquired earlier, not in the explosion. She has been unconscious since we found her a quarter hour after the blast."

The doctor leaned over Grace and pried open one eyelid, then both. He raked back her hair and checked her ears. He ran his fingers through her hair, pressing at certain points as Caine watched.

Then he straightened. "I believe she has sustained an injury to the brain, sir. I saw this in the war as you might have done yourself. There are signs the brain is swelling within her skull or loose blood is collecting there."

Caine had never felt such fear in his life, even when he thought he would die himself. "Will… will she live?"

The doctor glanced at Grace and back at Caine. "I can relieve the pressure. That will give her a chance."

"A *chance?* How much of a chance?" Caine demanded.

Samuels shrugged a shoulder. "I'm given to believe one out of four survive the procedure."

"*You are given to believe?* What procedure?" Caine watched as the doctor opened his medical case. He took out a vise of some sort. "What is that? It's not…"

"Yes, trepanning instruments."

Caine was already shaking his head. "You are not boring a hole in her head! Are you mad?"

"Sir, it is the only way!"

It took every restraint Caine possessed to refrain from tossing the man out the window. "You can't be positive her brain is swelling," he said, trying to sound reasonable. He looked down at the apparatus. "This looks brand-new. You haven't done this before, have you? Even if I were convinced this was necessary, I wouldn't allow a novice to do it!"

Samuels wore an expression of studied tolerance. "Sir, I have studied, apprenticed and practiced surgery on the battlefield. Be assured I know what I'm about."

Caine almost lost his reason. "You are *about* to be shown the door, Mr. Samuels. We don't require your services."

"She will probably die, then," Samuels warned, his expression dark.

"If so, it will be without another hole in her head," Caine declared. "Leave."

Samuels tossed in the instrument, snapped his bag shut and stalked to the door. "I shall send you the bill for my trouble."

Caine collapsed in the chair and rested his head on the bed beside Grace. Mrs. Oliver lay a hand on his shoulder and he looked up at her.

"Have I done wrong to refuse that?" he whispered.

She shook her head and smiled. "No, sir. The earl's physician will come soon. Our lady trusts him. He knew her da."

The hours crept by as Caine stood watch over Grace, alternately praying she would recover and cursing Wardfelton's murderous soul.

Grace struggled through the darkness, a viscous mass enveloped her, hampered her breathing, obstructed her limbs as she fought her way. One goal pushed her efforts. She had to find Caine. To save him.

The grayness swirled into shapes that moved and slowly, menacingly, features formed out of it. Wardfelton's smirking grin taunted her. His eyes promised a slow, smothering death. Grace tried to scream but her throat was so dry, her tongue so thick. She cried out for Caine, to warn him.

Dr. Ackers arrived at eight o'clock in the evening.

"She moved a little," Caine informed him as the physician entered Grace's room. "Tried to speak, I think."

Ackers went straight to the bedside and did exactly what Samuels had done that morning.

Caine's patience almost snapped. Did no one know what to do for her?

The doctor moved away after his cursory assessment and spoke to Caine. "There's little to be done other than wait. Dr. Samuels is still downstairs, convinced that relieving the pressure is the thing to do." He held up a hand to silence Caine when he started to protest. "I agree with you, sir. It's too dangerous. At times, these surgeons are a bit too eager to ply their trade. As it stands, she probably has an even chance to come around on her own when the swelling subsides. Her chances are reduced by half again if we proceed with surgery."

Caine breathed a sigh so deep it made him dizzy. "What can we do for her?"

"Cold compresses on the face, head and neck. Moving her limbs occasionally to encourage blood flow into them, away from the brain."

"Yes! That makes sense!" Caine felt vastly relieved at having something positive to do. And to have Ackers's agreement that he had not condemned Grace, but had done the best thing after all.

"The women can do what needs doing." Ackers beckoned to Mrs. Oliver and Jane, then continued to Caine, "My advice to you is to leave her for a while. Have some nourishment and rest. You aren't long out of a sickbed yourself."

"She might call for me. I need to be here," Caine argued.

"Then we shall find you on the instant," the doctor promised. "Go now and do as I say."

Caine crossed to Grace again and kissed her forehead. With a last lingering look at her, he left the room.

Others were depending on him, he knew, but he could scarcely think of anything but her. If she died, he feared nothing else would matter anyway.

Trent met him at the foot of the main stairs. "We have everything sorted down here. How is Grace?"

Caine shook his head, unable to answer. He clung to the fact that she had moved, slight as the stirring had been, it gave him hope. And her lips had opened, twitched a little. "I can't leave her for long," he told Trent. "How goes the search?"

"Neville's taken it to London. Harrell and I will commence here in the county at first light. God only knows where he went, but we will find him, Caine."

He found he couldn't discuss Wardfelton any longer or his blast of anger would erupt full force and convince everyone he was mad. Instead, he tried to concentrate on a lesser concern. "The house," he said as he surveyed the vestibule. "I think half must be brought down and rebuilt."

Trent took his arm. "But not tonight. Come

with me. Mrs. Bowden has a good stew and decent ale, everything's set up in the drawing room."

Caine went, noting absently that the doors to the damaged portion of the house had been closed and everything in the immediate area had been dusted. The floors shone. One would never guess from this vantage that nearly half the ground floor of the house lay in ruin with the floors over it highly unstable.

His entire life might lie in ruin if Grace lost hers. But if she recovered, as she must do, she would be furious if he had done nothing in the meantime but brace himself for grief. If their conditions were reversed, she would be taking charge, issuing orders and doing her duty. Hadn't she done precisely that when he lay abed with the gunshot?

He forced down a hearty bowl of venison stew, emptied a tankard of stout and went to compose a letter to a London architect he knew who had engineering experience. There at the desk in the library, he fell sound asleep.

"Wake up, sir!"

Caine stirred, catching himself as he nearly fell from his chair. Someone was shaking his shoulder. "What?" he mumbled just as full awareness hit. "Is it Grace?"

"Yes, sir."

Chapter Nineteen

"Mrs. Oliver shouted down just now for me to get you," Judd added in a rush. "Lady Grace called your name!"

"Thank God," Caine whispered. "Dr. Ackers is there?" he asked, hurrying out ahead of Judd.

"All night, sir. It's almost six now."

Caine dashed up the stairs and down the hall. He burst into the room and hurried to her side. She looked the same as before, not wide awake as he had hoped. He leaned over her, took her hand and kissed her lips, a brief touch only. "Grace? I'm here, love."

She moved her head and issued a sound, not quite a word. Her eyes opened slightly.

"You're back with me, aren't you! You came back," he murmured, brushing her brow with fingers that shook. "All will be well now. You will be well."

Her lips stretched into a weak smile and she spoke his name, a mere breath, but the most precious sound he'd ever heard.

She lapsed into sleep again, but he knew she would live. He kept her hand in his as he sank into the chair beside her bed, pressed his face into the edge of her pillow and wept soundlessly into the soft linen.

Grace woke hours later as the small mantel clock chimed ten. She remembered waking before or perhaps had only dreamed that. Caine had been hovering beside her, coaxing her awake, his hand holding hers, chafing it, warming it. She moved her fingers and realized he held it yet. When she turned her head on the pillow, his hair brushed her face. He was sitting in the chair beside the bed, leaned over so that his head rested next to hers.

She glanced around the room and noticed nothing had changed. Thank God the manor still stood and they had, by some stroke of good luck, avoided catastrophe. She figured she must have fallen and hit her head as she rushed to see if he had made it out of the cellar.

"Caine?" she whispered.

He raised his head immediately. "Do you hurt? Can I get you anything?" His free hand gingerly brushed her hair back, then cradled the side of her face. "God, I worried you would never wake fully! You've been in and out four times now. Does your head ache?"

"I fell. But I don't quite remember falling." She closed her eyes and tried again to think of what had happened. "Clumsy of me."

"It's all right, darling. You shouldn't worry about anything."

She swallowed hard. "The rain wet the powder then? Everyone's safe?"

"Everyone else is fine."

"My uncle?" she asked.

"Gone. You need not think of him ever again."

She sighed. "You...you have killed him then?"

Caine shook his head. "No, not yet."

She closed her eyes again as she heard the intent in his tone. They had no proof of her uncle's misdeeds and Caine would be arrested if he dealt out justice on his own. "You mustn't. I don't want you to."

"I know, love. I know you don't. Rest easy and it'll all work out in the end. You've had a terrible injury."

Her eyes flew open. "Do you believe I will die of it? You sound as if you do!"

He smiled. "Absolutely not. You will live to a ripe old age and bear us a few hellions just like yourself."

Grace tried to nod, but it hurt. "They might have to be bastards. I think fate is against this marriage of ours."

He patted her face gently. "We'll tie the knot as soon as you're able to stand upright without the headache. I promise."

"Tomorrow, then," she muttered as she drifted back to sleep.

Tomorrow did not work out. When Grace woke again, it was to overhear Mrs. Bowden and Jane discussing the damages to the kitchen wing and bemoaning the fact that the house would never be the same.

Grace was livid. Why hadn't Caine told her the explosion had happened? Damn the man for his coddling and cooing to her how everything was all right.

"Where is he?" she demanded in the strongest voice she could manage. The servants gasped and rushed to her side, but there was no calming her. Her home was ruined and no one had seen fit to tell her?

Her anger had cooled somewhat by the time Caine answered her summons, but she still resented his keeping her in the dark. "Why was I not told?" she demanded. "I want to see for myself how severely the house is damaged."

He sat on the edge of the bed and took her hands in his. "Of course you will, but later, when you feel a bit steadier. Not to worry, all can be repaired. I have someone working on the plans already."

She pressed him for details, but he ignored

that and cleverly guided her into a discussion of wedding plans. Grace allowed it, but only because she tired too quickly to sustain an argument.

Two days later, Grace was chafing at her confinement to bed. Dr. Ackers had insisted she rest until he gave her leave to resume her normal activities.

Caine kept her company most hours of the day and evening, letting her best him at cards, showing off his expertise at chess, teasing her with riddles and sharing stories of his childhood.

He acted as if everything was settled between them, almost as if they had been married for ages and well past the first bloom of passion.

She recalled how he had said he loved her when she was standing on his shoulders next to the barrel of gunpowder. Was that a momentary expostulation because she could climb like a monkey and had ripped out that fuse? Hardly the most enviable of circumstances to hear such a thing.

Caine never asked even once whether she loved him. Did he take that for granted? Well, she had told him only that once in the heat of anger. He must say it first and mean it before she would admit it again. But perhaps he really didn't love her, in which case, she shouldn't admit it at all.

Caine was totally unlike himself since the explosion. This playfulness of his, while endearing in its probable intent, now made her wonder if his brain had been affected by events, as well. She was bored, restless and also a bit annoyed by what seemed very like condescension of his part.

"We really should discuss what happened," she said, suddenly too impatient with him to avoid crossing swords. "Why do you always refuse?"

"I merely change the topic." He tapped her on the nose. "Because you need to dwell on happy things until you're well again. And there is nothing you can do that isn't being done to right matters. Wildenhurst is already under repair."

He traced the side of her face with his finger, peering at it as if to check for undiscovered damage.

She batted his hand away. "You know very well I mean we should speak of my uncle and what he's done, not of the house. What have you heard? Is there any news of him?"

"The search is still on. That's all I know."

He reached into his pocket and drew out a length of string. "Cat's cradle. Ever played that?" He began looping the string around his fingers. "Pull this one."

Grace groaned and closed her eyes. "You are impossible."

Chapter Twenty

Neville arrived at Wildenhurst that afternoon. Grace and Caine were having tea off trays in her chamber when Judd announced him.

"Come in, cousin," Grace said as she held out a hand. "Thank goodness for your company. This man is driving me to distraction!"

"My current goal in life," Caine admitted. "Hello, Neville."

Neville bowed over Grace's hand as he laid his other on Caine's shoulder. "I see you're both in fine form today. So happy to see you smiling, Grace."

After a few more pleasantries, he gave Caine a meaningful look and inclined his head toward the door. "You and I have a bit of business to discuss, if Grace will excuse us."

"If it concerns the incident with my uncle, I

wish you would include me," Grace said. "I'm quite well now, except for an occasional spell of dizziness and I promise not to swoon. Caine tells me nothing."

Neville looked to Caine for permission.

"Knowing nothing is definitely more trying than hearing the facts," she prompted. "I imagine the very worst."

Caine nodded with obvious reluctance.

"Very well. Wardfelton must have gone directly back to the town house," Neville told them. She could almost hear him grit his teeth. "He was there when I arrived to question his staff. They all swear he was there that entire night. When I accused him of setting the charges, he laughed."

"He denies it?" Grace asked, astounded. "How can he deny it?"

"That's no matter," Caine said. "Harrell can identify him as the one who delivered the gunpowder, the very one who put a barrel of it in the root cellar. We have him dead to rights."

Neville disagreed. "He has six employees who will vouch for his presence there in London at the time. You have only the one."

"What of his sympathies with the French? How did he answer that?" Caine asked.

"Unmentioned, because I have no proof whatsoever and it would have alerted him there is an investigation underway. When I said that you two would bring charges of attempted murder and testify against him in a court, he very patiently explained that you both have good cause to ruin him. That you, Caine, had threatened him with precisely that. And that you, Grace, strongly resented his assuming your father's title and having care of you because you are willful to the extreme. He cites your plan to marry a total stranger without his consent. And he further swore that you promised to slander him in the worst possible ways."

"What lies!" she cried.

"Of course they are, but a magistrate might not view them as such. He's quite persuasive. And he is an earl."

Caine smiled without humor. "He will never see a court. I vowed that from the beginning."

"You can't kill him, Caine," Neville warned. "I can't let you do that. You would hang."

"But he will be dead first."

"No!" Grace exclaimed, grabbing Caine's arm. "Listen to me. He dares not make another attempt. He cannot, without everyone knowing, now that he's been accused. You have to let it go, Caine."

Caine had grown calm. Deathly calm as he spoke. "Wardfelton is responsible for at least four deaths, including your parents', Grace. And he would have murdered both of us and possibly half this household. He is without conscience and was abominably cruel to you. How can I possibly let that go?"

"He must be stopped," Neville agreed. "Men convinced they are above the law will dare anything. But as it stands now, the law won't touch him. I can't prove his treason and you can't prove murder or even his attempt at it." Neville thought for a moment, then held up a finger. "We must let him hang himself."

"Get him alone. I have rope," Caine said, shifting restlessly, obviously eager to get on with it.

"No, no, that's not what I meant," Neville said with a half smile. "But I'm almost certain that if Wardfelton believes he's gotten away with everything, he'll want to gloat to someone. A man such as he will *need* to. His old cohort Sorenson is dead. Who will he boast to then?"

"Neville's right," Grace said, nodding. "That's exactly how he is. He won't be able to stand not crowing about his cleverness." She looked to Neville. "But to whom would he go? He hasn't any friends, or any acquaintances who would not be horrified by his actions."

"Precisely," Neville agreed. "It would have to be someone whom he knows could do absolutely nothing about it."

"Grace," guessed Caine immediately.

"Me?" she scoffed, crossing her arms over her chest. "He wouldn't dare show his face to me now. Not with all the protection I have about me. He would be mad to try."

"He *is* mad, Grace," Neville said. "Caine is right. It will be you he wants to taunt, to dare you to speak ill of him afterward and he will probably leave you with a threat for good measure."

"Only, he will never leave," Caine promised.

"Oh, stop it, Caine," Grace said. "Go on, Trent."

"We shall let him confess his cleverness to Grace, and there will be hidden witnesses," Neville said. "Reliable ones, with the authority to arrest him."

Caine took Grace's hand in his and gave it a fond squeeze. "I hate to put you in the position of bait, but I believe he will come eventually whether we do this or not. At least we can be in control of the meeting instead of having him spring a surprise visit in the middle of the night as he did before."

Neville added, "He won't be coming to kill you now that he thinks the threat of your accusation is over, Grace, so the danger to you is slight."

"It had better be nonexistent," Caine corrected. "So when should we do this and how do we get him to come when we want?"

Neville smiled. "Simple enough. Invite him to your wedding."

* * *

The Plan, as they now termed it, necessitated yet another delay in the wedding. Two weeks wait ensued so that invitations could be sent, received and replied to, and arrangements for three times as many guests could be made.

The Plan, in order to justify Wardfelton's invitation, required a larger guest list. Twenty or thirty at least would be included, many of them friends and peers of the Hadleys, other neighbors near Wildenhurst. Also attending would be the several gentlemen of Neville's acquaintance, one from the War Office. Caine wondered whether Wildenhurst would be too small to accommodate everyone.

Structural repairs on the cellar had been hastened and the kitchens were shored up, making the upper floors secure. Everything save a few minor surface fixes had been done. He had hired a bevy of workmen out of London who excelled in construction. The repairs and everything else had progressed so smoothly it worried Caine. He had grown so used to crisis on top of crisis, he kept wondering what catastrophe might happen next. The feeling left him on edge.

Now, on the day before the wedding, Caine wondered if the ceremony would really happen or if some other unexpected calamity would prevent it. But perhaps it was only frustration that plagued him. He wanted Grace so desperately and she had become as elusive as the holy grail.

Though she seemed well enough for anything now, Grace had not come to him again in the night. Mrs. Oliver had taken to sleeping in Grace's dressing room with the door left open. She insisted on doing that in the event Grace had a relapse.

All parties involved knew that was not the case. Mrs. Oliver had obviously guessed that he and Grace had anticipated their vows at some point and made it her business to see it did not happen again, at least not before it should.

Grace's injury had demoted her to Little Miss again, he supposed. Grace found all of this highly amusing, judging by her expression when he made the slightest suggestion that they needed to be alone.

"Patience, *love*," she would say and look at him as though he should reply to that in some way.

He thought he might go mad with the waiting and sorely needed more distraction if he was to endure.

The afternoon delivery of the mare he had purchased from a local trader proved a welcome interruption of his libidinous musings. The anticipation of giving Grace a gift lightened his mood considerably.

The roan was a beauty. He gave her a pat and

handed the reins to the groom. "Walk her around to the stables and make her shine, Jacky. Put on Lady Grace's new saddle, too."

He could hardly wait to present the mare to Grace, to see the pleasure on her face and to watch her ride. He imagined her flying across the meadows, wind in her hair, exultation on her face and in every line of her strong, slender body. Yes, just thinking of that expression of flying free she would wear, so like the one…

He shook himself sharply and whipped his mind back to the matter at hand. His gift to her.

While he searched for her in the house, Caine thought back to the first night they had met. He had promised her diamonds and she would have those in her ring. She had opted for a mare and new sidesaddle instead of the curricle and matched pair.

He had promised her freedom, too. He would give her more choices than most women had, but he doubted he could leave her alone for very long at the time. She didn't seem to want free of him anyway.

"Grace?" he called as he entered the kitchens, the last place he'd thought to look, of course.

"In here," he heard her answer. "The still room."

He entered and saw her, covered chin to knee in a large white apron and wearing gloves as she plied a mortar and pestle. "Stirring up spices?"

he asked. "Put it away and come with me. I have a surprise!"

She looked up from her task. "Will it wait a few moments? This has to be completed before I leave it or it will dry out."

Caine leaned against the wall to watch. "Of course. No hurry." Her efficiency impressed him. No wasted effort, no dithering, no pause to question her actions. "You seem to be doing everything yourself," he commented. "Should I hire more help?"

She worked the pestle as she glanced up. "No. Some things I prefer doing myself. Besides, we have taken on so many new people to serve as guards, more hiring would cut into estate profits. As it is, those are minimal at best."

"Are they?" How would she know about profits? "Harrell has complained to you?"

Her hands stilled. "Not at all. We discussed ways to economize, of course, once I studied the finances and began keeping the records."

Caine straightened, frowning. This was his fault. He hadn't had a chance yet to examine the Wildenhurst books. Straightening out Hadley Grange's affairs and dealing with Town expenses had consumed so much of his time and effort. He had assumed that Harrell had things in hand here. "Grace, I never meant you to burden yourself with that sort of thing."

"You said I might do what I would with the

place, and Mr. Harrell has been in a strut since I came, what with managing the guards' schedules, as well as seeing to the crops and tenants. Not to worry, my maths are quite adequate."

"I don't doubt it, but this is too much of an imposition."

"Nonsense." She tossed him a smile as she began bottling the substance she had mixed. "I enjoyed keeping my father's records and did a fair job of it. This is not so different. Only, on a larger scale. It's interesting to me, far more so than sewing, doing little watercolors, playing a pianoforte and the like." Her grimace at that list was endearing. "Mother despaired of me, but Father approved."

"What a delightful daughter you must have been!" Caine said with a chuckle. "Well, I approve of you, too, as you shall soon see."

She began clearing the table and called to one of the scullery maids to wash up. When she had discarded her gloves and apron, she blew a strand of hair from her eyes and raked another behind her ear. "Now then, you have a surprise you say?"

Caine offered his arm. "Indeed. I keep my promises."

And she exceeded hers. Perhaps having a wife might be a deal more advantageous than he once thought. A small weight lifted off his shoulders and he guided her to the stables with a spring in his step.

"Close your eyes!" he ordered her, and gave Jacky and the other grooms a jerk of his head to dismiss them. The boys scurried out, grinning at one another like little jackasses.

He led Grace to the mare that was tethered to a support post between the rows of stalls. The little mount's coat gleamed in the sunlight that streamed through the open doors. The groom had braided a portion of mane and secured it with a ribbon. *Nice touch, Jacky Boy,* he thought with a smile.

"Now, Grace, meet your newest friend, Sienna," he said.

Grace opened her eyes and the look on her face was priceless. In speechless wonder, she reached out and touched the mare. "For me?"

"All yours," he assured her with a grin.

Grace burst into tears, threw her arms around his neck and wept like a child.

Caine was unused to weeping women and hardly knew what to do. Grace never cried! He had done something really wrong. This had to cease! "Please don't!" He patted her back, held her head to his chest until she stopped. "I'm sorry, I thought you would like her," he muttered.

She grasped his face with her hands and kissed him soundly. When she released his lips, she whispered, "I *love* her and you are the *dearest* man!"

Caine's heart swelled as he kissed her back. Nothing wrong, then. Everything right. She tasted of cinnamon, nutmeg and tears, smelled of the spices and all that was Grace and felt as slender and pliable as a willow in his hands. *Everything* right.

A loud equine snuffle intruded on his entirely impossible hope of a quick roll in the hay. Taking his future wife to a hayloft and having his way with her was hardly the thing. Still, it was a worthy fantasy for all that. He released her with a half laugh of regret. "I suppose you'll want to ride?"

She laughed with him, not even attempting to deny her own arousal. It was so evident in her pinkened cheeks, the way her pupils nearly eclipsed the blue of her eyes and the rapid rise and fall of her breath. "I suppose I *should* want to."

He slid one palm over her breast. "We could go inside."

"The house is bursting with people," she replied.

He kissed her neck and whispered, "The accounting office will be deserted. And I should examine your figures."

She laughed low in her throat and pushed closer to him. "A *singular* figure is what you have in mind to examine…and it definitely could stand your attention."

She linked the fingers of one hand with his and gave the mare an absent pat with the other as they wandered out of the stables.

"I have this overwhelming urge to race you inside," he muttered to her as he nodded in passing to Jacky and the lads. They were punching each other and hiding grins behind hands.

"Tempting to rush, but that would draw attention," she replied. But her steps hastened a little even as she said it.

Caine delighted in her frank desire, her playful nature and her unabashed straightforwardness. He even appreciated her eye for propriety, no matter how inconvenient and totally useless it was at the moment. He knew *his* desire was evident to anyone who cared to look in his direction, but perhaps in her relative innocence, she was unaware of that.

They entered the house through the kitchen door and almost made it to the main corridor when Neville intercepted them. "We have an idea you'll want to hear," he announced. "Come in the library. Trent's waiting."

The library. Adjacent to the accounts office. Caine rolled his eyes and groaned as Grace squeezed his hand and murmured, "Patience. One more night."

One more lonely night to endure and she

would be his. The thought of that almost eclipsed his worry about the confrontation with Wardfelton. That remained in mind, however, and would until it was over.

Grace had taken to Neville's sly maneuverings like the proverbial duck to water. The four of them had spent a number of evenings secluded in the Wildenhurst library already, working out the details. Her suggestions proved exceedingly helpful, he admitted. Neville declared she should have been a spy herself, delighting her no end.

This was the last day of it. Tomorrow The Plan would either work or it wouldn't. Caine's nerves were so frayed, he could scarcely think. Grace excused herself, leaving it to them, but was gone only a few moments.

"Look!" she said, sweeping back into the library. She waved the paper she held and plunked it down on the desk. "At last, the expected missive from Uncle Wardfelton. Just as we first thought, he insists on coming. He left it late, though, didn't he! I'd almost given up on him."

Caine couldn't cheer her success as Trent and Neville were doing. They had decided that the invitations should be made by the Hadleys in London, so that Wardfelton's might seem to be a mistake. He had sent an acceptance, of course, unable to resist coming.

Grace had mailed a terse note explaining Aunt Hadley's mistake and warning him not to come, that he was not wanted here, which of course insured that he would.

Caine continued to protest about the risk involved. The closer it came to time, the more he dreaded it. "Neville, I want your men in place by the time we return from the church. There must be absolutely no chance that Grace will be alone with him, even for a moment."

"Not to worry. They want Wardfelton as much as we do, certainly enough to suffer confinement behind the false panels."

"And you, Grace," Caine said, hoping the gravity of his words impressed on her further the need for caution, "Keep the table between you at all times. Never let him near you."

Grace smiled and laid her hand on his arm. "We have been through this time and again. Nothing will go wrong." She gave him a comforting pat and headed out of the room. "Now, if you will excuse me, gentlemen, I have a final fitting on my wedding gown. I will see you all at supper."

Caine tried to imagine the worst that could happen, so he could prepare for it, but it seemed there was no detail left unresolved. "He might not reveal anything that could be used against him. What if he suspects a trap?"

"Then we are no worse off than before," Trent said. "We will try something else."

Neville agreed. "Yes, there's the investigation into his spending habits. Something could turn up yet. But, knowing Wardfelton, I do believe this will work. Grace knows exactly what she must do."

"She must be kept safe," Caine insisted. "Even if it means revealing everything before he's caught. Even if he goes free, laughing at our efforts. Grace must not be hurt again."

Neville sighed and reached for the brandy decanter. "Bridegroom's nerves," he stated as he winked at Trent. "You need a drink." He poured one and sat back. "Caine, leave this to us and enjoy your wedding. Tomorrow should be the happiest of your life thus far, eh? A quarter hour of it to rid England of a traitor and rid yourselves of an enemy is a small concession. The interruption will be over before you know it."

Trent raised his glass in a toast. "Just think how the excitement of it all will add to your wedding night. Grace will be over the moon, flushed with success, ready to celebrate!"

"And your relief will only add to the fervor," Neville added with a laugh.

Caine shot each of them a dark look. "You are both entirely too cavalier. And do stop drinking!" He slammed out of the room, more worried than ever. He knew Neville was right about the nerves, doubly on edge now. Two potentially life-changing events expected in one day were enough to ravel any man's constitution.

* * *

Grace slept quite late the morning of her wedding day. Sun streamed through her window and lay across her bed like a blessing as she drank the chocolate Jane brought her and nibbled on a toast point. Her calmness surprised her a little. She figured it was probably due to the two cups of valerian tea Mrs. Oliver had provided the night before.

Mrs. Bowden peeped into the room. "Good wishes from the staff, Lady Grace! Lord and Lady Hadley have arrived already and Mr. Neville's wife and the doctor have come with them."

"Thank you, Mrs. Bowden. I hope all is in order for the breakfast?"

The woman beamed. "La, you should see! The kitchens are like a hive of bees! They've worked half the night. It'll be grand." She gave a little wave and disappeared, closing the door behind her.

Jane was laying out Grace's wedding clothes, a wistful look on her face as she smoothed out the gown of pale blue taffeta topped with lace-trimmed sarcenet. It was very simply cut, but Grace thought that only added to its elegance.

"We did all right by it even without a proper dressmaker, don't you think?" Grace asked as she slid out of bed. She had not sewn a stitch on the gown itself, for that would have been bad luck, but she had supervised it closely.

She had a moment's thought of that long-ago time when she had dreamed of her future wedding at sixteen. This was real and happening today, though, not a young girl's grand fantasy of some fairy-tale affair. Her hopes and dreams now centered more on her future with Caine, not with fancy trappings or even the ceremony itself. She loved him beyond all reason.

"It's the loveliest frock ever," Jane replied with a misty expression.

Grace bathed quickly and Jane helped her on with the fancy clocked stockings, pantalettes, filmy chemise and brief corset.

All the while, Grace kept watch on the mantel clock. It bonged once at half ten. "A bit over an hour until we leave for the church. Best start on my hair now. Are the irons ready?"

Jane wound and heated the straight locks into curls and caught them up in a crown, surrounding them with a delicate edging of lace. She carefully added the sapphire combs so that they showed to best advantage. "There! More princesslike than a cap or bonnet!"

"I like it. You are a wonder, Janie." Grace peered into her mirror, daubed a bit of rose salve on her lips and smacked them together. She splashed on a bit of scent, pinched her cheeks for color and grinned up at Jane. "Will I do?"

Jane laughed merrily. "Not in your underpinnings! Time for the gown."

Mrs. Oliver hurried in, all aflutter, just as Jane finished buttoning. The housekeeper stood, hands clasped beneath her double chin, and watched as Jane fastened the sapphire necklace Caine had given Grace. "Oh, my lady, you look so *beautiful!* The carriage awaits. The captain's gone down to the church with the menfolk."

Grace gave her a hug. "You look wonderful, Mrs. Oliver. And doesn't Jane look pretty? What would I do without you two?"

"Very well, I should think, but we should go now. Hurry, Jane, and bring her flowers there." She bustled them out like a mother hen. "We shall go along first, Jane, then our little bride and the family will arrive with the church full, waiting to see her. This will be the nicest wedding ever had at Wildenhurst!"

Grace deliberately did not dwell on her uncle at the moment. She was determined he would not impose on this day any more than necessary. For the next hour, she would think only of becoming Caine's wife. The wait had seemed so long, the fear that it would never happen, so great. Now that the time had come, she felt like singing a hallelujah chorus to the world.

Repressing her longing for him and denying him what he desired of her these past weeks was the hardest thing she had ever done. Yesterday in the stables, she had given up trying. If Neville and Trent had not turned up, Grace thought she might have given a rather good account of herself in the accounts room. The thought made her laugh to herself. Caine's disappointment had mirrored her own, but it had worked out for the best, after all. Tonight would be the more perfect for it.

She was no longer an innocent, but she certainly did not regret going to him that night. If not for that, she would now be overset with worry about their wedding night and how it might go between them. As it was, she knew very well how things would progress and could hardly wait. With an entire day to get through, however, she mustn't let herself focus on that just yet.

The open carriage bumped along the drive and onto the road at a snail's pace to avoid throwing up dust. The Hadleys accompanied her, as did Neville's wife, Miranda. She was a lovely lady, and although they'd only just met, Grace hoped they would be friends. Neville had become one in short order. She prompted Miranda to describe their wedding and subsequent travels on the honeymoon as they rode to the church.

She noticed the earl gazing on her with appreciation while Lady Hadley remained her usual quiet self and stared out at the passing scenery. It was a pleasant ride and helped to calm Grace.

That calm ended too soon. When they arrived at the church, everyone was already inside. Except Wardfelton, who stood just outside the door. Waiting.

Chapter Twenty-One

Grace worked to conceal her panic as the Hadleys exited the carriage first.

Neville's wife grasped Grace's hand and whispered. "I shall stay between you. Chin up and smile."

Grace allowed the footmen to assist her down after Miranda. They walked to the church arm in arm as if they were close companions. Neville must have related The Plan and Wardfelton's significance to his wife.

Wardfelton opened the door for the Hadleys and watched them go inside. Then he turned to Grace. "You look rather washed out this morning, niece. Aren't you well?" He offered her arm, which she ignored.

"I feel wonderful," she replied. "Please step aside."

"I mean to escort you in, my dear. What is an uncle for but to give you away in the absence of your *father?*"

She stifled the urge to kick him, but only just. So the taunts had begun already. Why couldn't he have waited until afterward to bait her this way? She felt Miranda squeeze her arm in support.

They entered the vestibule and Wardfelton grasped her other arm, his fingers digging into her flesh. "Go on ahead of us, my lady," he ordered Miranda. "Let's do this properly or *not at all.*"

It was a threat and he was serious. Grace nodded to Miranda. "Go. I shall be fine." If her uncle did the least thing more than walk her down that aisle, Grace meant to scream down the church and claw out his eyes, even if it ruined the wedding and foiled their plan. The men would be on him within seconds. She was not afraid, she kept repeating to herself. He could do nothing to her here in front of so many witnesses. And he would be oh so sorry for this trick later.

Everyone stood as she marched to the altar. Caine frowned darkly at her unexpected escort and started toward them. Grace shook her head and he stopped, hands fisted at his sides. Damn Wardfelton, he was doing everything he could to spoil this for her. She held Caine's gaze and smiled defiantly.

There was no way she could conceal her deep breath of relief when her uncle deposited her at Caine's side and stepped a few feet away.

The ceremony became a blur, her responses instinctive, until Caine slipped the ring onto her finger and peered down at her, deep concern in his eyes. She swallowed and squeezed his hand to reassure him she was all right.

Thank goodness she had not even heard the vicar question whether anyone had objections. If she had, she might have expected Wardfelton to speak up. But now the words resounded that she had waited far too long to hear spoken.

"By the Grace of God and the Church of England, I pronounce you husband and wife together. What God has joined, let no man put asunder."

Indeed, that would be her constant prayer all day.

And then Caine was kissing her. Hungrily, desperately, as if they might never kiss again. She shuddered at the thought that they might not, even as she responded to Caine in kind.

Applause followed as they strode quickly down the aisle to the church doors. Guests had spilled out and were tossing flowers and rice as Caine rushed her to the waiting carriage and lifted her in. He climbed up beside her, tossed a handful of coins to the well-wishers, signaled the driver and they were off to the manor.

He threw his arms around her and held her close. "God help me, I thought I might kill him right there at the altar," he gasped. "Are you all right, Grace?"

"I will be if you cease cracking my ribs. Nothing he could do will spoil this day for me, Caine. Tell me you feel the same."

"I do, I swear. How did he get his hands on you? Guards were all along the way here. Where was Uncle Hadley?"

Grace sighed, pushing away a little so she could breathe. "It was so neatly done, and at the church door. I expect the earl hadn't time to think how to avoid it. Miranda tried her best." She shrugged. "It turned out well enough in the end. He did give me to you without a scene."

Caine picked up his hat, which had fallen off onto the carriage seat. "Ah well, we shall have to do vows again. I scarcely recall a word of what I promised you." His smile was wry as he met her eyes.

Grace appreciated his attempt to conceal his anger and concern. "Neither do I. Perhaps it's that way for all brides and grooms. Well, at least we know the gist of it." She stretched out her arm and looked at her wedding ring for the first time, a gold band set with five sparkling stones.

"I did promise you diamonds," he reminded

her. "Though, the sapphires suit you perfectly."
He touched the gems of her necklace. "I suppose
I should have thought to buy you pearls for the
wedding. More appropriate and sedate."

Grace laughed. "Pearls are boring little
things."

"Which you never are, so I forgive myself."
He settled her against him and sighed. "So it's
done. Here we are, wed at last. Hard to believe
after so much going on to prevent it."

He would believe it soon enough, Grace decided, smiling to herself. In a few hours time,
perhaps not that long, they would have nothing left to distract them from a future together,
a future as shiny and as full of fire as her new
diamonds.

Mrs. Bowden, Cook and the staff had out-
done themselves. Grace had never seen such an
array of food as was presented at the wedding
breakfast. She counted at least thirty guests in
attendance and likely missed a few with all the
milling around. Most were strangers to Grace,
friends and peers of the Hadleys.

Tables had been set about the drawing room,
as well as two buffets laden with food. Musicians played softly so as not to interfere with
conversations. Huge arrangements of roses
scented the air and added festive color.

Grace refused to let the imminent confrontation with Wardfelton detract from her immediate happiness and pride in her new home and the Wildenhurst people who had made it all possible.

Once the meal concluded, toasts had been made and cake had been served, the event took on the attitude of a ball. Tables were being cleared for dancing. The musicians began playing and the day wore on. Grace stayed on edge, her only comfort Caine's nearness. She wanted Wardfelton gone so she could enjoy what was left of the day.

Finally, Neville caught her eye and gave an almost imperceptible nod. She nudged Caine. "Time to ignore me. Go."

He clutched her hand. "Take care, Grace. Promise?"

"I shall."

"I love you," he whispered, then left her side.

Why in Heaven's name couldn't the man declare that when she wasn't poised on the edge of some cliff? Grace threw up a hand and blinked with frustration as he walked away to join Trent and Neville. She let herself appear annoyed, as indeed she was.

That was precisely when she saw Wardfelton across the room, smirking. Her cue to proceed, she figured. She began to weave her way through the crowd of guests until she reached the vestibule. It was deserted at the moment. As planned, even Judd was not hanging about. The south end of the house was closed off to guests, including the morning room they had prepared for the confrontation.

She glanced back and saw her uncle heading in her direction. A moment longer and he would be able to see exactly where she was going. Grace waited, then went into the morning room across the vestibule's corridor from the drawing-room doorway.

She closed the door, crossed the room and waited. "I'm here," she said in a low voice, alerting the men behind the false wall panels constructed for this purpose alone. That had taken two full days, but they looked perfectly normal, as if they had been there since the room was first built. "If you hear me well, knock twice and hurry." The knocks came. She knew that Caine and Neville would be just outside the windows in the event of trouble. She should be perfectly safe.

One deep breath, followed by another and another before she heard the door latch click open.

"You have deserted your guests," her uncle said, an amused reprimand.

"I felt stifled, but now I find it even more so in here," she retorted.

"Grace, Grace, you were once such a delightful girl, quite likeable, and I was glad to have you around. So industrious, so helpful."

"You tried to kill me!"

He laughed. "I could have, at any time, you know. I kept hoping you would relieve me of that necessity."

"I hate you!" The angry exclamation had slipped out. Grace knew she needed to make him confess, not leave in a huff. She took a deep breath and clenched her eyes to regain her composure.

"Oh, Grace. And here I came to do my duty," he said as he pulled a cigar from his pocket. "And to warn you not to persist in your wild accusations." He proceeded to light the cigar and puff on it, pausing only to add, "I will ruin your life and Morleigh's if you do."

"Ha! You'll be found out soon enough. Caine is going to the gunpowder company. They will remember that you were the one who ordered it and took delivery. That will *soundly* implicate you in the plot to destroy us." She moved around the table as he tried to approach her.

"They won't recognize me, Grace. People see only what they expect to see," he said with an evil grin. "I went there in disguise. With an eye patch. A private jest, you see. A former soldier who needed the job. He gave me work." Wardfelton laughed. "And so did your Mr. Harrell here. As a guard. Imagine that."

"You think you're so clever, don't you? Mr. Sorensen obviously thought himself so, too.

Well, neither of you were." She shot him a sly look and repeated the words she had looked up and memorized. Her own idea, an added prod. *"Ceci va exactement comme vous avez prévu? Peut-être ma mémoire est meilleure maintenant."*

His expression of shock was worth memorizing every word in the French language, not only the few she had committed. Grace smiled, eyebrows raised, awaiting his response.

For a long moment, he remained silent. When he did speak, his words were calm. "So you *were* taught. Not very well, Grace. Your French is atrocious."

"A bit lacking, perhaps, but you may be assured that I comprehend far better than I speak it," she lied.

"I suppose this is meant to let me know you did overhear us that evening. To answer your poorly phrased question, yes, things are going exactly as planned with only a few minor diversions. And your memory of it is of no consequence at all. I warn you, repeating what you heard between Sorenson and me will gain you nothing. No one will believe it," he snapped. *"No one."*

"That you are a spy? That you committed treason? Oh, I believe some will listen to me!"

He tossed down the cigar and moved around

the table toward her, but Grace moved, too, keeping her distance.

"I was never a spy," he said, clearing his throat, straightening his sleeves and staring down his long straight nose. "The funds I provided the French were only for insurance."

She pursed her lips and trailed one finger along the tabletop, as if pondering what he said. "Insurance against what, pray tell?"

"In the beginning, I believed that revolution here was imminent. The unrest, the rabble siding with the citizens of France against the nobles posed a credible threat. My inheritance was new then. I merely sought a way to keep what was mine if it ever happened."

"So Sorensen collected it from you for the French," Grace said, willing him to admit everything in detail.

He glared to one side, as if remembering the arrangement, perhaps justifying his actions to himself. "Soren Sennelier promised me I would lose nothing after the revolution reached England if I supported Bonaparte beforehand. He nearly beggared me, the bloody fool."

"Sennelier? So your Mr. Sorensen was a Frenchman," Grace said, waiting for him to elaborate.

He scoffed. "Yes, but I never *spied,* Grace. The very thought is ridiculous. Say as much and you'll be laughed out of London. I am a peer of the realm and I would never *spy!*"

"You gave the Corsican financial support that aided his cause," she argued. "That sounds very much like treason to me. What happened when the war ended? Did you refuse to pay when the man blackmailed you? Is that why you killed him?"

He puffed out his chest, indignant. "I did not kill him!"

"Hired it done, did you? And that gunpowder for Caine and me would have provided you distance. What about my parents, *Uncle?* Your own brother and sister-in-law? Did you distance yourself from that death scene, as well? With poison, perhaps?"

The very thought of it incensed Grace. "Haven't you enough evil in you to murder face-to-face?" She felt such hatred for him at that moment, such livid anger, she cared nothing about proximity. She saw a trace of regret flicker in his eyes. "How could you kill your own *brother?*" she demanded.

He looked away from her as he moved around the table. "He should never have threatened me." His eyes met hers again. "And neither should you!"

She was close enough to strike him, so she did. She dealt him a resounding slap that numbed her hand.

Wall panels flew open and three men emerged, two armed with pistols. Grace yelped as Wardfelton grabbed and turned her back against him. The arm on her neck choked off her breath. "Back away or I will kill her!"

And they did! Grace clawed at his arm to no avail as the three men watched, tensed to interfere, but not moving. "Help!" she cried, struggling.

He was too strong, nearly lifting her right off the floor by his grip on her neck. She cursed the temper that had led her to carelessness. Caine would be furious with her!

Wardfelton was dragging her near the windows. "Open one!" he demanded of the man standing closest to them, the one unarmed official.

Grace could not let the traitorous murderer get away and she certainly didn't mean to let him take her with him. Why didn't the men overpower him? He only had an arm around her neck!

She fought, trying her best to twist away or reach behind her and hurt him somehow. Nothing she did broke his stranglehold. Next thing she knew, he had backed through the open floor-length window and dragged her with him.

She didn't know how he planned to leave with her. Or maybe she did. Teams were tethered to graze at the side of the house, out of their traces for the duration of the celebration. Break her neck, take one horse, scatter the others and he could get away!

"Nooo!" She screamed and kicked backward, hitting his knee. His hold loosened as he cursed her and she bit down hard through his sleeve. The moment his arm jerked, Grace dropped to the ground and scrambled away.

She looked back in time to see Caine plant him a facer worthy of a boxing champion. She winced as Wardfelton stumbled backward and fell against a window left closed, smashing the panes with his head.

Caine rushed to her and helped her up. "Are you daft, woman?" Furious. Just as she had known he would be. He must have come out the front to watch through the windows and would have seen how she disobeyed, letting Wardfelton get too close.

"I went a little mad, yes!" She looked down, extremely put out with herself at her lapse of caution.

Her shoulders drooped as she exhaled sharply. The danger was past but she was a wreck. Shaking with relief, yet angry that the entire day was spoiled. She flapped her arms once in frustration and brushed a hand over her grass-stained gown. "I've ruined it."

"To hell with the dress, Grace! You nearly got yourself killed!" Caine shook visibly, huffing like an angry bull about to charge. "God, when he raised that knife…"

"Knife?" Grace squeaked. "There was a knife?"

Caine caught her as she swayed. "Steady on, Grace. This isn't over yet."

Grace leaned against him, holding fast to the front of his coat for a moment. Then she straightened and glanced over at Neville, who was kneeling beside Wardfelton. "How is he?"

Neville shook his head. "Neck's severed." Others, including Trent were spilling out the front door to see what had caused the commotion

Explanations must be made. Caine and his family must not suffer the scandal of having a traitor in his wife's family. She refused to let Wardfelton's perfidy ruin them.

She ran to Neville and leaned close. "Bury this, Neville. Do not let Caine's family suffer for it."

Pretending hysterics, she rushed back and grasped Caine's arm, muttering swiftly so that none but he could hear, "Clear everyone away as soon as may be. No one must remark the window was broken inward instead of outward." She pushed away from him, waving her arm in distress as she cried out, "My poor uncle has fallen through the glass! Hurry! Someone fetch the doctor!"

Grace hoped Neville had the presence of mind to remove the knife from her uncle's hand before anyone happened to see it. "A distraction," she ordered Caine. "Remember Cavanaugh's?"

Hand to her head, Grace collapsed against him with a loud, tortured moan. He grabbed her up in his arms and met the gathering crowd with her in his arms, pushing through as he exclaimed in a loud voice, "Please, men, get the ladies back inside! It's a bloody sight they shouldn't see! She's fainted from it! I need help!"

The guests trailed him en masse, hurrying to keep up, concerned for the bride, murmuring sympathy, offering suggestions. Caine carried her into the drawing room, laid her on the divan there and knelt beside her. "Someone, smelling salts, please!"

Grace suffered the sharp smell as he shoved the bottle under her nose. Her sneeze wrecked her attempt to revive with any dignity. She peered up at Caine and sobbed. "Uncle should not have had so much to drink," she moaned. "I was too late to save him!"

"There, there, dearest," Caine said, brushing her hair from her forehead and laying a kiss on it. "You cannot blame yourself!"

"No, no, gel!" the earl piped up. "Tippling even before the wedding, he was, and after, too! Hardly ate a bite to soak it up! Damned shame, that, but what can be done?" He began pontificating to the others about the evils of drink, drawing much of the attention away from Caine and Grace. The countess stood by the earl, nodding.

Ten minutes later, Trent strode in. "There was nothing to be done for him," he announced. "I am very sorry, Lady Grace, but your uncle is dead."

Grace buried her face in Caine's vest since no tears would come. Damn Wardfelton. Even in death he had almost ruined her life. She would don no black for that man, no matter what society might expect of her.

Caine stroked her hair. "It is over now, sweetheart," he crooned. "Let me take you upstairs to recover."

"Yes, let's put the poor child to bed. I'll bring up something to help her sleep," Mrs. Oliver declared.

Caine lifted Grace again and spoke to the guests in a sorrowful tone, "Thank all of you for coming today to share our joy. I regret such a tragedy marks the occasion for all of us. Please have care on your way home."

It was a kind dismissal, Grace thought. And necessary. Caine took her to her room and Trent followed them up, closing the door behind him.

"Trent! Get out of here!" Caine ordered. "This is the first chance I've had to kiss my bride since the ceremony."

He laughed. "Kiss her, then, but hurry. You haven't time to…do anything else…much. The earl insists we meet him in the master suite's sitting room within the hour, and I wanted to give you my gift before I have to leave." He handed over two wrapped parcels. He waited. "Well?"

Grace tore off the paper wrapping of hers. Trent had captured Caine at his worst, unshaven, hair tousled, the old eye patch turned up on his forehead. He wore an expression of absolute ennui. It was a perfect likeness, yet so totally unlike the Caine she knew, Grace couldn't control her laughter.

Caine rolled his eyes at the sight, but he laughed with her. Trent preened at their responses as he pointed to the parcel Caine held.

Caine ripped the paper off and his laughter died. He looked at the picture for several moments, then at Trent and nodded, obviously pleased. "Now *that* is Grace. A labor of love, wasn't it?"

"For you both," Trent said.

Grace tipped the picture so that she could see. "But it's not funny!" she said, surprised at the way Trent had portrayed her. "Why, I look so…I don't know…sort of windblown and transported! *This* is how the two of you see me?" Perhaps how they *wished* she appeared.

"Exactly the way you look when you ride," Caine said, nodding.

Grace grinned. "Then I might decide to *live* on a horse! Thank you!" She gave Trent a quick hug and kissed his cheek.

Trent cleared his throat. "On that pretty note, I believe I shall make my exit. See you in a quarter hour. Earl's orders."

Grace barely had time to tend Caine's fist, repair her hair and brush off her gown. And have that kiss. She could barely tear herself away when Caine ended it.

"We have to go," he said, "and say good-night to everyone. Then I want you all to myself."

All the guests had already departed Wildenhurst, except for the Hadleys, Dr. Ackers, Trent, Neville and his wife. The three men who had come at Neville's behest had taken Wardfelton's body away to London. Mrs. Oliver kept the staff busy in the kitchens preparing a light supper.

Everyone who remained now repaired to the master chamber's sitting room as the earl requested. Grace thought it an odd place to gather, but figured his lordship must be too exhausted from the day's events to meet downstairs.

Hadley took charge once they had all assembled. "This will be brief and to the point," he declared. "We will put what has happened with Wardfelton behind us now. Life is too short to dwell on unhappy doings."

No one objected to that— Least of all, Grace.

She smiled her thanks to the earl, who looked very like a king holding court.

He smiled back at her as he continued, "I suppose each of you knows that, according to Dr. Ackers, Grace has saved my life, or at least prolonged and improved it. Also, Caine has had the goodness to keep me informed of everything despite my frailties. I thank you, my boy, for your continued deference to the title and for your trust. My wedding gift to you both is joint title to Wildenhurst."

He handed Caine the deed. Grace curtsied as Caine bowed and thanked him.

"Neville," the earl said in a strong, sonorous voice, "you and your Miranda shall have the hunting box in Northumberland, since you loved it so as a little lad. Refurbishments were begun when you married and now have been completed."

He handed Neville the documents for that. "Apologies for my lies to your cousin concerning your character. I had to do something to get him hopping after that Thoren-Snipes debacle." He grunted a rusty laugh. "If not pushed to wed, I feared he might give up on women altogether."

"Never the smallest chance of that, sir," Trent drawled, "but I grant you, he might not have married."

"All is forgiven, sir," Neville assured the earl. "Miranda and I thank you for the gift."

"Now, briefly back to this business with Wardfelton," the earl said to Neville. "Buried now, is it? I hope maybe you might prevent a scandal?"

"Not a single rumor will emerge," Neville promised. "I was assured today by my colleague from the War Office that the Regent will be most grateful if treason by one of his nobles is never brought to light." His questioning gaze went to Dr. Ackers, the only one among them who might expose the truth.

Ackers nodded. "The earl of Wardfelton bled out from a glass cut through his jugular vein after stumbling through a window. There was liquor on his breath when I examined the body. An accidental death with no indication of foul play that I could ascertain."

The earl smiled and slapped Ackers on the back. "Fine then, that concludes the business of the day. Everyone who is hungry should repair to the dining room, partake as hastily as possible and be off to London!"

"It will be full dark before you reach Town!" Grace said quickly. "Surely you'll wait until morning!"

Hadley was nearly to the door, leading the way. "Not possible, gel. The master's bed here is no longer mine to occupy. Besides, I am still earl and have matters in London long neglected. Come along, Bewley dear, mustn't dawdle, eh!"

The countess did delay, though, stopping beside Grace. "She was a fool, wasn't she? You know, the pretty one?"

"Quite right, ma'am, indeed she was," Grace replied.

"I thought so," the countess said in her odd, pensive way. "Here." She handed Grace a small piece of embroidery still stretched in its little frame, then followed everyone else out of the room.

Grace looked down at the gift so off-handedly presented. A ring of jagged and mismatched roses surrounded Grace's name. The letters were crooked and oddly worked, but the fact that the countess had done this just for her brought tears to Grace's eyes.

Caine was looking at it, too. "Not the most beautiful thing in the world, is it?" he commented when they were alone.

"Perhaps not on the surface," Grace replied, holding the piece to her chest and loving it. "But beyond that…"

"So, Mrs. Morleigh, are you hungry?" Caine asked, still standing with his arm around her.

"For once, food is the last thing on my mind," she replied, her heart full of happiness, anticipation rushing through her like a wildfire.

"Then perhaps it's time for bed," he suggested, sliding his arms around her and drawing her close.

She cut her gaze to his teasing one. "Don't you think we should wait for darkness to fall?"

He grinned, swept her off her feet and into the adjacent master's chamber, kicking the door shut behind him. "I think we've waited quite long enough."

Grace laughed as he tossed her onto the massive bed and followed her down. His mouth was hot as it found hers, his body insistent as he pressed her into the counterpane. He finally relented, breathless as he rose to his knees and tugged off his coat.

Grace watched with fascination as he undressed. Nothing meticulous or methodical about it, thank goodness. She reached up and toyed with the buttons on the flap of his trousers, undoing them one by one while he dispensed with his waistcoat. He yanked his shirt over his head as she reached the last button.

"Now you," he growled as he flipped her over and unbuttoned her gown. His impatience delighted her, fueled her eagerness as they wrestled her out of her clothes.

He kissed her again, thoroughly. And unexpectedly released her. Grace watched as he ran a hand through his hair and laughed a little.

"Better give me a minute to marshal my senses, or this will be too swiftly done," he advised as he lay down beside her, holding her more gently against him.

Grace looked into his eyes. She touched the scars that surrounded them with her finger. "I treasure every line of these marks. Without them, I would not have you. You do know that I love you, Caine? That I chose you freely that first night I came to you? It had nothing to do with gratitude."

"I hope that's true," he murmured, kissing her finger as it traced his lips. "For there's no going back, ever."

"There never was any question of that," she admitted. "Not since you first asked me to dance."

He kissed her again, tenderly, sweetly as his hand slid over her body. "We'll dance often, then. A ball every week if you want. Fox hunts, house parties, whatever you wish." He nipped her earlobe.

"But the time involved in all that, Caine. What of your work, your duties and dealings for the earl? I know your worries about that and I refuse to be an impediment."

He pulled her on top of him and framed her face with his palms. "You are no impediment, Grace. You're a part of me, the very best part. You remind me to live life and take it as it comes, good or ill, instead of driving myself mad trying to impose order on everyone and everything. You keep me sane, even as you drive me mad."

She moved sinuously beneath him, sliding her arms around his waist. "Then say you love me when I'm not poised to die, would you please?"

He leaned to press his lips to hers for just an instant. "I do love you, Grace. I think from the first time I saw those eyes of yours speaking to me from across Cavanaugh's ballroom."

He wore a serious look as he softly repeated words once spoken so loudly for all to hear. *"You've quite stolen my heart and I cannot live without you.* I said it then, Grace. But I *know* that I mean it now."

"And I simply cannot wait to be your wife," she said, echoing her own words of that fateful night in a slow, suggestive tone. "It's not a done thing yet, you know."

So, in the earl's enormous bed covered with a deep yellow canopy, they made it so.

Epilogue

April 1816, London

"She's making up for lost seasons," Caine remarked, nodding to Grace from across the room as he watched his uncle Hadley lead her sedately in a quadrille. "Danced every dance. I had to call in reinforcements."

Trent smiled and pointed with his glass of champagne. "The most beautiful of the lot, as it turned out. Not exactly what you once asked me to find for you."

"Not in any respect." Caine laughed. He did that often these days and with excellent reason.

"Oh, my, would you look there?" Trent said, keeping his voice low. "Miss Thoren-Snipes herself, pirouetting so grandly under the hand of Lord Logan. What an absolutely off-putting sight!" He made a face and shuddered.

Caine followed the direction of Trent's gaze. "Off-putting? That's ill said of you, man." He remembered when the very people around them were probably saying the same of him. "The fellow can't help being old and wrinkled."

"Oh, not Logan." Trent shook his head. "I meant *her*." He grinned at Caine. "Watch when she turns around."

Caine looked, squinting to focus better. The couple danced closer and Belinda made the turn. "My God, what is that on her bare back? Looks like a terrible boil or something. Two of them, in fact!"

"Pustules, yes." Trent sighed sorrowfully. "Too bad they aren't real."

"Look genuine to me," Caine observed.

"Hmm. Amazing what a half-baked sculptor can fashion with globs of soft rosin, a bit of paint and rabbit-skin glue, isn't it?"

"I daresay you have missed your calling." Caine drew his mouth to one side and considered. "Must have been damned hard to apply."

"Had to dance with her twice," Trent admitted. "Ruined my left glove." He polished off his champagne and reached for another as a servant passed by with a tray. "But I do love the waltz."

Trent would never grow up, Caine thought with a chuckle, just as the music dwindled and

Uncle Hadley brought Grace back to him. Trent made his bow and reached for her hand. "May I?"

Her cheeks were flushed with pleasure and she was a bit breathless, cooling herself with the new silk fan that perfectly matched her dress of azure blue. Her eyes sparkled like the sapphires she wore and the beautifully tortured curls danced as she shook her head. "That has to be my last turn for a while! Sorry, Trent."

"She's danced quite enough for tonight. In fact, we should be leaving soon," Caine declared, laying down the law with a look directed at Trent, his uncle and Grace.

"Will you let this bounder order you about that way?" Trent demanded of her. "What a bully he's become!"

"Well, we must forgive and indulge him, you see. After all, the man is…" she said, pausing for a second before whispering the rest, "in an *interesting way*."

Trent's mouth dropped open as his gaze shot from her to Caine, to Hadley and back again to Grace. "You don't say!"

Caine grinned ear to ear as she leaned forward, fan open to shield her next whisper as she confided to them, "He's to become a father."

Trent and his uncle whooped, disturbing the crowd around them as they slapped him on the back and kissed Grace's hands.

Caine decided he rather enjoyed these social

events again, but would be even happier when they could return to Wildenhurst.

Fortunately, he would not need to worry about taking up the mantle of lord anytime soon. The earl seemed hale enough to last a good while.

Grace had been a godsend, putting in order the Hadley finances and numerous other tasks Caine had thought so overwhelming when faced with them alone. How could he ever have thought she would be a hindrance?

Each day when he looked into his mirror to shave, his scars were still there, unchanged. But he saw a new man who bore them, thanks to her, a very happy man full of hopes, dreams and plans. Ironically, Grace's appearance was so different, no one recognized her as the sad wallflower of almost a year ago. And yet, she was the same inside herself, a force to be reckoned with and a joy to all who knew her.

He wished with all his might that she now carried a tiny Grace within her, because the world, and especially he, would be exceedingly glad to have two such marvels. However, an heir would be perfectly acceptable this time around.

They said their good-nights at twelve, left the ball and strolled the short distance to Hadley House, arm in arm. "Uncle and Aunt Hadley won't be home until the wee hours," he said. "What shall we do with ourselves?" He had ideas.

She squeezed his arm with both hands and peered up at him, her expression very serious. "You have a mad craving for strawberries, don't you, my darling?"

"Strawberries." He nodded. "Mmm-hmm. And perhaps some cream?"

"I knew it. I could sense it," she said, nodding emphatically, hurrying him along. "I'll order a tray sent up for us the moment we get there. For the life of me, I don't know how we shall get you through these next six months with all these unusual cravings of yours." She clicked her tongue and shook her head.

Caine smiled, loving her so dearly he ached with it, an ache she sensed and soothed quite often. She was the one with a taste for the strawberries, of course. And the oranges out of season. And cucumber slices with jam. He winced and wondered if he could hide his portion under the pillows next time they were required.

All he ever really craved was Grace.

* * * * *

A sneaky peek at next month...

HISTORICAL

IGNITE YOUR IMAGINATION, STEP INTO THE PAST...

My wish list for next month's titles...

In stores from 3rd August 2012:

- ❏ A Not So Respectable Gentleman? – Diane Gaston
- ❏ Outrageous Confessions of Lady Deborah – Marguerite Kaye
- ❏ His Unsuitable Viscountess – Michelle Styles
- ❏ Lady with the Devil's Scar – Sophia James
- ❏ Betrothed to the Barbarian – Carol Townend
- ❏ Montana Bride – Jillian Hart

Available at WHSmith, Tesco, Asda, Eason, Amazon and Apple

Just can't wait?

Special Offers

Every month we put together collections and longer reads written by your favourite authors.

Here are some of next month's highlights— and don't miss our fabulous discount online!

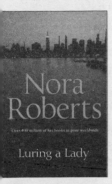

On sale 3rd August

On sale 3rd August

On sale 3rd August

Save 20% on all Special Releases

Find out more at
www.millsandboon.co.uk/specialreleases

0712/ST/MB381

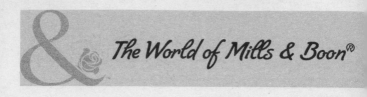

Have Your Say

You've just finished your book.
So what did you think?

We'd love to hear your thoughts on our
'Have your say' online panel
www.millsandboon.co.uk/haveyoursay

- 🌹 Easy to use
- 🌹 Short questionnaire
- 🌹 Chance to win Mills & Boon® goodies